STONE MAN

J M BEEVERS

For Mom.

And for all the rest of you, too. You know who you are.

ONE

Gydrocc Castle is, if I do say so myself, one of the loveliest places in world. Not that I've seen many other places to say so myself, but everyone that visits spends much of their first fortnight gushing about the loveliness of the cliffs and associated waterfalls that come crashing down into the lake beside the castle, the neatness of the forest the other side of the village, and the invariably beautiful sunrises over the Gray Mountains in the distance.

The only person I've ever met in my life who never even seemed to appreciate the loveliness of Gydrocc is the very person who should have appreciated it most.

She didn't even ride through the castle gates with the windows open like a good Clovian noblewoman would, intent on surveying the kingdom that would one day be hers. Instead she was seated in a wagon with the curtains drawn tightly shut, not even peeping out for a first look as it rounded the last bend before the castle.

Typical of those with both wealth and standing, it couldn't just be a normal old wagon transporting this foreign princess. Normal, in this case, meant something with wheels. No, this was some strange Marchant contraption supported on two poles that ran front to back. There were two horses, yes, but one was in the front between the poles and the other was in the back so no part of the wagon itself touched the ground.

I watched from above the main gate with the court alchemist and several guardsmen as a poor fellow on foot led this strange contraption across the drawbridge to the castle wall, a guard of honour riding in front and behind. Another wagon, this one a normal covered wagon with wheels, trailed along at the very back, presumably carrying everyone other than the guest of honour.

'Ridiculous,' I said, as I leaned over the wall to watch as the foreign guards at the front of the procession greeted the gate guards. 'How unbelievably pretentious.'

'It would be bad form for the descendant of a fairy queen to have transport that touches the ground.' Philip leaned forward on his stick as the procession entered our gates and he recited the ancient though decidedly strange tradition. He continued his recitation like a well-schooled boy, though too many years graced his wrinkled brow to make that comparison easily. 'The Royal Family of Marchant take their family history very seriously.'

'The horses are still touching the ground even if the wagon isn't,' I replied as I straightened up and turned to the stairs. 'Personally I think that's cheating.'

'Well unless you can find pegasi in the forest as an alternative I doubt your complaint will ever be addressed.'

I might have glared at Philip, but it was hard to show annoyance at the frail old man stooped over a stick, no matter how much he deserved it. Instead I settled for a shrug and led the way down the stairs without another word.

Princess Amanthea Diann Sidorra Delee has always had too many names for my liking. For months before her arrival I had been calling her Sidorra the Squid, or 'The Ugly, Fat Princess', ever since her portrait had been chosen out of the dozens sent along for Prince Caleb's perusal. I had seen that portrait, and knew the plain face on the little painting wasn't the reason for Prince Caleb's choice of bride.

Ever since Prince Caleb was a boy various courts in the neighbouring countries had been sending miniature portraits of any unattached young ladies of good families in hopes they might be the next queen to sit in Gydrocc. Of the ones sent since the prince had come of age two years ago, Princess Amanthea's portrait barely ranked in the top dozen.

Though the portrait was of a girl with lovely blonde hair and a nice smile, she had nothing on some of the other girls put into consideration. Her portrait landed near the bottom of the heap, right between a remarkably chubby duke's daughter and an elderly princess from the fens.

That is, until my uncle saw it.

According to the serving maid who'd been taking the wine around to all of the king's advisors while they were examining the portraits, he'd said, 'Wrong. Wrong, wrong, wrong.'

He picked up Amanthea's portrait, swept the others off the table with a great clatter and cracking of fine wooden frames, and placed hers face up in the very centre of the table. 'This girl is the key to Clovia's future. Ignore how she looks and think about the trade connections.'

Since my uncle, Lord Ruben, is the king's first advisor and one of the wealthiest Lords of the Realm, they listened.

Six months and a trade agreement later, here she was in the flesh, this princess who was apparently so important, and there was not a soul in the castle that wasn't curious about her. Philip and I reached the last steps of the gatehouse in time to see the pretentious wagon pull up in front of the main doors into the castle.

Prince Caleb stood outside the doors with his mother Queen Isabelle and a selection of noblemen as the foreign contraption came to a halt in front of them. Prince Caleb stepped forward, as a good prince should, to greet the woman he would take as his wife at the end of summer. Even from here he looked nervous at the thought.

The man who led the horses came to the side of the wagon, knelt down on the cobbles and placed a well-used stepping stool down beside the door. With a flourish, he flipped the catch and opened the curtained wagon door.

I glanced at Philip, who motioned for me to go ahead without him. With a quick smile I hurried along the edge of the courtyard as quickly as I could without running to see this princess that everyone had talked about for so long.

I expected to see someone who resembled the portrait, only uglier. Court portraitists are very nearly contractually obligated to beautify the truth just to the edge of recognition in order to keep in favour with their masters.

My last court portrait looked rather like the Goddess Freia, but with dark hair instead of red. For that reason my expectations of this princess were already very low. The only people who could in good conscience compare me with any goddess were the people who couldn't see clearly past the end of their nose.

A drumroll sounded in my veins as I rounded the courtyard to come up behind other curious onlookers hoping to catch the first glimpse of the foreigner. The first thing I saw over the shoulders of a crowd of jealous competitors for the prince's attention was her foot.

It was dainty. So she wasn't a fat princess. Oh well. Ugly Foreign Princess rolled off the tongue just as well.

Next came her hand, equally dainty, placed in the palm of Prince Caleb's hand. I glanced at his face, to see what he was thinking, and could see immediately that he wasn't. Dumbstruck would be the appropriate word to describe his expression.

And then she stepped into the light and I could see why.

The curtains weren't closed because she didn't want to see Clovia.

They were closed because she would have dazzled the living daylights out of it.

Naturally I had to be there for the official welcome in the Great Hall, where the Princess Amanthea was to be introduced to King Stephen. That didn't, however, mean I had to go quietly.

'Have you seen her? She's like a doll. A terrifying, magical doll. She can probably enchant people with her gaze.'

'I doubt that, Tara,' Lord Ruben chided me, striding

swiftly along the corridor on the way to the records chamber to get the official scrolls, where Princess Amanthea's arrival would be recorded for posterity with a record of the occasion.

'She is descended from fairies, which has something to do with her—ahem—appeal, but I doubt she has inherited anything more than their good looks. Perhaps a touch of mischief.'

I hauled my skirt out of the way as I followed Lord Ruben up half a flight of stairs, both of us taking them two at a time. He stopped in front of the door on the first landing so quickly I nearly ran into him, but he didn't notice.

I gasped out my objections with distaste. 'She's pretty enough she could persuade an ogre to turn cartwheels in a field of daisies. What do you think she'll persuade Prince Caleb to do, given half a chance?'

Lord Ruben rolled his eyes but didn't respond, only unlocked the door and went in long enough to get the necessary scrolls for the upcoming ceremony. After a moment he reappeared, locked the door behind him, and brushed past me on his way back down the stairs. I followed, trying to find words for what I was thinking.

'You've been telling me for the last five years that Marchant is no friend to us, and that their way of life is completely incompatible with ours.' As I struggled to find words, the thought at the front of my mind is what managed to tumble out. 'What on earth do you have to gain from this?'

This time Lord Ruben responded, by turning on heel so quickly I nearly ran into him a second time. Again, he was unperturbed by my proximity, and took the opportunity to lean close to my face. He apparently did not merit the accusation that he would arrange the prince's marriage for personal gain to be worthy of a reply, because his next words were focussed on me.

'Your fate is not to marry a prince of the realm. Learn that now and it will make the next few years much easier.' The words were harsh, but his tone was bland, as if he did not care particularly either way. He straightened. 'Better to be an advisor to a king than to be emotionally invested in one. Trust me. What you can do as a friend to this foreign princess is far greater than what you can do as her rival.'

He turned as if to leave, then added over his shoulder, 'By the way, we've hired a new portraitist. You're to see him tomorrow. Perhaps with a new portrait we'll actually manage a reasonable proposal for you.'

I could feel myself turn red as he walked away around the corner to enter the Great Hall. My uncle certainly wasn't one to mince words. My last portrait was an unqualified disaster. It had resulted in only one offer of marriage, that from a grandfatherly Lord of the south countries who had already run through four wives and all of their property.

Lord Ruben gave me an impatient look at the door of the Great Hall as I stopped to shake out my skirt. I had to hope it wasn't dusty or wrinkled. The Great Hall had been designed for receptions of the finest sort and was lined with tapestries rich enough to empty the coffers of the wealthiest men in the kingdom; much as anyone might consider themselves above worrying about their appearance, the Great Hall was not a place for dusty skirts.

When I was finished Lord Ruben pushed the heavy oak door in front of us open with one hand. It was a small side door that let us in behind a press of other members of the court. The room was impressively full, though most of the courtiers were there without an invitation. The moment Prince Caleb's bride was introduced to the court was not something anyone wanted to miss.

The press of bodies was such that I never could have made my way through on my own. This was a time I truly appreciated being in the company of my uncle, as the crowd parted easily for him. He was one of the few in this room now who was both invited and expected, as was true of his presence at almost any event in the Great Hall. As the royal recorder he was both needed and wanted.

I still had to fight my way through the sea of silk and satin to keep up with Lord Ruben, though not as hard as I might have otherwise. It took a quick step to keep up as the crowd closed almost immediately behind him, but I managed to find my way without too much difficulty. I knew where I was wanted and made my way there with some determination. Today was the first time I was to be given any court responsibilities, and that knowledge lent me confidence.

When we arrived at the front of the room Lord Ruben took one step up onto the lower dais, which was mercifully uncrowded. He then stepped up to take his usual place next to the upper dais, where the two thrones of state overlooked the room. I positioned myself a few steps away and hoped no one would notice as I attempted to refasten my veil. It was making for escape off the back of my head.

A low murmur of voices accompanied the short wait for the princess. King Stephen and Queen Isabelle, already seated, spoke quietly to Prince Caleb who stood between and behind their thrones. I watched the three of them intently, wondering what exactly they made of the princess who had arrived in such style earlier.

It was obvious from the queen's intent expression and Caleb's dazed smile that they were not disappointed in her looks, but I knew there would be more to think about than just her immediate appeal.

I didn't get a chance to wonder long. The doors at the other end of the room swung open and all eyes turned to see what sort of a show the foreigners would put on.

First through the door were two guards of honour

carrying flags on long poles. Atop one pole was the blue and white flag of Marchant and atop the other the crest of the Marchant royal family. The soldiers' grips were steady enough that though their eyes stayed aimed directly forward, the flags stayed uncannily level with each other.

Behind them came four guards in a single line, each with large ceremonial shield on the left arm. They were knights, judging by the fineness of their shields, but the detail that caught my eye was the greying hair that peeked out from the brim of their round helmets and the deep lines across their faces.

Their best years were clearly come and gone. It was a strange comment on the value of this princess; here was the stunningly beautiful eldest daughter of a powerful kingdom, but her guard of honour on the way to her betrothal was a small group of knights well past their prime.

The couldn't keep anyone's attention long. In the middle of the procession, flanked by four maids, walked the princess.

TWO

A gentle breeze of whispered admiration stirred through the room when she came into view. It was hard not to gasp or sigh as Princess Amanthea glided into the room, golden hair streaming uncovered behind her. No amount of corseting, hairstyling, or artifice could ever make me or anyone else in the court look as gloriously ethereal as she did in that moment as she glided forward to meet her fate.

Her foreignness was as much on display as her beauty. She wore a wide skirt, obviously bolstered by several petticoats, which made for a very pretty but very impractical ensemble, and her hair hung free for anyone to see instead of being modestly covered by a veil. I reached up to my own veil to check that it was still in place, her beauty making me self-conscious, and saw that I was not the only one to do so. Several women stood up straighter, and others looked down at their own dresses as if to compare them to those of the foreign princess.

When the princess Amanthea reached the raised dais where the thrones stood, she swept the most perfect curtsey I have ever had the misfortune to observe. Her delicate hands swept those voluminous skirts out to either side as she sank down, head bowed demurely.

She paused at the lowest point of her curtsey, not a moment too long or too short, and rose again with a rustle of fine silk to view the family she was marrying into.

It has been my experience that many people are only capable of properly paying attention to one of their senses at any given time, especially when one of those senses is being dazzled. For this reason, I don't know that anyone was listening while my uncle made the official introductions, so distracting was the princess' appearance. Even the king seemed a little awestruck, as there were several moments of silence after Lord Ruben finished before the king spoke.

'We are pleased to welcome you, Princess Amanthea, to Gydrocc Castle and to the great kingdom of Clovia. We hope you will enjoy our kingdom, our customs, and our people, as we are certain we will enjoy your company.'

The princess offered a gentle nod and a smile so sweet it could melt stone.

The king waved a hand toward Lord Ruben. 'We would like to offer the services of one of our ladies of the court as companion and help to you. She will, at your pleasure, be your lady-in-waiting. Let us introduce Lady Tara of Dynnan, granddaughter of the late Lord Samson and niece to my advisor Lord Ruben.'

I offered the best smile I could muster and stepped forward. I was supposed to curtsey, but after having seen Princess Amanthea curtsey, it seemed like a bad idea. I didn't want to be hanged for disgracing my country in front of important foreigners. I dipped my head deeply instead, and stayed that way until the king was done speaking.

'We will leave you in Lady Tara's capable hands now to lead you to your rooms, which we hope you will find to your liking.' The king smiled at her in a fatherly kind of way and gave my uncle an approving nod.

Princess Amanthea curtseyed again, but did not speak. She was not required by court etiquette that she do so, but usually foreign dignitaries would make a comment on the beauty and comforts of Gydrocc. Certainly everyone in the room seemed hopeful that she might open her mouth to embarrass herself and prove that she was indeed human.

Or perhaps that was just wishful thinking on my part.

The princess turned to me with an expectant look. I dipped my head again and motioned to the side door I had entered through with Lord Ruben. 'After you.'

She glided toward the door, maids trailing after her. The knights stayed to make their own bows to the king and be introduced to Hawkins, the captain of the guard. I looked back at Lord Ruben to see if he had any instructions for me, but my gaze was drawn instead to Prince Caleb, who was watching the princess leave with that same dumbstruck look from earlier. I felt a red flush on my cheeks and hurried out after the princess without a second look at my uncle.

The princess had not gone far. I found her standing halfway down the corridor, maids waiting silent at her side. The four of them looked rather like they'd been cut from a mould labelled 'average sort of woman', but with some hair colour variation. Like the princess, they were young, slim and fair, with golden hair hanging loose behind them. Any one of them could have been mistaken for the princess' sisters, though none shared their mistress' stunning good looks. While they had been in the procession, they had in fact gone completely unnoticed behind the princess, pale shadows of the young woman they followed.

'This way,' I said evenly as I sized up the group of fair women in front of me, and motioned down the hallway. Princess Amanthea followed me around the first corner into a blessedly empty side corridor and gave a brief sigh of relief.

'I'm so glad that's over,' she said, and put both hands over her stomach as if she felt queasy. She gave me a terrified smile that could have charmed a rabid dog out of the idea of biting her. 'I was very nervous.'

My last thread of hope for the princess being someone I could like vanished as I heard the perfectly articulate tones, made only more pleasant by her slight accent. She sounded as beautiful as she looked, and the comments on her nervousness were endearing. The moment she spoke to Prince Caleb he was going to be so lost in her perfection it would take all the king's hounds and a hunting party to find him again.

'I wouldn't have guessed,' I replied blandly as we turned another corner to face a tower door. I pulled this open and began to ascend. 'Your room is in this tower, up three flights of stairs,' I explained. 'I hope you don't mind climbing.'

The only reply to this was silence. When I looked back, I couldn't see anyone behind me on the tightly curved staircase. I groaned inwardly. If she was going to object to the room she was allotted, it would mean rearranging half the castle to find something more suitable. I descended with an annoyed step until I could see the doorway we had just come through.

There stood Princess Amanthea. She wasn't objecting to the climb. Instead, she had her skirts and what must have been two layers of petticoats gathered in both hands as she struggled to keep her balance on the narrow spiral staircase.

I briefly considered the forty-six towers of Gydrocc Castle and their associated spiral staircases. A good quarter of my life was spent climbing stairs, and now hers would be too.

I felt a little mischievous grin spread across my lips.

'Shall I give you a tour of the castle?'

Over the next two hours I spent most of my time waiting at the top or bottom of staircases for the princess and her retinue. The remainder of my time seemed to be spent waiting for the princess' dress to be untangled from banisters or tapestry hooks, occasionally both at the same time.

'The great houses in Marchant have wider hallways,' she said in a sort of apology-complaint as her maids worked another tapestry hook out of the hem of her wide gown. 'That way we can wear wider skirts without fear of having them catch on every passing thing.'

'In Clovia we wear narrow skirts so we can navigate the halls our ancestors were kind enough to build for us,' I retorted, the grim smile still lingering at the corners of my mouth.

Somewhere between the dining hall and the east wing, the princess decided getting me to engage in small talk might be more pleasant than the slightly aggressive silence I had been favouring her with up until that point.

'Your uncle is an important man,' she opened as we

walked down the hallway more slowly than I would have liked. 'Is your father also?'

'My father is dead,' I replied, a little more harshly than I meant to. Unapologetic, I added, 'But no, he was not politically important, aside from the fact that most of the king's advisors wanted him dead.'

A very loud silence followed my statement. As no responses seemed forthcoming, I thought I'd explain something else. 'I'm my uncle's only heir, so was brought here when I was young to learn the ways of court. Someday I'll own half of Clovia. Your future husband will own the other half,' I added, sending the princess a wry smile. This was an exaggeration, but not much of one.

'Unless your uncle produces an heir,' the princess said in reasonable tones. 'He is young enough still.'

'Of course.'

In my mind, I added, *He won't let me inherit anyway. I'll be disowned long before then.*

That night I retired to my room above Princess Amanthea's with a kind of mental exhaustion that had nothing to do with the princess' questions about Gydrocc's history, or her rather more irritating attempts at sparkling conversation.

No, the exhaustion was more to do with the fact that we spent most of the rest of the day listening to someone complain about the fact that Clovia was different from Marchant. The princess herself wasn't too bad, but her maids were considerably less tolerable than she was of the fact that things did not run exactly the same way here that they did at home.

Even at dinner they had not ceased their complaints. I sat through two hours of listening to those four maids whine to anyone that would listen about the apparent inferiority of Gydrocc compared to any castle in Marchant. This they did, of course, underneath a sheen of politeness that fooled no one but made their comments more acceptable as dinner conversation.

In the quiet darkness of my own room I flung open the window to let in the night air. I closed my eyes and let the wind strike my face, cold but refreshing after a day like today. There was only so much grovelling and scraping I could manage before I thought seriously about throwing myself into the nearest fireplace, and today had me feeling as if sitting in the flames would be more comfortable than another moment of feigned politeness.

The thought of fire made me remember my mother's most recent letter. With a sigh, I closed the window and turned to my table. It took only a moment to light a candle and find the folded bit of paper in a pile of missives I had yet to answer.

Darling Tara,

I miss you and hope you are doing well at Gydrocc. If Ruben is treating you unfairly please do let me know and we can do something about it.

Bryn would very much like to meet you. He requests that you come when the moon is full next, at the place you know. He would apparently like some assistance in a matter of some delicacy and also to hear your opinion on another matter.

Cousin Celia sends her love, as do the Sisters here. I hope Ruben can find it in him to allow you to return to me sooner rather than later.

All my love,
Mother

I glanced out the window to assure myself that yes, I had one more day until the full moon. At least that was some small consolation. It would have been unbearable to have to leave now after having dealt with the princess all day. If there was any one thing I needed right now, it was a chance to rest without anyone's expectations weighing on me. Anyway, I had no desire to meet Bryn without a chance to see Philip for advice first.

The meeting with Bryn was a secret between myself and my mother, and had been a long time in coming. I had definite qualms about it. These qualms covered everything from being abducted and never seeing Gydrocc again to dying a slow, painful death by fire because I didn't live up to Bryn's expectations.

Of course there was always the possibility that everything would go well with Bryn, but that my uncle would find out about the meeting and promptly see to having me disowned and banished, if not worse.

Somehow this made absolutely everyone else's arranged marriages seem gloriously enviable. No matter how bad the fiancé, most well-bred young women's futures didn't include both the possibility of being exiled by their family and the possibility of being burned to death by their potential future husband.

Mother's missive went back into the pile with the rest, hidden but not forgotten, at least until the morning.

Hopefully everything would seem brighter by daylight.

THREE

Early mornings are not usually a friend to me, but I was spurred out of bed at sunrise by the knowledge that if I didn't get up before the princess, I would spend the entire day disentangling her from the furniture without even a sniff of a chance to see Philip.

The first glow of dawn crawled through my window as I washed and dressed. I stood in front of the mirror to affix a pale grey veil over the tight knot of dark hair at the back of my head in the Clovian fashion and wondered if I would ever be able to attract attention the way Princess Amanthea did.

It seemed almost as if the princess needed to expend no effort at all on her appearance, she was so naturally beautiful. She would still look beautiful wrapped in brown sacking. Certainly if I looked like her I would not feel the need to spend very much time beautifying; the job had already been done quite remarkably by Mother Nature.

Another look at my reflection said that I should keep dreaming. Even if the princess had been average looking instead of remarkable, she carried herself with a grace that I could not compete with, and her foreignness made her beauty more remarkable. I was a true Clovian with dark hair and olive skin that only turned more brown in the sun, a complete contrast to the pale, blue and gold princess. My uncanny ability to walk like a man, my prominent chin, and my uneasiness in my own skin meant I could never be competition to someone so graceful.

I glanced at the growing pile of missives on my table in an effort to clear my head and thought of mother. She had been intentionally vague in her message, in hopes of avoiding suspicion should Lord Ruben read the letter, but I wished she had given me more of an indication what I should expect from this long-awaited meeting with Bryn. It was difficult enough to prepare for this meeting without being given any hint what might happen. As it was I was going in completely blind.

My mother had her reasons not to trust her brother, Lord Ruben, and therefore to be careful in the letters she wrote to me. On the topic of Bryn she trusted Lord Ruben so little that he had not even heard

Bryn's name, let alone news of the marriage agreement forged when I was a child.

Lord Ruben had been known to read my letters before now, it was no secret. Mother's letters were now vague in an attempt to protect me from his displeasure, and in this case, I had to deal with the consequences of that.

With a sigh I turned from the mirror and headed for the stairs. In the morning silence, I could hear nothing from the rooms above or below me in the tower as I opened my door, meaning that the princess and her maids hadn't yet stirred. Perfect. I didn't want to explain myself to them if I didn't have to.

I made quick work of the stairs down to the main floor of the castle and headed for the Alchemist's Tower. The first King at Gydrocc had built the Alchemist's Tower for one of his favoured advisors, the legendary Edden of Vail, the first alchemist to successfully transmute wood to stone. Ever since then the tower had housed dozens of alchemists, all the best at their work, all eager to please the kings of Clovia.

Philip was the only alchemist currently in attendance at Gydrocc, and had been for nearly twenty years.

He was also the first alchemist not to ever set fire to his tower. After the third such event, the tower had been rebuilt near the castle wall rather than in its old position next to the castle. It was now only connected to the main body of the castle by a stone hallway that acted as protection from rain and mud for those passing through.

I rounded the last corner to the passage that would take me to the Alchemist's Tower just as the sun made its way over the mountains to cast an orange glow across the courtyard, where the castle guards were stretching for their morning exercises and kitchen maids were running from the standalone Kitchen Tower to the cellars and back again with armloads of food.

In the din I stopped for a moment, breathed in the cold morning air, and looked around me carefully. The courtyard contained no one that I need worry about; they were as uninterested in me as I was in them. Even if they saw me getting up to something they were unlikely to report it to my uncle, as they rightly deemed me to be mostly unimportant.

With a glance behind me I could see that the halls were empty, though I heard the rustling of cloth and voices in the distance as the earliest risers of the court headed for an early breakfast in the Second Hall.

Thoughts of breakfast in mind, I hurried down the hallway to the lower door of Philip's tower. If I was quick I would make it to breakfast before anyone noticed my absence.

At the door to the Alchemist's Tower hung a bell pull, which I hauled on to make as much racket as possible until someone answered.

It seemed as though I stood for ages on the cold

stone floor of the outside hallway before the door finally creaked open and I could hear Philip's grumbling.

'These old bones aren't made to get up this early, especially on a day like today,' he moaned as he pushed the door open for me and turned to the stairs. 'If I didn't like you so much I do believe you would be spending today as a frog.'

I smiled at Philip's retreating figure. No one else would dare visit him at this hour of the morning. He was not a creature of the early morning and made it very clear to those who disturbed him before midmorning. He made an exception for me only after several years of friendship.

'You don't know how to turn people into frogs, Philip, that's wizard's work.' I ducked through the low door and followed him past the stairs into the main living area.

The inside of the tower was pleasantly warm, and I could see Philip's young page scurrying around the living quarters as he built a large, roaring fire. Beside him was a plate of sausages ready to be cooked and a large loaf of bread that would certainly be toasted in the sausage drippings. Philip was of the opinion that he'd lived as long as this by consistent daily intake of large amounts of fat, and had no intention today or ever of eating the castle breakfast of porridge and stewed vegetables.

Philip motioned me to follow him into his upstairs workshop instead of the warm living area. 'Not today,' he said as he directed me upstairs. Disappointed, I turned to follow. He closed the stair door behind me and leaned forward to present his cheek. I favoured him with a quick kiss as payment for calling him down so early and smiled.

He smiled back and started up the stairs. His workshop was on the next floor, but it took twice as long as it should have to ascend the stairs with Philip at the front. He pushed open the door to the workshop to let us both in.

I looked around the workshop with interest. While I had been in many times before, there was always something new to look at. The first time I entered I had been overwhelmed by the sheer amount of stuff. The room was more full of breakable objects than any other I had seen in my life, along with crates, barrels, strange and rather fantastic ingredients for spells, and what must have been the largest collection of animal skeletons in Clovia.

As Philip closed the door behind us I said, 'I'm supposed to meet Bryn tonight.'

'Tonight?' Philip looked surprised, and counted on his fingers with a glance out the window. 'Yes, I suppose it is the full moon, isn't it. Did your Lady Mother send any further instructions? Any hint what you should expect?'

'No,' I admitted. 'Whatever it is, I'm not looking forward to it overly.' I shuddered at the thought of being carried off captive by a great green dragon. 'I won't have time to come by later, but I don't want to go without something to protect myself. What do you recommend?'

There was a thoughtful moment as we both wondered what chance I could ever have against a grown dragon. Philip tutted. 'I'll send you with a charm for burn protection. You'll certainly need that. I've found a way to make an arrow always hit its mark, if that helps. Are you any good with a bow?'

'No. Lord Ruben doesn't approve of me learning weapons play.'

Philip made his way to a bookcase at the back of the crowded room. There he pulled down a familiar box of charms. 'Here's burn protection,' he said, pulling out a small jar on a string that held a piece of burnt charcoal. The little black lump flaked every time the jar was moved. 'I'm sure that charm for never-miss arrows is in here as well. At least take it with you, you never know if it might come in useful.'

As Philip rummaged through his boxes of charms, I picked my way carefully across the room to view his latest collection piece, a unicorn skeleton. 'Are you going to tell me where you got this yet?' I asked, leaning down close to the table, where the bones were arranged anatomically, ready to be reassembled into a standing statue. I had asked almost daily for weeks, but Philip was not forthcoming. Unicorns were flighty, fragile creatures, not the kind to let themselves be found by hunters.

'If I thought you really wanted to know I would tell you,' Philip said, setting aside yet another box. 'Ah, here it is.' He reached to the back of the shelf and pulled out what looked like a gold coin painted with a red bullseye. He held it out to me.

'I suggest that if you decide to use this, you get a crossbow from the armoury. Hawkins will show you how to use it. Just secure the charm on the back of the crossbow and you should find yourself hitting everything you aim for.'

'Do you think a bow would be enough?' Visions of dragons the size of houses danced in the back of my mind.

'Do you think anything would really be enough?' Philip scoffed. 'We hardly have time to train you in swordplay and get you enchanted armour.'

Comforting. I'd just have to hope my new fiancé wasn't too moody. 'Thank you, Philip,' I said as I picked my way across to where he stood, skirt gathered up around my knees to keep from brushing against anything accidentally. 'I'll send you a nice bottle of wine from the cellar tonight to keep you company until I get back and I'll tell you all about it.'

I dropped another kiss on his cheek, took the two proffered charms, and left as quickly as I could. Time was not on my side today. The princess was likely to notice my absence, especially if I missed breakfast, and explaining to her was at the bottom of my priorities list.

At the bottom of the tower I bid farewell to the page, closed the door behind me, and looked out to the training field, where the soldiers were in the middle of warming up for a day of drills. There are no doors connecting the hallway where I stood to the outside, but the many large arched windows served well enough.

I tucked the charms from Philip into a pocket and sat on the low windowsill. There was no glass in any of the arches along this corridor, as no one wanted to risk installing something so expensive next the highly-flammable alchemist's tower. With a quick swing of my legs I landed lightly on the grass and started across to the training fields.

As I passed the kitchens I caught a maid by the arm. She turned and curtseyed shortly, but I didn't have time to deal with formalities or annoyed maids.

'Please send some nice wine up to the alchemist tonight, compliments of Lord Ruben's household.'

'Yes'm.' The girl dropped a curtsey and ran on. It was not an unusual request, and one Lord Ruben allowed me to indulge in on occasion. I kept Philip happy, and Philip kept the king happy. Anyway Lord Ruben took it as a sign I was following in his footsteps toward being a political influencer. What better way to start my bid for future power than to bribe a talented alchemist into liking me?

I found my way back into the castle with no time for breakfast. By the time I arrived, the food was being cleared away and the room was almost empty. Princess Amanthea stood talking with a couple of other ladies of the court. When she spotted me looking around for anything left to eat, she smiled brightly, excused herself, and hurried over to my side.

'I got lost on the way to breakfast this morning,' she said excitedly, as if that was a major accomplishment.

'Where are your maids?' I asked, and glanced around the room for the four forgettable faces. I didn't mind not having them around, but there was something strange about seeing the princess all on her own.

'Still sleeping.' She smiled just enough that she looked embarrassed. 'We don't rise nearly so early in Marchant but I couldn't sleep any longer.'

'Look, Squid—er—Princess Amanthea,' I corrected hastily, 'you probably shouldn't go wandering off around the castle yet without someone who knows the way. There are places you could get lost and not find your way out for hours. This castle isn't the friendliest of places if you don't know your way around.'

'I didn't go alone this morning,' she protested with an innocent shake of her head. 'I followed you when you went down earlier, but I lost track of you somewhere after you turned left by that big yellow tapestry.'

My mouth dropped open with surprise. She had followed me? First thing in the morning, before the sunrise, to the other side of the castle? The yellow tapestry she spoke of was the last turning before the

Alchemist's Tower, where I had stopped to see if anyone was following me.

Either she was a better sneak than I could have imagined or I was losing my touch.

I took her arm and gently led her out of the Second Hall toward our tower. 'I went to visit a friend this morning. I didn't think you would be awake.'

'May I meet your friend?'

With those big doe's eyes, it was hard to believe this princess was six months older than me. She certainly didn't act it. I smiled gently and shook my head. 'Not today. Today we need to wake your maids, get you dressed, and I need to go see the court portraitist.'

Princess Amanthea nodded agreeably and together we went back to her rooms.

FOUR

The new court portraitist had set up camp in the Long Gallery, below the portraits painted by his predecessors. There wasn't always a court portraitist in residence, but when there was they tended to take up rather a lot of space and cause more disruption to the schedules of the servants and therefore the courtiers than was strictly necessary.

The current portraitist was no exception, what with the fact that he was constantly spilling paint, which required a lot of extra cleaning.

I led the princess and her maids into the Long Gallery around mid-morning to see to my first sitting for a new portrait. The gallery was a long, airy room with massive windows on one side and a series of paintings on the other, ranging from oldest near the door to the newest at the far end of the hall. As we walked along underneath representations of Gydrocc's historical rulers, I pointed out the most recent royal portrait at the far end of the uncrowded hall.

'It was the last commission from Grennon of Loree before he died last summer,' I explained. 'King Stephen, Queen Isabelle, Prince Caleb, and his two younger brothers.' I gestured to the two sprigs of lavender in the queen's hand. 'The queen also bore two daughters, but they died in infancy long before I came to Gydrocc.'

'They are all very handsome,' the princess offered, though she didn't look long at the portrait. Her gaze moved down to the crowded tables at that end of the room and the figures bustling among them. 'Is one of those the new portraitist?'

'Yes, but I've not been introduced to him yet.' It was true. Though I'd heard many a complaint about him from the maids, I'd not actually met the artist in person.

There were three people working at the end of the gallery, a girl and boy on the edge of puberty, and a thin man with a carefully trimmed beard. The children were grinding and mixing paints while the man rearranged a chair and table near the wall. He did not look up as we approached, though he could not have missed the echo of our voices.

'Are you Liam?' I asked, directing my query at the

bearded man, though I could not help watching the children out of the corner of my eye. The girl was carefully adding beetle shells to a mortar already full of glistening scarlet powder.

'I am,' the man said, not looking up. 'I assume you are Lady Tara here for a portrait? Your uncle said—'

Whatever it was my uncle might have said was lost as Liam looked up and caught sight of Princess Amanthea. His eyes widened, his breath caught, and he dropped the chair he was holding onto the stone floor with a clatter.

I glanced at the princess, who seemed unperturbed. Apparently this was a fairly standard occurrence for her. I cleared my throat. 'I am Lady Tara. This is Princess Amanthea of Marchant and she has no need of your services.'

Liam's gaze went to me, back to the princess, then to me again. 'No, I can see that.' He looked down at the chair he dropped. Rather abruptly, he shoved it out of the way against the wall and bowed. 'My apologies for staring, princess, but you are very beautiful.'

'Thank you.' She inclined her head graciously and turned to me. 'Tara, I believe we will have a look at the other portraits and leave you to get on with things.'

Mercy, at least she understood she was a distraction. Her kind smile as she turned away made me think she might have some redeeming qualities after all.

Liam set about studying my face for half an hour, first having me sit this way, then that, pulling at curtains, lighting and blowing out candles. Finally he threw his hands up into the air in exasperation.

'Natural light. We'll put you next to the window.' He didn't seem pleased about this. 'Wear something colourful, not that thing. Maybe red, or pink? And a white veil. No grey.'

I rolled my eyes. It was the same with every artist. Unless you were as beautiful as the princess, and she was the only one I'd ever met of that calibre, an artist would never be completely pleased.

'Can you please make it actually look like me?' I asked as I stood to leave. 'The last portrait I had looked like someone else.'

He shrugged. 'If that's what you want,' he said doubtfully.

I grimaced. Of course I wanted to look more like a dark version of Amanthea and less like, well, me, but didn't we all?

The moment we were turned loose after dinner I bade Prince Caleb a polite farewell and herded the princess up to her room. My mind was on the upcoming hours and I wasn't about to be distracted.

We arrived at her bedchamber just as one of the maids came out from having lit the fire for the evening. I scowled. It was a waste of wood to have her own fire when there were feather blankets stacked a foot high on her bed.

'I hope you had a pleasant evening with the prince,'

I said formally as the maids undressed the princess from her multi-layered evening costume. Again, she wore multiple layers of skirts and petticoats, as well as a heavily embroidered vest with a collar that stood up as far as her ears.

I sat down on the edge of the bed and immediately sank several inches through the fluffy bedding. I would rather have been preparing for my midnight ride with destiny, but I did have duties to attend to. Anyway, the sheer silliness of the princess was somehow calming. She was a distraction from the seriousness of my situation that I very much needed right at that moment.

'He is very pleasant,' she agreed calmly. She was watching the progress of her maids in the silvered mirror and I could see her occasionally glance at me as well. 'Though I think he likes the sound of himself talking more than he's interested in the conversation.'

I blinked in surprise. I had always thought Prince Caleb perfectly charming, and if conversations with him were a bit one sided, I was usually too busy thinking about the colour of his eyes to notice. The princess glanced at me in the mirror when I didn't reply.

'Oh.' She turned, looking apologetic. 'I didn't mean to offend you. It's only that it was a bit difficult to steer the conversation onto more pleasant topics than horses running into each other.'

'I'm not offended,' I said as I stood from the bed.

'Surprised, but not offended.'

It wasn't like a courtier to simply speak their mind in front of someone they didn't know very well, especially when the result was to say something unflattering about their future ruler. Perhaps princesses were by nature different from the average courtier—I hadn't known enough of them to be a good judge of that—but this was not the first thing about this particular princess that said there was more to her than beauty.

Silence stretched out as the maids peeled another layer of skirts from the princess, finally getting down to her underdress of fine peach silk.

'What do people call you?' I asked as the princess turned to face me.

'What do you mean?' She asked as she strained to pull a heavy ring from one finger. Behind her the maids were now working to undo her hair from its intricate braiding.

'Your friends can't possibly call you Princess Amanthea all the time. What do your friends call you?'

She looked at one of her maids, who studiously avoided her gaze. With something that was almost a frown, she looked at me again. 'Things are very proper in my father's court. Nicknames are not looked upon kindly.'

I was getting tired of thinking of her as Princess Amanthea, and my more adjective-ridden nicknames weren't sticking as well as I thought they would have.

'What would you rather be called, then?'

The princess looked down at her handful of rings, then at the maid next to her. The maid accepted the rings and put them in a jewellery chest on the table. The princess nodded to the maids one at a time and they filed out of the room a moment later to leave the two of us alone.

When the door shut behind the last of them, the princess walked over to the bed and leaned against the footboard next to me, her gaze wistful. 'If I could pick anything? Something exotic. Elizabeth, maybe. I would have loved to be a Tara.' She ducked her head, flushing pink.

Again I was surprised, but this time far more pleasantly. I laughed. 'A nickname is usually something that has to do with your normal name. Like…we could call you Thea.' I thought of Sid the Squid and laughed. 'Or Sid.'

She laughed too. 'Thea sounds terrible! I like Sid better,' she said with a shake of her head.

'Sid it is, then?' I teased. She smiled so broadly I knew there would be no going back. At least if she knew I was calling her Sid it technically wouldn't be impolite, though I wasn't about to tell her why I'd thought of the name. I sobered slightly.

'But while the court here doesn't frown on nicknames, Sid wouldn't be thought of as a very nice one. Is there something more…polite,' I said slowly, 'that would roll off the tongue better than Princess Amanthea?'

Her eyes almost sparkled. 'I like Sid. And if you can't call me Sid around other people, so be it. I don't mind. We're going to be spending a lot of time together, just the two of us, and I like the idea of having a secret name.'

'What do you mean just the two of us?'

If she was going to surprise me this much in normal conversation I was going to need something to calm my nerves.

'My maids are leaving in three days, with most of the guards. Only one maid and two of the guards will stay.' She shrugged. 'And I don't mind if Alois hears my new Clovian name. She's the closest thing I have to a friend.'

That's how the princess came to be known as Sid.

I glanced at the window and saw from the gathering darkness that I had a while longer before I needed to leave to meet Bryn. The thought of the upcoming meeting made my heart sink.

With a glance at Sid, I decided that if she was amenable we could sit here a while longer and she could hopefully distract me.

'So how do you like it here?' I asked as I sat back down on the bed, one arm wrapped around the bedpost to keep me from sinking down too far into the softness of it. 'Clovia. Gydrocc.'

'They're fine,' she said cautiously as she sat down next to me. 'I haven't seen enough of them yet to say otherwise.'

That was probably a fairly standard answer from someone who really hasn't seen much of a place. If I really wanted to get her talking I would need to start with something more basic.

'So what do you know about Gydrocc?'

'It has far too many stairs,' she said with an exhausted laugh. Her smile drooped for the first time all day. 'I'm not used to it. The palace in Marchant is much more on one level. My legs are already sore from so much climbing up and down.'

That was fair enough, and her tone made it obvious that she didn't mean to complain. I tried to offer a smile, but it died on my lips. A conversation about stairs wasn't enough to keep my mind from my task later.

Well. If it was on my mind anyway, I might as well let off a little bit of my anxiety by talking about it.

'So,' I said with an attempt at nonchalance, 'Have they told you about the dragons yet?'

'Dragons?' She straightened as if shocked. I grinned inwardly at her reaction, but her next words caught me off-guard. 'You mean they're real? The stories? The people of Gydrocc really are connected to the dragons?'

She sounded so excited I wondered exactly which stories she'd been told. Probably not the ones about people getting bitten in half or maidens getting carried off by force.

'The stories are true,' I said, and the desire to scare

her a little rose up like a wicked imp in my breast. Perhaps if I managed to scare her it would draw the fear out of me a little. 'Do you want to hear what happened the last time a dragon came to Gydrocc?'

'Absolutely,' Sid breathed, and she leaned toward me with eyes wide as a child's.

So I had an attentive audience. Good. I considered the best way to tell the story.

'So the story goes,' I started, and lowered my voice enough that Sid had to strain to hear me, 'That when Gydrocc was first inhabited by the ancestors of the throne, dragons lived in the cliffs on the other side of the lake.

'This was hundreds of years ago, when there were as many as a thousand dragons in this part of the world alone. The first king of Clovia was a knight who settled this area, and he slayed a dozen dragons with his sword in an attempt to make the land safe from the dragons who ate men like they were cattle. But his was the only arm strong enough to slay a dragon, and many of those who followed him were killed in battles against the beasts.

'As the death toll grew greater and greater on both sides, the king decided to make a deal with the dragons. He would offer them peace, and would no longer seek to drive the dragons away, as long as the dragons would not kill any more of the people who sought to stay in this area.

'The dragons did not take kindly to the offer. Why

would they? It was their territory to start with. But there was one thing they did want that the king could give them.'

'His daughter,' Sid breathed, her eyes wide.

So she had heard the story before. That wasn't surprising. There weren't many places that could boast a story like this and it had long ago passed into popular legend. I nodded.

'The dragon king, who was himself a powerful sorcerer, wanted to be able to deal in the courts of men, to use the tools of men, and to walk among men to garner their wisdom without striking fear into the hearts of everyone who saw him, and he wanted his posterity to have the same. He thought that if he could turn himself into a human, and father a child, that child could have the ability to be both a dragon and a man, to walk in both worlds without fear.

'The human king did not like the idea, and refused. So the dragons attacked. For weeks they flew over the villages, eating cattle and burning down houses, until finally the human king had no other choice. He offered his daughter to the dragon king.'

I shifted a little on the bed. The only sound in the room was that of the fire crackling and my skirts shifting. Sid was completely entranced. It was a good sign that we might get along. I had always liked this story, and thought it was fascinating, though people dismissed it as a myth. Considering that Sid was allegedly descended from a fairy queen herself, I could see why she would find it interesting.

'Years passed, and decades, and the dragon king's wishes were fulfilled. His children, and theirs, and theirs after, were able to change between human and dragon forms as easily as we might change our clothing. But it wasn't enough for there simply to be one marriage between the dragons and the humans; every couple of generations, they needed a new human to marry into their line.

'So they took them. And, for the most part, the human kings cooperated without complaint, at least for a couple of hundred years. A maiden would be chosen and sent up to the cliffs as sacrifice. Sometimes there would be a hundred years between sacrifices, sometimes as little as twenty. Eventually, though, memories dimmed, and people forgot that the dragons only stayed away from Gydrocc because some brave soul had volunteered, or been chosen, to be a sacrifice to the dragons.'

I hesitated at this point. This is where the story ceased to be a legend and became considerably more personal.

'And?' Sid said when I didn't proceed immediately.

With a sigh, I continued. 'And the last time the dragons came, the only reason they didn't destroy Gydrocc completely was that a woman scaled the tallest tower and tied herself to the roof, waving a red flag to draw the attention of the dragons. She was a cousin of the king, and remembered far better than the other members of the court that there are indeed dragons still living on this earth, and that they carry a grudge far longer than human memory can last. She knew that the only way the dragons would stop would be if someone sacrificed themselves to the dragons, as the king in his pride would not ask anyone to volunteer, nor would he even explain what the reason for the dragon's attack was.

'The woman drew up a scroll in her last hours before going up to meet her destiny, reminding those of us in the courts of Gydrocc that the dragons will come again. She reminded us that they will seek another sacrifice, and that we would do best not to forget the agreement that the first king of Clovia made with the dragons. They still hold that agreement to be valid, and they do not mind causing what they deem to be a little bit of mayhem in the human world.'

I paused to gather my thoughts again and felt a cloud of stress and worry descend. 'It's been over a hundred and twenty years since the last sacrifice to the dragons. They've never been more than two hundred years in asking for another, and more often the gap is less than a hundred years. That means that they will be back, sooner rather than later. They may come tomorrow, they may not come for twenty years, but they will come.'

Sid's jaw was hanging open. Somehow, even gaping like a complete fool, she was still beautiful. How that was possible, I didn't know. Surely it was against the laws of nature for someone to never look at least slightly awkward.

'Generally,' I added lightly, 'They take the most beautiful woman in the kingdom, given the choice. They have been known to throw less attractive candidates back.' I grinned. 'So you might want to watch yourself.'

My last words seemed to break the spell, because Sid laughed, genuinely and heartily. She leaned back on her hands. 'I think I'll be safe enough,' Sid said with a shake of her head. 'I'm not from Clovia, after all. Surely the dragons—if or when they come—want someone from Gydrocc? A descendant of the first king who made the deal with them?'

'Perhaps.' I shrugged, disappointed I hadn't managed to worry her even a little, but having told the story somehow seemed to lift a bit of the worry I had been holding onto. 'Perhaps not. I'm not sure anyone would resist your face, regardless of where it's from.'

Sid made a sour face and shook her head before offering a little smile again. 'So Gydrocc really does have a relationship with the dragons? They actually come here, and people have seen them?'

I hesitated. 'Not in a long time. Perhaps on the borders, closer to the cliffs at the northern edge of the kingdom, but not generally this far south.' I considered. 'Perhaps the dragons today have less tolerance for the waterfalls and rain in this area than their ancestors did.'

'Dragons,' Sid breathed, looking completely starry-eyed. 'I can't believe it. I mean,' she corrected, 'I can. I've seen stranger things. Or at least things as strange as a dragon.' She straightened again. 'So who would be the next sacrifice if the dragons did come? Surely someone has been chosen, or volunteered.'

'Oh,' I laughed, smiling weakly. 'The king doesn't believe that they'll come during his lifetime. And Lord Ruben, my uncle, doesn't believe they'll ever come back.' I shook my head as the princess considered, and the thought crawled across the front of my mind: *They have no idea how wrong they are.*

FIVE

I spent almost an hour chatting with Sid before I managed to leave for my own room. It might have been a more enjoyable use of my time if I hadn't been so busy thinking about the fact that I needed to sneak out of the castle, not for the first time, and get to the other side of the lake before midnight.

Admittedly, now that I had spent a bit of time with Sid, she really wasn't that bad. Once I got used to the fact that she was so stunningly beautiful, and that she spoke a little differently, she seemed to be pleasant enough company. Perhaps the coming months spending days with her wouldn't be as painful as I had imagined.

I shook the thought off as I dressed in my riding

clothes in the dark of my room. This was not the time to get distracted. I had a long ride ahead of me in which to dream of the future.

Uncle Ruben would likely have me dunked in the moat if he knew where his second-best coat disappeared to. Over the last two years, the dark blue coat had seen more than its share of night-time hikes up the falls and excursions to the forest to go hunting for unicorns—none of which my uncle, or anyone else in the castle aside from Philip, was aware of.

I slipped the thick wool coat over my tunic and fastened the front, then slipped my feet into my riding boots as I prepared mentally for this excursion.

It isn't difficult to sneak out of Gydrocc Castle, if you know the right way to do it. The only real danger of discovery comes when getting into and out of one's own tower. It's the only place in the castle where there's no chance of escape if someone comes on you unexpectedly, as there's only up and down. There's nowhere to hide on a spiral staircase.

After that the only thing to worry about are maids and soldiers on patrol in the hallways, but there are never very many in the middle of the night. Most of them hole up in front of a fire somewhere and wait to be called. A courtier coming out of their own room at night was completely unheard of, so I didn't even bother worrying about the possibility.

There was a tense moment as I descended past the princess' door; I didn't want a repeat of the morning's surprise of her following me. She managed it once, and that was more than enough. Likeable as she might be, I wasn't prepared to let anyone in on certain secrets.

When I was certain—really certain, this time—that no one had followed me, I made my way swiftly through the corridors to the door leading to the Alchemist's Tower passageway. It was the easiest way to get outside without going through one of the servants' entrances, as the alchemist's corridor was left unlocked in the event of a fire.

It took little time to find my way out to the stables and saddle Niggle, my mare. Together, she and I had a sure method of getting out the castle wall. First I would sneak in the first door of the barracks and take the key to the guard gate from the hook above Hawkins' bed. He was a notoriously heavy sleeper so there was little worry of waking him. Second, I would unlock the heavy oak and iron guard gate door and coax Niggle through, making sure to lock up after myself. I had never been late enough getting back to need to worry about the key being missed, although I realised that someday I might be.

Hawkins was, as always, snoring away in the anteroom to the barracks so it was easy to slip into the small room, grab the key, and get out without causing any disturbance.

I took Niggle's reins again and led her to the door of the guard gate. It was the only door through the main wall of the castle that wasn't guarded on both sides, this because most people thought it was sealed shut. The other factor that made it an ideal choice for a night-time escape was that the incomplete moat didn't come around this side of the castle wall so there wasn't a drawbridge of any sort to contend with.

At the door, I pushed the key into the keyhole and turned it with some difficulty. Sealed it wasn't, but enough rust had accumulated in the locking mechanism that it did produce quite a lot of scraping. After a struggle, I pushed the door open with one shoulder and pulled Niggle through. She shied a little, and I glanced at the gap between her flanks and the man-sized door.

'Apparently someone has been giving you double helpings of oats,' I whispered accusingly as I eased her out the doorway. 'Much more of that and you won't fit into your saddle, let alone through a door.'

Niggle gave me what could only be described as a withering gaze. I scratched her behind the ears with a little smile. 'Sorry,' I whispered.

Niggle stood patiently as I eased the door shut again and locked it carefully. I was sneaking out, yes, but I wasn't about to leave a hole in the castle defences. The key safely in my pocket, I mounted Niggle and we started our journey.

The chill of early spring bit at my hands and face, not bitterly cold but enough to keep me awake as I steered us to the lakeshore. Out in the freedom of the wild, Niggle and I could take off and ride as we pleased. On any other night we might have used the strong moonlight to explore the woods around the lake or perhaps looked for pixies in the trees, but tonight we had other duties to attend to.

I breathed deeply of the lake's freshness as we approached and looked up at the cliffs that rose precipitously from the other side, where six waterfalls roared endlessly year round. It was beautiful, even to the most cynical eye. Certainly even Lord Ruben had been known to tear up when listening to poetry about the Six Great Falls.

The place I was to meet Bryn was a secret clearing at one of the falls that my mother discovered when she was my age. At the time she, like I, had chafed at the constraints of court life and made it a habit to explore the land around Gydrocc with all of her spare time. That was how she discovered the clifftop meeting place.

Gydrocc Castle is at the east side of the lake, and on the west are the cliffs with The Six Great Falls. It is the second smallest of the Six Falls that conceals our secret place. That particular waterfall is the only one that is actually comprised of two falls, one directly above the other. The first waterfall tumbles off the high edge of the cliff, down nearly two thirds of the distance to the lake, where it meets a shorter outcropping of rock just large enough to make a small pond, before the water pours over a second cliff and makes its way down to the water's surface.

That shorter cliff cradles a small clearing, lush with undergrowth where the rocks give way to soil and there is enough space that a cottage could be built there without fear of the occupants tumbling off the cliff when they open the front door.

The clearing was, once, the place where my parents courted in secret, away from mother's family in the castle. For that reason it has always been special to me; I can clearly envision my parents sitting on the cliff, appreciating a distant view of the kingdom and planning their future.

A part of me always wondered if they had seen tragedy coming when they made those first promises to each other. From the stories my mother told, she and my father were very much in love. Perhaps it had made them blind to the risks they took in marrying each other.

At the foot of the cliff I steered Niggle toward a secret path that could hardly be counted a path unless it was well known. It led behind one of the waterfalls and across a small beach to a little place where I did not bother to tie Niggle but let her roam around the small grassy embankment. I didn't worry that she would wander; she was afraid of passing behind the first waterfall without me so would not leave.

With a quick stroke of her neck I left her and began to climb the cliff. It was a steep path, and at this point it could barely be called a path even if you knew it was there. I knew which rocks to climb and which to avoid so I would not be left stranded but that was it. Halfway up there appeared a more well-established path of hairpin turns that must have been maintained by the colonies of mountain goats that lived on the cliffs.

By the time I reached the meeting place after climbing the rocks and navigating nearly twenty hairpin turns, it was past midnight. I slowed as I came to the last turn before I would come in sight of the clearing and hoped my lateness would go unnoticed, or at least not be considered offensive.

Bryn's disposition was uncertain, but from what I knew of his kind, he was likely to think that my tardiness was a product of a lack of respect for him, however unintentional it might have been.

As I approached I could see scorch marks on the cliff above my head. My hand went to the small dagger I carried, though I knew there was little point in drawing it out from my belt. The burns were new, and not a promising sign. In the silence of the night the occasional crackle of a still-burning twig could be heard over the hum of insects.

This was a good time to stop and take stock of the situation. Over the top edge of the cliff there was a dragon. This particular dragon had apparently seen fit to start spewing fire for some reason. He was here to meet me, and I was late. While it seemed imprudent to go into a first meeting with a dragon with a knife in hand, it seemed suicidal to do otherwise.

In the dark I fumbled for my knife. Next came several deep breaths, in anticipation of making a quick escape back down the side of the cliffs.

Not that one can run from an angry dragon.

Not successfully, anyway.

Very carefully, and as quietly as I could, I edged up the path and took a quick peek over the edge of the cliff to the little rocky meadow. The knife shook treacherously in my hands as my head cleared the last of the rocks and the meadow came into view.

The meadow was normally lovely and green, if quite rocky, but what I could see from that quick look told me that the ground was churned up all over and several of the larger boulders had been disturbed. Their normal resting places were now patches of dark muddy earth, and previously large and bushy plants had been mown down underneath the newly displaced boulders.

In several places there were long, parallel gouges in the singed grass, some of them running along for several feet. At the edge of the cliff quite near to me, a good sized tree hung precariously from the edge, its roots newly exposed to the air, branches smoking and charred.

And in the midst of the destruction, sitting on a rock underneath a particularly burnt out section of the clearing, was a young man dressed in the scarlet robes of a magician. From a distance in the dark, he was just a man a few years older than me, unimpressive and distinctly average. This was somehow comforting, especially in light of the destruction that had been wrought on the clearing.

With great care, I inched forward along the path until I judged myself to be close enough to speak but still far enough away to run.

'Who are you?' I demanded as loudly as I could manage.

The man stood to look at me, saw the knife in my hand, and laughed.

I lifted the dagger that was little more than a letter opener in what I hoped was a menacing fashion and tried to act as if I knew what I was doing. 'Who are you?' I repeated.

He grimaced. 'Not someone you should attempt to stab,' he said seriously. 'I'm Bryn.'

'Do it properly,' I demanded. 'Wizards are known liars.'

The man visibly bristled and drew himself up in what could only be described as a pompous manner. It looked a little ridiculous coming from someone who didn't appear to be very much older than me.

'That's a good way to get yourself scorched. Dragons don't lie.'

'Then do it properly.'

I heard an exasperated huff of breath, then heard, 'Dragon's blood, dragon's tooth, by dragon's hide, naught but truth. I am Bryndessnyl, son of Chessins the Lord of the Mountains, and Lady Mysselna of the

Sea Cliffs.'

Even in the darkness, I could see him make a circular kind of movement with one hand. Once the gesture was complete, a ring of fire large enough to circle my wrist puffed into existence and gently floated forward, burning in the nothingness. The floating ring of fire was bright enough to illuminate his face briefly, but not enough that I could see his features clearly.

The fire floated towards me as it was bidden. As it neared I lowered the knife and extended my other hand toward the glowing circle. If he spoke truth, the fire would not burn, or so I had been told.

The ring of fire slid around my hand and onto my arm. It had grown slightly on the journey and did not touch my skin until it reached my elbow.

Then it burned.

SIX

I yelped, raised the knife again, and gritted my teeth as I prepared to run.

'Look at your arm,' He said calmly. My knife was apparently not enough of a threat to even look worried.

One glance was enough to tell me that while I had felt the burn, it left no mark on my skin or clothing. It had burned, yes, but it hadn't burned.

I let out a relieved breath. This was indeed Bryn, not some impostor trying to take advantage of me.

'Why can't people be just a little more specific when they talk about these things?' I muttered under my breath as I sheathed the knife, still staring at my arm, a little offended at my own ignorance. Mother had warned me about this magical ritual once, a long time ago, but she hadn't been terribly specific. The few historians that wrote anything about it hadn't been either.

When I looked up, Bryn was standing quite still at the other side of the clearing, as if waiting for me to make the next move. I looked around at the tormented grass and trees.

'Why did you tear up my meadow?' I demanded. 'I wasn't that late.'

Bryn looked around, and I could hear something that could either have been taken for pride or sheepishness. 'This place is a bit small for landing on.'

I looked around again, and my mouth made a little 'oh' shape.

The sequence of events became clear on closer inspection: a great dragon had flown in, tried to land, missed, then slid over the edge of the cliff, leaving the long gouges in the grass. He must have grabbed at and uprooted the tree I had seen as he fell. The boulders looked to have been used for traction on the way back up.

Laughter bubbled up my throat as I envisioned a large dragon scrambling like mad to get over the cliff into the clearing, eyes bulging, fire spewing out of its mouth in frustrated embarrassment.

A glare from Bryn turned my laughter into a cough. I cleared my throat, held back a giggle, and reached out a hand.

'Forgiven,' I said diplomatically.

He walked toward me, grasped the offered hand, and frowned.

Up close I could see what the darkness was hiding.

He was, well…attractive, but…

It wasn't beauty like that of Prince Caleb, whose face was like the melody of a harp wafting over a pond on a sunny day and the smell of mahogany and alfalfa. Nor was it the traditional handsomeness of his father the king, bearded, stately, and perfect as an oil painting.

Bryn's attractiveness was the kind that clubbed the viewer into submission with the nearest blunt object. He sported brutally short golden hair, a strong jaw, an icy glare, and a row of large golden studs through his left ear. The impression of being beaten into submission by his beauty was only added to by the width of his shoulders, which put me in mind of packhorses.

Or dragons.

I almost didn't notice that he gave me the same type of appraising look.

'You'll do.'

It was a dismissive kind of statement, and I flushed. I should have expected some kind of statement on my appearance, given the circumstances. Perhaps if I'd been thinking more about the fact that Bryn might approve of me rather than that he might turn me into toasted Tara, I would have put more effort into my appearance.

'I'm so pleased to meet with your approval,' I replied sarcastically. In the awkward silence that followed, I cleared my throat. 'My mother said you have something important to speak with me about.'

'Aside from finally meeting you, after all these years? Yes.' Bryn turned back to the pool and motioned for me to follow. We moved carefully across the now muddy clearing. As we approached the rock he had been sitting on when I first arrived, I could see that he had placed several items there, laid out for inspection.

Bryn sat down on the large flat rock and reached for the large piece of parchment he must have been examining when I arrived. It had become damp from the near constant spray of the waterfall not far away but Bryn seemed unconcerned.

He held the parchment up for me to see, expertly angling it to catch what little light there was from the still smouldering tree above us. Though it was a strain, I could make out the lines of a map and some of the larger written notes.

'This is a map of the land under Our sky,' Bryn said. He managed to capitalise the 'our' even in conversation, and by that he undoubtedly meant his kind. Who was to argue that dragons were the masters of the sky, especially to a dragon himself? Bryn traced the borders of what I recognised as Clovia, Doria, Marchant, and Fremont.

'It's a very nice map,' I said primly, though I couldn't see it very well. If I wasn't mistaken, the parchment was warm. Quite warm. I put my hands underneath it and immediately felt relief from the cold damp that had my fingers screaming for relief. I put a finger out to trace the borders of Clovia and felt steam rising from the surface of the map. Dragons. No wonder he wasn't worried about the map getting wet.

'Thank you. I made it from my own observations.'

'Spelling needs work.' I pointed to Gydrocc, misspelt Gidrock, one of the few words I could make out in the darkness.

Apparently this did not merit a response. Bryn drew my attention to the forest east of Clovia, on the border with Fremont.

'If you look here, these woods are experiencing some kind of human interference. There is a great deal of tree cutting, up the edge of the Gray Mountains, and they are doing something strange to the mountain. Like dwarves, digging tunnels.'

'Is that something to worry about?' I asked, puzzled at what he expected my reaction to be. Humans did, on occasion, cut down trees and dig holes. This was rarely for sinister purposes, but Bryn seemed worried at the possible reasons behind it.

Bryn paused, apparently unsure how to respond. 'Your mother was always one to investigate these things for us, and of course your father, before…' he trailed off with a significant look at me. 'My father said you would be the best person to ask, and your mother seemed to agree with him when he inquired.'

'Ah.'

There was little else I could say. Mother had something of a reputation from her years of adventuring, and I knew only half of the things she had done. While she had made attempts to educate me as to magic and logic and the defence of other creatures, I had only gone so far as occasionally freeing pixies from rabbit traps while out on my midnight jaunts. The jaunts themselves were as far as I had gone in any kind of rebellion like that of my mother. This meeting aside, of course.

Apparently mother wanted me to follow in her footsteps. The thought came like a somewhat unwelcome bolt of lightning through my veins that set my heart throbbing, as I could clearly recall the details of the stories she told me of her own adventures. Most of them ended with her barely escaping with her life.

'I don't mind helping,' I said honestly, and took a deep breath in preparation for my disclaimer. 'But I'm not my mother. I don't have any skills to speak of other than a decent bit of horsemanship. I can barely defend myself, even with the help of charms and enchantments. Even those I have to borrow from other people as I can't do them myself. I'm a lady of the court, not a lady of the wood.'

The words tumbled out of me in a rush and hung in the air like biting bugs. A feeling of being very small and unworthy crawled up my spine like a spider. It had perhaps been a bad idea to meet Bryn at all. He was obviously expecting someone more like mother, and that I was not.

Bryn frowned at me across the parchment. Again it took him time to decide on a response.

'Your mother said you would be able to help, and we trust her.' He paused. 'More than we trust most humans, anyway. If she says you can help us, I believe her word.'

There were another few moments of silence. What difficult situations had I ever faced to make me worthy of that trust? Mother's faith in me was kind, I thought, but unrealistic.

To distract myself from these pessimistic thoughts, I looked to the space between us on the rocks. All I could see was the occasional glint of fine cloth laid out to cover several items as the fires above us in the trees died down to nothing. 'What's under here?' I asked, leaning down to get a better look.

Bryn headed me off by handing me a rock he produced out of a pocket. 'First I want to know what this is.'

'I didn't think a dragon would be unfamiliar with granite,' I teased as he placed it in my hand. Immediately I rethought that as the weight of the stone fell into my hand—this was not just a normal rock from the cliffs here, judging by its heft. It weighed considerably more than it would have if it was granite, given its size. My brow furrowed as I brushed dirt from the surface and held it up to the light of the moon, now the only source of illumination that remained.

After some inspection, I gave my verdict. 'Iron ore.' I looked at the map and put together what he had told me about the cutting of the trees on the Clovian border. 'Is this what they're digging out of the mountain?'

'Yes. What is iron ore?'

Only a dragon could manage to remain completely ignorant of iron ore in the days of plate armour and steel swords. It was only reasonable, I supposed. The only exposure dragons had to iron ore was in the finished form of weapons and armour. Perhaps they thought we magicked those things into existence.

I hefted the stone again. 'Humans melt it down to make weapons and armour,' I said.

Bryn made a little 'Ah' sound.

Well, if I was going to help there was at least one other thing I could offer. 'Do you mind if I take it? The court alchemist will know more than I do. He can say if there's something unusual about it, anything more than the fact that it could one day be part of a sword.'

Bryn nodded and watched thoughtfully as I pocketed the rock. When he spoke, his voice was quiet. 'The place that rock has come from is…not somewhere that the dragons go. I do not know why, but it is treated as a cursed place.' His voice betrayed confusion. 'Why the humans would want to go there to take this iron ore, rather than someplace safer, is a mystery.'

'What kind of curse is it?' My curiosity was piqued. 'I've not heard of such a thing as a cursed mountain.'

He shook his head. 'I don't know. Only that we don't go there. We do not speak of it. When I asked my father he would not—or could not—tell why.' Then, rather unexpectedly, he grinned. 'I think he means to test me by giving me this assignment.'

Then, as if suddenly remembering something, he picked up a branch from between his feet and held it up close to his face. With one swift movement he cupped one hand around the end. He watched me with a little grin and blew on the end of the stick. In a moment, the stick burst into flame.

At my gasp, Bryn laughed, his skin glowing as golden as his hair, as if his whole body were cast in bronze.

I scowled and made an annoyed gesture. 'Why couldn't you have done that when we were looking at the map?'

Bryn only smiled. 'I have something for you,' he said, and moved the flaming stick over the rock between us. With his other hand, he took hold of the cloth I had noted earlier and pulled it away to reveal Treasure.

SEVEN

I f ever my eyes had been dazzled, they were now. Even in the moonlight, the spread of jewels lying on the rock were a match for Sid's beauty. They were an obvious testament to the riches of the dragons. My mind went blank as I viewed what would have been, to humans, an absolute fortune in gems and jewels.

The moment I could think, I put a hand to my throat as if to help me remember to breathe and leaned forward to look more closely at what Bryn had brought with him.

There were seven pieces of jewellery, all gloriously wrought in silver or gold or both, each sporting different decorations, some of them jewelled, others plain precious metal.

My hand reached out to touch them, more by reflex than by conscious thought, but Bryn caught my wrist several inches from the jewellery.

'These are not ordinary jewels, and not something to be taken lightly,' He warned.

Still holding my wrist, Bryn leaned closer to me. I looked at him, and could see that he was concentrating, as if what he was about to say was of great importance and he didn't want to mess it up.

'As this our first meeting, I have brought you a gift of binding in honour of the agreement that was made over us three years ago when your mother sent us a lock of your hair and my father sent your mother one of mine. The agreement has always been binding, but this gift tonight is one that is made in our own names, not the names of our parents, and will make fuller the contract that was drawn between our families.'

Bryn's eyes seemed to glow red in the darkness, brighter than the bits of flame around us and far more strongly than the moon above. I felt my face redden as he lifted our hands up close to my face. I could feel heat flowing from him like a fire, and his eyes watched me with an intensity that seemed like magic. They drew me in, until all I could see were his eyes burning an angry scarlet ringed with gold.

'By choosing to take one of these gifts you choose to accept this contract, of your own free will, and by my acknowledgement of the gift you choose, I accept this contract of my own free will. If I do not acknowledge your choice of gift as being consistent with the one I have chosen for you, you may keep it and be freed of all obligations heretofore entered into.'

His grip on my wrist tightened, and the place where our skin touched became hotter and hotter until it began to burn, but Bryn's grip was unshakeable. Just as the heat became unbearable, he released me, and both of us leaned back quite suddenly. I rubbed my wrist, gasping, as my mind caught hold of what Bryn had just done.

It was an enchantment. I recognised the form. Different from a regular spell, an enchantment affected the soul, not the body, and was normally very dangerous magic to be dabbling in.

This particular enchantment was one of binding, not altogether dissimilar to the one that had accompanied the original agreement between our parents. This one, however, was stronger and far more personal than what had been performed fifteen years ago when we were children. In fact, the only time I had ever heard of this enchantment was in legends and stories.

'So this is genuine Dragon's Treasure, then?' I asked as I looked at the jewellery between us. The wrist he had been holding felt strange. My skin was unhurt, but I could still feel the warmth of his grip radiating up my arm. Again, this was a spell that burned, but did not burn.

Bryn only smiled at my question. It was not a particularly friendly smile. It was more predatory than anything else and for the first time I could truly see that this was indeed a dragon I was dealing with. I offered a weak smile in return, and attempted to focus my attention on the objects before me. I should have realised that this was coming; mother had warned me, after all, that I would be required to accept or reject the contract on my own at some point.

Somehow it hadn't ever occurred to me in advance to consider whether or not I would *want* to accept the contract. Even now, it seemed like it would simply be wrong to reject something that had been arranged for so long, not least because it would lead to political complications that could be potentially deadly for more than just myself. It could put Clovia at risk, as it would mean another generation of violence between the dragons and men.

I had no practical reasons to turn down the agreement, in that I had no other suitors, and would never get a better offer. True, Lord Ruben would disown me the moment he discovered the pact, but I somehow doubted I would live long enough to see any inheritance from him anyway. I knew full well that his distrust of my mother extended to me as well.

I looked at the treasure in front of me. Dragon's Treasure, as it is known, is like a complicated game of choices. It was always 'played', as it were, between a Dragon and a Subject. The items placed before the Subject all had a different nature and meaning, and the object chosen was meant to represent the Subject; the

Dragons claimed that fate and destiny would not allow the Subject to be steered toward choosing any object that was not truly representative of them.

The point was that one of the objects had already been marked by the Dragon, and if that was the object Chosen, the contract or agreement, whatever its nature, would be binding between the two parties. It was the Dragons' favourite way of making sure a deal was not only destiny, but that it would be respected by both parties. It was powerful magic, and not something that could easily be tampered with or broken after the fact.

In front of me was a selection of jewellery, all of it beautiful, all of it very probably priceless judging from the workmanship, though the raw values must have varied considerably. Least expensive was undoubtedly the plain silver filigree armband that was nonetheless highly beautiful, and would be a credit to any woman who wore it. At the other end of the spectrum was a necklace, so short as to almost be snug around the neck, encrusted with enormous oval diamonds and so expensive that I could not imagine Queen Isabelle herself wearing it for anything other than her own coronation.

Neither of those items drew my attention for long. Others caught my eye. One was a pair of emerald stud earrings, the emeralds the size of my smallest fingernail, and so perfectly cut that they would certainly throw glimmers around the room anytime they were in the light. The other was a bracelet made of thick gold links, with a single ruby gleaming like an eye in the middle of one of the links.

Surely the point was to take the one that I was immediately drawn to? If one of these items was supposed to represent me surely I was meant to choose the one that I could most easily see myself wearing.

I looked at Bryn and wondered what he was thinking. He gave no indication that he wanted me to choose any one of them. Those eyes, still startlingly glowing, stared right back at me with no regard for the treasures between us.

So much for hints. Bryn's face was impossible to read. Did he even want me to make a choice? Would he be relieved if I chose wrongly? I looked down to examine the selection of jewellery again. My eyes fell again to the earrings and ruby bracelet.

The enchantment was designed to be foolproof, a sign of fate. Surely, then, it didn't matter what I chose? Whatever I was fated to pick up, I would pick up, regardless of how long or how deeply I thought about it. This was somehow both comforting and terrifying.

With my heart beating so loudly I was certain Bryn could hear it, I decided to let fate decide. My hand reached out again, and with only a spare glance down, I let it drop.

It was with some surprise that I found myself fingering a very fine chain. I looked down, confused. My thoughts had been on the ruby bracelet, perhaps because it so seemed to match Bryn's appearances. The ruby was a mirror for the hypnotic enchantment in Bryn's gaze; certainly that item represented him, and by choosing it I would be acknowledging that I would accept the contract.

Instead I found myself lifting a long, fine chain of indeterminate colour, at the end of which hung a pearl the size of a quail's egg wrapped in fine swirling fingers of the same unattractive metal that made the chain.

I glanced at Bryn again, to find that his gaze had shifted to the pearl. He didn't look overly pleased, but neither did he look disappointed.

'Not the one you chose?' I asked, and I could have kicked myself for sounding hopeful. Bryn didn't seem overeager to relieve my worries.

'It isn't the piece I placed in for consideration,' Bryn acknowledged. He pointed to the ruby bracelet. 'I have always been fond of red.'

'So I figured.' I continued to stare at the pearl. 'Who chose this?'

'My aunt,' Bryn said. He could not seem to take his eyes away from the swinging pearl. 'She is fond of pearls. She believes that the only human that can survive a dragon is one who is as cool and fresh as water. Hence, the gem of the sea.'

'She makes an interesting point.' I eyed the pearl, unable to put it down. There was something attractive about it in spite of the look of tarnish on the metal. The milky surface glowed gold in the firelight. Some part of me wondered if I would get to keep it even now that the contract was broken.

Bryn wasn't finished. 'I did not place the pearl in the selection,' He said slowly, 'but when the jewels were placed in front of me, I selected the pearl as well.'

The pearl hung between us, swinging in small pendulous movements, first toward me, then Bryn, then back again.

My mind was blank again, and all I could do was look from Bryn to the pearl and back.

'So does the contract still stand?' My voice was shaky, and I swallowed a little compulsively. Did I really want to hear the answer?

Bryn reached out solemnly and clasped my hand that held the chain. His hand still emanated that inhuman warmth. 'I acknowledge your choice of gift and declare this contract valid and binding until the day that it is fulfilled, by our marriage or by our death.'

His grip went icy cold, and a chill ran through me for an instant as the enchantment sealed itself. At that same moment a gust of wind blew out the now dim flame of the torch in Bryn's other hand. In the darkness I couldn't see him shaking, but I could feel it in his hand. He released me almost immediately and began to wrap up the other treasure.

Now that the enchantment was finished, there seemed to be an emptiness to the evening. The contract was sealed, and we still knew nothing about each other.

I licked my dry lips and watched as Bryn picked up the other jewels. 'Who chose them all?' I asked, watching as the last little glimmers disappeared into the folds of the fabric.

'My father chose the diamonds,' Bryn said wryly, sounding as uncomfortable as I felt. 'A true Dragon, him. Your mother, the sapphire ring, and the silver cuff in honour of your father. My mother, the emerald earrings. The amethyst ring was chosen by the seer who approved the match.'

The pearl still hung from my outstretched hand, unwelcome but somehow terribly satisfying to hold, until Bryn said, 'Put it on, then.'

My hands trembled as I lifted the necklace over my head. The pearl settled heavily against my chest, the chain long enough that it could easily be hidden beneath the neckline of any of my dresses. There was something odd about the way it sat, though, almost as if it was heavier than it should be—or else magnetized to my chest. I lifted it in my hand again and could feel its strange heaviness.

'The enchantment is fairly simple,' Bryn explained without looking at me as he bundled up the rest of his things. His tone was business-like and his movements quick, as if he wanted to be done with this as soon as possible. 'It will give you basic protection, and also serve as a warning to me if ever you are in danger. Do not remove it,' He said firmly, and turned to face me again. I could see his eyes glowing in the darkness.

'Once it is removed the protection and the warnings are gone, so I will have no idea if something has happened to you. I am now ultimately responsible for your safety so please keep it on.'

'Lovely,' I said, looking down at it. 'Can I take it off at night?'

Bryn shook his head. 'Night is the time of assassins and thieves. If you remove it during the hours of darkness I will be at your side as swiftly as I can.'

What could he possibly be worried about? The only real danger to be faced in Gydrocc anytime soon was that of embarrassment in front of the court. Perhaps being a dragon bride was more dangerous than I thought, though I didn't know how it could be, as it was going to be a secret from almost everyone. Or, maybe it was protection for the journey ahead, for whatever help he wanted me to provide in the forest.

Another thought occurred to me as I looked down at the pearl. There were very likely to be times I would need to take it off for at least a few minutes, namely while bathing or getting dressed. That would be an embarrassment—a dragon showing up at Gydrocc because I had spent too long in a warm bath before bed.

'How about you let me take it off for half an hour at a time without overreacting?'

Bryn considered this. 'I will not come if you replace it within that time, but I will begin to worry the longer it is away from your person.'

'Fine. I can handle that.'

'Good.' Bryn looked up at the stars for a few moments to gauge the time. 'Wait here for a moment. We're going to go see the forest I showed you on the map.'

I looked up, the pearl momentarily forgotten. It slipped between my fingers and dropped down to the end of the chain, where it settled unnaturally quickly, without a single swing.

Surprised, I looked at the pearl, then at Bryn. My thoughts untangled themselves and I pushed the strange pearl to the back for the moment.

'What do you mean?' I demanded, thinking of the map. 'That forest is hours away at a full gallop.' I motioned to the sky. There were not many hours of darkness left before dawn, certainly not enough time to get to the forest and back.

'It is, if you are on foot,' Bryn agreed. 'But I think you need to see what is happening yourself. There may be details I overlooked.'

He moved toward the trees and disappeared into the darkness without another word.

'But…' Words failed me. What could I really do? Say no to a determined dragon? I glanced again at the sky, hoping that this would not take as long as I feared.

Waiting in the cold, misty air, I could only wonder what he was doing hidden in the trees. First I could hear the occasional cracking of a twig, then as moments passed a deep rumble and a loud slithering noise.

It occurred to me what had happened just in time to keep myself from jumping in shock when Bryn returned. He came coiling out like a great metallic snake in his natural form. Scales gleamed gold even in the dim light, and his eyes like red hot coals glowed bright enough to read by. Four narrow, muscular legs propelled him along the ground while great leathery wings rustled impatiently against his back.

He was as long as three houses butted up against each other with a head the size of a cow. It was immediately obvious why he had churned up the ground so much in making his landing; he was almost as long as the clearing, so must have nearly run into the cliff upon entry.

This is who I had just agreed to marry.

Maybe we could negotiate a long engagement.

'You look better as a dragon,' I blustered with fake confidence as Bryn moved toward me, not quite a slither but not quite a walk either. On that long serpentine body, legs almost seemed a hindrance. As his body swung back and forth his legs bounced backward and forward, giving the impression that for every step forward his body was fighting against the movement, wanting to go back.

It was definitely less than graceful, but dragons are not meant to be graceful when they walk. They are creatures of earth and sky, where they find their greatest swiftness underground in tunnels and their greatest agility in the air above.

Bryn shook his massive head briefly and shrugged his shoulders, which drew attention to the pack laced around the base of his neck. It didn't take any stretch of the imagination to understand what he meant. The only way we were going to get to our destination quickly enough was to fly, and that meant I needed a place to sit and hold on.

I moved toward him gingerly. The thought crossed my mind that I wasn't any good at riding an unsaddle horse, let alone an unsaddled dragon. The thought scurried away like a mouse, terrified by the impatient snort from the direction of Bryn's head. With a grimace, I hauled myself onto his shoulders gracelessly.

Bryn's scales were thankfully smooth instead of the razor-sharp things of legend. I found a not too uncomfortable seat in front of the joints of his wings, my legs hanging down in front of his front legs.

Bryn. This was Bryn, the frighteningly handsome golden-haired man I had been talking to for the last half hour. I stared at the scaly neck for several moments, uncomprehending. It was only a second shake of those shoulders as he waited for me to take hold of something that brought me back to reality.

I took hold of each side of the pack, which gave me a decent grip, and tightened my knees around Bryn's neck. Then I prayed.

It went something like, Please don't let me die from terror. Or lose my grip, which would amount to the same thing. Or let Bryn do anything stupid that will make me fall off. I stopped there because the more I thought about it the more I realised that the possibilities for disaster were pretty much endless.

Without any further excuse to hold us up, I looked forward at Bryn, who was watching me with one great coal-eye.

I swallowed a sudden lump in my throat and nodded.

He nodded back, and turned to the edge of the cliff.

And then, in one stomach wrenching moment, he dived off it, taking me with him.

EIGHT

There are writers in Gydrocc who tell stories of the exhilaration of flight. They speak of excitement, of pounding hearts, of the view from high up in the clouds. They make liberal use of words like 'silken', 'majesty', 'gloriousness', and other things that I might use to describe a particularly delicious pudding.

It took me exactly half an instant after we plunged off that cliff to decide that the so-called 'exhilaration' of flight is primarily composed of the terror of falling.

For several long moments that seemed like an eternity, we fell, the dragon and his fool of a human rider.

Wind whipped at every part of me that wasn't firmly tied down. The leather band in my hair was brutally torn out after half a second, along with what felt like a significant portion of my hair. It didn't matter. We fell so swiftly there was no chance of my hair getting to my face.

My uncle's heavy coat whipped painfully at my skin and my eyes filled with tears so quickly that I could not even see the surface of the lake rushing up to meet us. The only thing that seemed unaffected by the fall was the pearl, which continued to weigh as heavily on my chest now as it had on the ground.

Then, in an even shorter instant, vast wings spread out with a snap on either side of us and caught the wind so sharply that my stomach plunged down to my feet. The laces on my boots seemed to strain as if not tied tightly enough. The deceleration was so sudden and forceful I was flung forward onto Bryn's neck with a resounding slap.

Dragon scales aren't soft, especially when one's face makes contact with them at high speed. I would have reached up to rub what would certainly be a massive bruise come morning, but I didn't want to remove a single finger from the harness. If I let go for even an instant, my very active fear glands told me, it would spell my immediate death.

In my imagination, I let go with one hand long enough to rub my chin, just at the moment Bryn decided to swerve off to one side. My imaginary feeble grip with a single hand proved insufficient; and so my imagined self fell to a swift death, bones crushed to a pulp on impact with the ground that we now flew over.

Morbid thoughts like that were hardly something I wanted to accompany me for the entire journey, so I did my best to pretend this was all something I could observe from a safe distance. Face stinging with the impact and the cold, I looked up at the sky, across to the low clouds, and occasionally down to the ground, though that never proved reassuring.

I don't know how far we flew, as the moon did not give enough light that I could distinguish the trees on the ground very well, but I do know that I became cold very quickly and wished for either a fire or about three more coats. Bryn's flesh had seemed very warm when he was in human form in those moments he had touched my wrist, but as a dragon all of his body heat was contained beneath those smooth scales.

Distractions were few on the flight. I mostly stared at the moon and tried to think about breakfast in the morning. When that became too nauseating, I tried to pretend I was riding Niggle across a grassy field.

The illusion was shaky, especially as the wingbeats of a dragon are nothing like the quick up and down of a horse, but the mental image was enough to keep me from sobbing in terror.

After what seemed an eternity of white-knuckled flying, Bryn finally glided down to treetop level, and I could feel the wind become gentler against my face. He slowed so much after a while we seemed to be hovering in place, and I opened my eyes to Bryn's head swivel gently at the end of the long neck as he looked for a place to land in the thick forest below us.

This close to the ground I could watch with fascination as one of Bryn's forelegs reached out to grab a treetop. The great claw closed around the thin trunk of the tree, and then I felt his wings close behind me. There was no time to brace myself as we fell, but my still-tight grip on the pack around his neck was enough that I wasn't jerked free. The fall was not long, but was enough to coax a scream out of me, as Bryn's grip on the tree was tested and we swung inward.

In none of the storybooks are dragons said to be tree climbers, but they are well designed for it. Bryn grabbed the tree with another leg and scrambled down so quickly the tree never had time to bend to its fullest. If the tree could so easily handle the weight of a grown dragon clambering down its trunk it was either a very strong tree or dragons were far more lightweight than I ever thought.

Bryn's legs came into contact with the ground quite heavily, though this time I managed not to hit my face on his neck. My fingers still wrapped around the straps of Bryn's pack in spite of safe ground underneath us, I took quick stock of my body parts.

Every bit of exposed skin was ice cold, and my fingers seemed to be completely stuck gripping the pack. Now that we weren't moving, all of my limbs felt leaden. It was almost like the feeling of stepping onto land from a boat after a long voyage.

Bryn planted his feet more solidly and shrugged to motion me off. I grimaced as I straightened my sore, half-frozen fingers. There was little to do but get off as gracefully as possible. I hiked one leg over Bryn's neck and slid down his side. Once my boots hit the ground Bryn brought his head around to face me.

He hesitated.

With a confused blink, I looked down at myself and wondered what was wrong. As I lowered my head to look, the muscles in my face throbbed, and torn skin began to sting. That was when I remembered the impact with Bryn's neck.

I reached up to touch the cold skin and immediately regretted it. The freezing air had numbed the pain of impact, but the right-hand side of my face felt like one massive bruise. I grimaced and regretted it immediately as it made my face feel even more like a macerated pulp.

With an accusing stare at Bryn, I said, 'Just show me what you brought me here for.'

Bryn continued to look at me with those massive red eyes for several moments, just long enough that I wondered what he was thinking before he turned and slithered away through the forest.

I followed and tried not to think about how much my face hurt.

It was easy enough to follow Bryn as he was the only brightly coloured object in the whole forest.

Anything with any desire to track him wouldn't have needed to resort to looking for tracks or broken twigs. He almost glowed, even in the dim light that filtered through the trees. His bright golden scales somehow magnified moonlight into a warm golden glow like a fire.

It might have been unnerving to know that we were so easily followed, but there are advantages to keeping company with a dragon. The contract Bryn and I had just formed was enough to reassure me that he would protect me in the event of any hostilities from man or beast.

All the same, as we walked through the dark trees I could feel myself become uneasy. It was as though our progress was being observed by someone—or something—in the trees. Even the trees around us almost seemed to have a presence and personality all their own.

Bryn knew where he was going, and stopped walking after less than fifteen minutes. He twitched a wing at me, and I slowed my pace. It took me a few moments to catch up with him, occasionally casting glances around at the trees. Bryn didn't seem worried about the forest, but trees unnerved me. I shuddered a little and edged closer to Bryn, who stood still in the undergrowth.

When I looked forward, I could see that we stood not far from the beginning of the Gray Mountains themselves. We were at the top of a rise with a view across a little valley. The trees thinned and stopped not far in front of us, before the ground dipped down and rose again to form a sudden, steep rise that formed the first foothill of the Gray Mountains. They were, I knew, some of the highest summits in this part of the world, and unique in the way they thrust their way almost vertically out of the ground in what was otherwise a fairly flat landscape. They were a popular subject for artists due to their unique shape. At least one painting of them hung in Gydrocc Castle.

Small fires lit up the side of the mountain, the well-tended fires of human encampments. The light they cast on the mountainside was sufficient to see that the ground had been stripped completely of trees in a large swathe up the embankment.

The woody casualties stood in a heap at the bottom of the valley, no small number of them carved into heaps of firewood. They had been replaced by the occasional dark hole leading down into the side of the mountain.

Strangely, armed sentries stood at intervals along the mountainside, next to the fires, watching the treeline with a vigilance that seemed unnecessary for such a secluded area. Some even faced the tunnels, never wavering or looking elsewhere, and yet more were standing guard over carts full of rocks, all covered in what looked like thick tarps.

I thought of the chunk of ore in my pocket. 'Mining tunnels,' I said, uncertain what to think of what lay before me. 'And lots of them. You say this is recent?'

The dragon nodded. I studied the scene, and mentally marked out the size of what they had cleared. 'Say we return at half moon,' I said, thinking forward nine days' time. 'We'll see how much progress they've made and I'll try to find out in the meantime if anyone knows what's happening. It is strange that they've started mining so suddenly, especially if it's cursed.'

Bryn looked at me for a long moment, but I didn't know what he meant by it. Finally, I said, 'Shall we go, then?' And he slithered off in the direction from whence we came.

NINE

It was, much to my surprise, nearly dawn when I arrived back at the castle. Niggle was tired, but not overly exhausted by our night-time jaunt, though the same could not have been said for me. After the adrenaline-pumping nightmare of flight, my body felt the exhaustion of several days all piled into one and I nearly fell asleep on the earthbound part of the ride back to Gydrocc.

I pulled Niggle to a halt at the edge of the forest, before we entered the cleared area that separated the lake from the castle. Standing atop the tower was a sentry, fully visible from where I stood. It took several moments to determine that he wasn't looking towards the trees. In fact, based on the way he was slumped against the wall, I would guess he was asleep. If Hawkins saw that, there would be a whipping, but Hawkins himself probably wasn't awake yet. In the pre-dawn twilight, few were conscious enough to comment on other people's sleeping habits.

Semi-conscious as the guard was, I could probably make it back to the door without alerting him to my presence, provided we moved slowly and quietly. With a glance at Niggle, I nudged her forward at a walk.

Compared with riding a dragon to the border of the next kingdom, riding a horse across a completely unguarded field was hardly daring, but my heart pumped wildly anyway. There was only so much more time left before I would be missed. I was not supposed to be out of the castle grounds at night, especially alone, and my sudden appearance outside the main castle would set alarm bells ringing, and that was without the unmistakable smell of brimstone that surrounded me.

It took spare minutes to cross the field, but I watched the sentry the whole time. About halfway across, he moved, but only far enough to push his helmet back and scratch his head. I breathed a sigh of relief as we moved beneath the shadow of the wall to the heavy wooden door.

The keys were, now that I checked, still looped through my belt and not lost somewhere over the forest. Luck was kind to me today. I unlocked the door with as little noise as I could manage and led Niggle back through, locking up behind me.

In the courtyard there were few people awake, and those few were not looking in the direction of the stables as I led Niggle back along the wall. I paused only long enough to slide the keys deftly back onto their hook just inside the barracks. Hawkins let out a huge snore as I withdrew to the door. I giggled and stuffed my fist into my mouth; exhaustion tended to make me giddy.

Once Niggle was unsaddled and happily drinking in the stables, I turned wearily to the kitchens.

One of the castle wells was located right next to the kitchen, with an assortment of buckets. I could hardly explain to anyone the reason I needed a bath drawn up so desperately, and so early in the morning, so would have to make do with a bucket and rag. I smelled of sweat and dirt, and undoubtedly looked a fright.

With a bucket of icy cold water in one hand, I trudged back to the castle, making good use of the least trafficked hallways. It was a stroke of good luck that the castle seemed well and truly abandoned at this hour. I made it up to my room unnoticed just as the first rays of morning light came flooding across the plains.

I made quick work of stripping off my clothing and boots, all quite filthy after the mud in the clearing and the detritus in the forest. Even swifter was my sponge bath. The water was freezing, and woke me up more easily than anything but a full night's sleep could have. By the end of it, I almost felt invigorated. Almost.

Dressed again, with the pearl in place around my neck under my dress where it wouldn't be noticed, I left my own room with a wistful look at the bed. I wanted nothing more than to lay down and go to sleep; the world seemed unfocused, like I was viewing everything through a goblet of water, but there was no chance for me to sleep now. If the princess had been up early enough to follow me yesterday it stood to reason that she would be up early enough to dress for breakfast today.

My knock at her door was answered by one of the maids, who looked as tired as I felt. She didn't even look at me, too busy yawning behind her hand. Apparently it wasn't everyone's habit to be awake this early. But, as I suspected, the princess was up, seated in front of the mirror having her hair done.

'Ah, Tara. Good morning!' She said, turning around in her chair. The moment she saw my face, she gasped, one dainty hand going up to cover her mouth. 'What happened?' She demanded, horrified.

'What do you mean?' I demanded, a little affronted. Then I saw that hers was not the only gaping face. I caught a glimpse of myself in her mirror for the first time this morning and remembered what had happened hours ago.

I could see from my reflection that half of my face was swollen, parts of it a deep, angry red. The bruise I had felt growing all night was now a solid field of purple around my eye and all across one cheek. It looked rather as if I'd been punched in the face by someone with a very large fist.

'Oh.'

The princess watched me, waiting for an explanation, and I could feel the gaze of her maids as well. 'I must have fallen from the bed in the night,' I offered. 'I sleepwalk sometimes.'

Half-truths are usually more successful than lies, but this was not a situation where I had a decent half-truth to tell. I had never sleepwalked before in my life. If I had told this to anyone else in the castle, they would have raised an eyebrow and immediately started a new bit of gossip.

Sid only turned back to the mirror, her eyes still on me in the reflection. There was something strange about her expression. Confusion and…what? Admiration?

My guess was that she was simply surprised I could be so nonchalant about something so visibly unattractive across my face. I wasn't worried; my appearance was not as lofty a thing as that of a fairy descended princess. I wouldn't mourn a couple of weeks not looking my best. After all, it had happened before with normal things like facial spots, something the princess looked as if she had never suffered from.

This is what I told myself, anyway. She wasn't going to be the only one giving me suspicious looks today.

'Let me know when you're ready for breakfast,' I said as I stepped away from the mirror and her gaze.

'We can go. I'm finished.'

Breakfast was uneventful, more so than usual because Prince Caleb was not there to talk to. I looked around for him for a few minutes, but could not see him. Some friendly conversation would have been a welcome distraction from my own exhaustion and the princess' indomitable cheeriness.

There was nothing for it. It was all I could do to stay awake until the princess and her maids were finished eating. I cleared my throat once Sid stood to leave and motioned her aside.

'I need to go visit a friend this morning. You are not obliged to come but I need to speak with him for a time. Would you like me to show you to the library, or perhaps the gardens, while I speak with him?'

Sid clapped her hands together, excited. 'Oh, no, I'd like to meet your friend! Is this the same friend that you went to see yesterday?'

I winced. My head had begun to throb with headache during breakfast, and interacting with someone so vibrant was not helping.

'I'm afraid he's the court alchemist, and he doesn't welcome strangers into his realm. Not five of them at once, anyway. He fears his experiments would get disturbed.'

'Oh, my maids don't need to come.' Sid turned and shooed the other girls away. 'They can entertain themselves with the other ladies. I want to meet your friend.'

There is, unfortunately, little a lady in waiting can do to dissuade a determined princess from whatever course of action she might put her mind to. It would be rude to say she couldn't come, and there were no other options or excuses I could offer.

I wondered how on earth I would be able to tell Philip what had happened last night with the princess in the room, curious and asking uncomfortable questions.

But, with no other options ready at hand, I had no choice but to take her along.

We walked the route she had already seen yesterday morning. When we came to the 'yellow tapestry', a scene of sunrise over the Great Battle of Recovery or the Driving out of Doriann, she laughed and pointed it out.

'This is where I lost you yesterday.'

She sounded absolutely delighted at her failure to continue following me. Every time she spoke to me she seemed more and more of an enigma. She wasn't simply cheerful and open with a mind like a leaking sieve, as I had long thought. The more I was around her the more I thought that her excessive cheeriness was a cover for someone considerably more complex.

We walked down the covered pathway to Philip's tower at a sedate pace. At the foot of the tower, I knocked loudly.

'Funny to think you were so close to arriving at your friend's,' Sid said calmly once it was obvious we had arrived at our destination. Something about her voice got my attention, and I looked at her sharply. She was still smiling, looking around, apparently completely unconcerned.

I got the feeling if she had wanted to, she could have followed me anywhere without my noticing, and had perhaps stopped yesterday simply because she didn't want to learn too much too quickly.

Philip's boy, Rue, answered the door at the bottom of the tower and waved me in without hesitation. What did make him stop for a moment was the angelic vision of Princess Amanthea standing beside me. It was obvious from the look on his young face that he thought he was seeing a vision instead of reality.

Sid smiled at the boy, who began to turn red, and followed me through Philip's living quarters. Rue watched her pass with a slack-jawed regard, frozen on the spot.

'Ah, Tara,' Philip said, looking up from his book as I came in. He was seated in a comfortable chair in front of the fire, wrapped in a warm dressing gown with a woolly hat pulled low over his ears for warmth. His breakfast was cooking over the fire. 'You look terrible. What happened?'

I shook my head minutely and stepped aside to reveal Sid. The cheery look on his face dimmed when he saw the princess. His eyes narrowed and he added, 'You've brought a friend.'

'You can call me Sid,' the princess said, walking up

to Philip and extending a hand. 'That's what my friends call me.'

Her innocence, whether feigned or not, combined with my exhausted giddiness, made me giggle. With a glance at me, Philip took her hand cautiously and waved for her to sit.

'I am pleased to officially meet you, Sid. It's a very nice name, but not your usual one. I didn't know that the people of Marchant took on nicknames.'

'We don't, usually.' Sid smiled very pleasantly and wafted gracefully into the chair that I usually occupied when I came to visit. It was the only comfortable chair in the room aside from the one Philip was sitting in himself. She sat with her back ramrod straight, completely negating the purpose of a comfortable chair. I rolled my eyes and brought up the nearest wooden stool.

'Tara and I watched your arrival. It was very grand.' Philip gave me a sympathetic look as I settled myself a little sorely onto the short wooden stool. I had spent half the night on either a horse or a dragon and my sore legs were now reminding me of this fact. If I sat down for too long there was every chance I wouldn't be able to stand up again.

Something in Sid's countenance dimmed slightly, but she recovered with another blazing smile. 'My family likes to do things in a grand way.'

Philip noticed the hesitation as well and changed the subject. He turned to me to examine the bruises on my face. 'Was all well last night?'

Sid looked at me with an unreadable expression. I tried a reassuring smile, but by the time the sore muscles in my face processed the expression it probably looked like more of a grimace.

'Aside from a bit of bruising, it was alright, I suppose.'

I glanced at Sid. Philip recognised the evasion immediately with a raised eyebrow but seemed to know what it was about. At this point, though, I needed to get a few things across to Philip that were a little more sensitive. I would just have to be as discreet as possible and hope that Sid wouldn't follow the conversation.

I looked down at my hands as I considered my words carefully. 'Mother didn't tell me all of what to expect from the full moon. Some things were a surprise.'

Intrigued, Philip placed his book face down in his lap. 'Ah. I see.'

Sid looked from me to Philip, obviously confused. 'What were you expecting from the full moon?'

'The full moon has particular alchemical significance. Tara was experimenting.' Philip seemed unfazed by the question and the diversion rolled off his tongue easily. He turned his attentions back to me. 'Anything in particular?'

The memories were a hazy flood in my exhaustion. The only things I could think of were the sweet, smoky smell that hung around Bryn as he held my wrist to seal the contract, a newly discovered terror of flying, and the fact that I hadn't gotten any sleep.

'I wasn't expecting the bruises.'

Philip smiled grimly. He knew more than anyone else in the castle about my predicament, so was well aware that I had met with a dragon. The details were relatively insignificant, given that I returned alive. If things had gone badly, the castle would simply have been one young lady short this morning.

'How did they come about?'

'By accident,' I said truthfully. Aware of Sid, I added, 'I sleepwalked into a wall, apparently at rather high speed.'

I considered a moment and decided to continue with the theme of dreams. 'My dreams were adventurous, and things weren't what I expected. There was no malice. Only a fulfilment of the things that have already been prepared for a long time. I came out of it with something, and it was the thing that was agreed on. Also, there was…' I hesitated. 'It was…like going on a journey. Like seeing the Gray Mountains for the first time.'

A look of surprise crossed Philip's lined face, and he considered this, obviously taking my meaning. He knew that I had never, before last night, been to the Gray Mountains. After a moment, he drummed his fingers on the arm of his chair. 'And what was he like?'

Sid perked up. Philip ignored her, so I did the same. The thought of Bryn's iron grip on my wrist came to mind, this time accompanied by the image of his face, with red eyes burning bright in the darkness.

'Beautiful,' I said honestly. 'And terrifying.'

TEN

Philip directed me to see Riann, one of the castle's cooks and its unofficial healer, after only a few more minutes. With a recommendation for a salve to go on my gradually worsening face we left the Alchemist's Tower with a promise to visit again. Sid insisted on following me down to the kitchens to see a new part of a castle but I was able to beg off after collecting the salve with an honest claim that I had not slept well last night and could do with some rest.

Sid promised to collect me for the midday meal before she left me in blessed silence to smear salve on my face and collapse into bed for a while. She bustled back in at noon, flanked by her maids, and roused me with a hateful cheeriness. I bustled her right back out again and spent ten minutes sitting in front of the mirror massaging my temples with my eyes shut.

In the Second Hall on my way in to lunch I spotted Philip by the arched entryway, lingering like a cat wary of a pack of dogs. He leaned heavily on his stick as he eyed the rest of the diners, suspicion written all over his face.

Philip didn't often come down to the main castle for meals. This was partly because he preferred solitude and the food he chose himself, but also partly because of his sometimes disabling paranoia. It was a surprise to see him in a place with so many other people.

Sid spotted him as well, and with no knowledge of the peculiarity of Philip's presence here, approached with her usual brightness. 'My good alchemist. Your company this morning was very enlightening.'

Philip looked up at Sid with both hands still clenched on his stick. She stood slightly taller than him but his presence and personality still dwarfed her. Without a word, he directed a questioning look at me. *Enlightening?* I could see him think.

'Glad to be of service.' Philip said bowed his head ever so slightly in her direction.

'Please go on to luncheon, Princess,' I said gently. 'I'll catch up.'

Sid smiled brightly at the both of us and walked into the main room, her maids like a trail of ducklings behind her. She greeted everyone she already knew with every bit of the grace one would expect from a princess.

I moved to Philip's side and watched Sid's progress through the room. 'I'm glad you came down.' I took his arm and slowly turned us away to walk in the corridor. Both of us would be more comfortable holding this conversation out of sight of the court.

'I could hardly help it,' Philip said as we made our way to a quieter part of the corridor. 'What really happened last night?' His lined face was curious and worried in equal measure.

I glanced back at the door to the hall to see that Sid had not returned to look for me. Seeing that we were alone, I took my time in explaining the events of the previous night in full and presented the chunk of iron ore Bryn had given me. Philip listened intently and accepted the stone with a curious look. When I described the mountain stripped of trees and dug out for mines, he looked away, but did not say anything immediately.

'It would be wise to ask your uncle about it if you get a chance,' he offered after a moment. 'Not immediately, as it seems to be a very new development, and not directly perhaps. Once word comes around to the castle about the mining, as it will, you could make oblique reference to it and see what Lord Ruben knows. Pay attention at the court meetings; there may be mention of something going on.'

'Are you worried? About what it might mean?'

Philip considered, watery eyes fixed on the empty hallway ahead of us. 'Not myself, no. But Bryn and his father are right to be. In all likelihood the ore is going to be sold to someone with more of a capacity to forge it than we have. What you're talking about is enough ore to start a conflict, if not a war. The end result may be weapons that get used on the dragons.'

The idea of anyone being dumb enough to think about declaring war on the dragons caught me off-guard. 'Why would anyone in Clovia be interested in making war with dragons? We have a truce already.'

But Philip didn't get a chance to respond, as Lord Tyburn spotted us from down another corridor and hurried over. 'Ah, Philip,' the large, ruddy-faced man huffed. 'How good to see you in the castle. I wonder if you might help me with a dilemma.'

'My Lord,' Philip said with a gentle incline of his head as he extracted his arm from mine, 'I must apologise but I'm off to my workshop for a busy afternoon. It is pleasant to see you again.'

The tone of his voice said otherwise, but rudeness was, after all, Philip's trademark. Lord Tyburn could only watch as Philip, with his usual slow, shuffling gait, made his way back to his tower.

The task I had given myself was to find out whether the king and Lord Ruben knew about what was happening on the slopes of the Gray Mountains. The difficulty with this is that they didn't know that I knew what was happening on the slopes of the Gray Mountains, and there wasn't a good way to ask unless I had an excuse for knowing about it.

As Philip had suggested, unless some news came from the Gray Mountains to the castle about what was happening there, I couldn't ask about it, and with no news immediately forthcoming, I could only wait and listen.

Sid was surprised and her maids not very pleased when I announced that we would be attending the thrice-weekly court meetings where the king addressed business with the nobles and heard from peasants. It wasn't my first choice of how to spend my mornings, but there was a chance that the events at the Gray Mountains would be mentioned, so it was my first choice of a place to go for evidence.

When Lord Ruben saw me at the first of these meetings, he stared for a while, then gave an approving nod. It was his job to attend and record the events of the morning, and he had been trying to get me interested in the meetings for a good long while. I suspected he wanted me to get interested enough that I would take over the note-taking so he could spend more of the meeting advising.

With that in mind, I tried to leave quickly after the meetings finished so he wouldn't catch up with me and ask what had caused my change of heart about attending. I wasn't a good enough liar that a consummate deceiver like Lord Ruben wouldn't see through my thin façade of interest and I didn't want to end up as assistant court recorder. At least I had Sid as an excuse for running off.

I spent the rest of my days helping the princess get to know both the castle and the other inhabitants thereof. Of the forty-six towers, we explored nearly half. I was pleased to see over the course of several days that the princess became more practical about her choice of clothing so that she could more easily manoeuvre through the narrow passages without getting caught on anything.

Somehow she only seemed more elegant for having disposed of her wide skirts in favour of something more practical.

On the mornings there weren't court meetings we would meet with the ladies of the court before we spent the afternoons in the library or touring the castle and countryside.

It surprised me how quickly Sid learned her way around. She had a very good sense of direction, enough that it seemed a single visit to a place was enough that she would always be able to find it again, no matter the distance or direction of approach.

This uncanny ability coupled with her skill at following without being noticed made me worry a little and wonder a lot. How any lady of court, much less a princess, learned to follow someone in complete secrecy, or to build such accurate mental maps of a place, was a mystery. I could only guess as to what events in her life had led to the development of those skills.

At the end of the first week of Sid's stay, her maids and the guards packed up to go, apparently having fulfilled whatever duty they had been sent to do. Sid and I walked down to send them off with Alois, the lone maid who was staying behind, to bid them farewell.

Sid didn't seem at all perturbed that her last major connection to home was leaving; in fact quite the opposite. She positively beamed as they packed themselves onto horses and wagons and trundled out the gate in procession around midday.

'Wonderful.' She clapped her hands together as they disappeared around the first bend and turned to me with a bright smile. 'Would you care for some lunch?'

Her excitement struck me as odd. Her relief at being left alone by her own people was obvious and strange. I tried to understand what her motivation was but didn't have time to wonder long.

The quick drum of hoofbeats the other side of the castle gate drew our attention. I thought at first it might be one of Sid's guards returning, but this particular rider pulled up short at the castle gates without entering. The rider was filthy from a long hard ride and wore the green feathered cap of a messenger.

He waved a groom over. One of the grooms, a young lad, fairly new to service in the castle, detached from his work and hurried over. Messenger and groom held a quiet, hurried conversation accompanied by much excited hand-waving and a few furtive glances toward the castle.

After a few moments the messenger shoved something into the hands of the groom and pulled sharply on the reins of his steed to turn about. He was gone from sight in moments, as if he had never been there save for the sealed message now held by the groom.

The young groom looked at the parcel in his hand for a moment, a bit overawed at the manner in which the message had been delivered, and hurried toward Sid and me. He gave me a curious, respectful look as he handed over the small parcel.

'Compliments from Dayton,' was his crisp message as he bowed and stepped back.

I grimaced as he walked away, and the blood drained from my face. I turned to look at the castle, for any sign that Lord Ruben or any of his servants might have seen what had happened through a window or an open door. The young groom was obviously not aware that Lord Ruben demanded that all letters from Dayton be delivered to him and only him.

Letters from Dayton Abbey only ever came from one writer, and they rarely made it to me, the intended recipient, unopened, unless they were delivered in the middle of the night by someone who could get into the castle unseen. Most of the time letters simply appeared underneath the door to my room sometime in the night; it was rare to see one arrive by the light of day. It was a massive risk to think that this letter would reach me without being seen by Lord Ruben, and I hoped appropriate care had been taken to see this message guarded.

'Who is that from?' Sid leaned over to look as I inspected the outside of the message, my name and location written in looping letters. The handwriting was so familiar it might as well have been my own.

'My mother.' I said shortly as I tucked the letter into a pocket. 'I'll read it after lunch while you're working on your embroidery with Alois.'

Sid watched the letter disappear into my pocket, curiosity written all over her face. I couldn't blame her. It took the best of my self-control to wait until we had eaten and gone back up to Sid's rooms before reading the letter. The parcel was small, no more than a couple of sheets of paper, but it weighed heavily in my pocket throughout lunch. No doubt this letter contained news from the dragons, and hopefully words of wisdom from my mother on how to deal with them.

We returned to Sid's room without delay after lunch. She seemed as eager as I was to open the letter and see what had been worthy of such an unusual and hurried delivery. Sid was obviously disappointed when I seated myself on the opposite side of the room to where she and Alois sat to do their embroidery.

The moment I was seated I broke the wax seal and carefully unfolded the papers with a glance at Sid. She made a show of being engrossed in her work, but I was certain that once I started reading she would be watching me, not her fingers.

With a deep breath, I scanned the letter. Mother had not been careful about writing this particular missive, that was obvious. If Lord Ruben got a chance to read it he would have understood as much of it as I did. Perhaps that was why the horseman who delivered it was so vehement in his conversation with the groom; he wanted to be sure this letter went only to me.

My Dearest Tara,

It pleases me greatly that you were finally able to meet with Bryn and that all is going ahead according to what your father and I planned for you all those years ago. We owe Bryn's family a great debt of gratitude and I cannot imagine having to disappoint them when all they have wanted for so long is a union between our families.

I snorted. There were other reasons that mother couldn't imagine disappointing the dragons—they weren't generally terribly friendly if they didn't get their way. Not to mention that if there wasn't a sacrifice already arranged, they were known for carrying off virgin damsels as brides in addition to terrorising the countryside.

Your choice of gift is also very pleasing, though I'm certain you don't yet understand why. There is great magic attached to the choice of gift, and it is a telling sign of your future. I cannot explain more at the moment.

I have also heard of what is happening at the edge of the Gray Mountains and I must say I am perturbed. It is no light thing to tear up a forest that houses so many magical things, and I worry that the person responsible for this destruction does not know what they may cause.

I would recommend that you find a copy of Fionnuel's History of the Dark Woods. There is a great deal of information there that you may find useful. The writer talks about the woods around the Gray Mountains in great detail and if there is any information that could help you, it would be there.

It has now been a year since your last visit. Might you consider pleading with your uncle that he allow you to come to me for a few days? I would ask a fortnight but fear that he will want you close by his side and not mine.

All my love,
Mother

Sid watched me closely as I finished reading the letter. I could feel her eyes on me the whole time, and a glance at her embroidery confirmed that she hadn't been concentrating on it as deeply as she pretended to.

I turned the letter over to read the postscript—*The messenger was told to deliver this letter only when he could see you in the courtyard so as to get it directly to you. I do not know how long he had to wait but I hope it was not days.*

I smiled a little. How very like my mother to give someone a task like that, even if it meant a long wait and more than a little discomfort. There was a reason that messenger had looked so scruffy.

'How is your mother?' Sid asked cheerfully.

'Fine, thank you,' I replied, my mind on Lord Ruben. Mother's mention of visiting her at Dayton was just what I needed. I couldn't think of a better way to help figure out what was happening in the forest. If anyone would be able to figure things out, it would be her.

Perhaps I could persuade Lord Ruben to let me go, even if only for a few days. It had been nearly a year since my last visit to Dayton, so the request would not seem strange. If he were to give his approval it was possible I could make the visit just after the spring festival in a few weeks. That would probably be soon enough that I could get her help on behalf of the dragons. I folded the letter again and stood.

'If you'll excuse me, I need to go see my uncle.'

Sid's eyes followed me all the way out of the room. I could feel her scrutiny even as the door shut. The moment I was alone on the tower stairs I took the letter up to my room to stash it away under my mattress. The letter would need to go in the fire as soon as possible, but there weren't any burning this time of day. It would have to wait.

As I descended the tower again, I thought of mother's mention of Fionnuel's History of the Dark Woods. I had heard of the book, but never read it; histories were not generally something I used my spare time to read. Books were sometimes difficult to get hold of, but there was one person in the castle who would know where to find it.

After a moment of indecision, I continued down the stairs past Sid's room to the main halls.

ELEVEN

The library was located in one of the larger towers, where it occupied the three upper floors. Bookcases were packed in so tightly it could be difficult to navigate the narrow walkways to get to the spiral staircase at the centre of the room that went up to the upper floors and roof.

An elderly man named Felton had run the library for as long as anyone could remember. He was a portly old man near Philip's age who walked with a limp and knew what every book in the library was and where it was located.

Felton was a fount of information who had proved his worth repeatedly with his encyclopaedic knowledge of not only the contents of the library but the important details of many of the writings held therein.

When I arrived at the library I entered with caution. Lord Ruben often frequented the library tower and Felton's company to discuss matters of law, and I didn't want to stumble on Lord Ruben without a bit more of a chance to prepare myself. However, when I pushed through the stacks of books to the bottom of the spiral staircase where Felton did most of his work it was to find not Felton and Lord Ruben, but Felton's daughter Amelie.

Amelie was an upright, angular woman of middle age with a thin face and permanently ink-stained fingers who was in the process of taking over Felton's place as head of the library in the event of his death. She had a perpetually tired look from the dark circles under her eyes that never completely went away even when she'd had plenty of rest. While not as full of information as Felton, she was still a force to be reckoned with.

'Good afternoon,' I said politely as I stopped at the side of the table she was working at. It was spread thick with books, scrolls, and notes for some project that apparently had to do with the rites of spring.

Amelie nodded to me without looking up from making an annotation in one of the large library records. 'Good afternoon. Is there something I may help you with?'

'Yes. Fionnuel's History of the Dark Woods, please.'

Amelie held up one dark, ink-stained finger for silence as she finished scratching the note, then set down her quill and disappeared between the shelves of books. It wasn't long before she returned, a medium-sized book bound in ageing, cracked leather held easily in one hand.

'You're far swifter than your father,' I commented as she made a note of my name and the book I requested. The last time I had requested a book I had to wait several minutes while Felton wheezed his way up and down the spiral staircase.

'They aren't normally so close at hand,' Amelie replied in her dry voice. 'Someone else has been reading this recently.'

I looked again at the leather-bound book in her hand. Not only had mother made a very good guess of what information would be useful, but also it appeared that I wasn't the only one in the castle interested in what was happening in the mountains.

'Have you seen Lord Ruben today?' I asked carefully as I gathered up the book to peer inside the cover at the beautifully inscribed front page.

'No, I haven't, but that's where my father is. He was asked to report to Lord Ruben's rooms.'

I nodded calmly and bid her good day though I could feel the gentle tide of worry rise in my chest at the thought of speaking with my uncle.

Amelie waved me away soundlessly, already absorbed again in her book-keeping, and I left with the book clutched to my chest.

Lord Ruben's rooms were, rather unusually for Gydrocc Castle, not located in a tower. Instead, they were on the south wall, where he would have good light year round, on the top floor so as to be well out of the way normal castle traffic.

One definite advantage of being the king's favourite advisor was that Lord Ruben had some say in where his rooms were located, and no place was too lavish. Lord Ruben's rooms were located just down the hall from the king himself, a sign of his importance, and it was a rare soul that was allowed to enter those halls unquestioned.

I knew the way, and walked past the guards at the entry to the corridor without difficulty, though they did watch me closely as I ventured down the wide hallway of the Royal Suite. Here, there were guards stationed at every doorway as a deterrent to trouble-makers. I did not have to go far before I could see the entry to Lord Ruben's rooms, again guarded by two liveried soldiers.

As I approached I saw Felton waddle out of my uncle's suite, his gait rather unsteady as was his way. His dingy brown robes with their inky sleeves looked out of place in the airy, clean hallway, and put me in mind of a dog come in from the street. Felton spotted me and gave a nod as I passed, along with a possessive glance at the book in my arms.

I tightened my grip on the leather spine. Felton knew that someone else in the castle was interested in this book, and my curiosity about who it was almost got the better of me as he passed. It was all I could do to bite my tongue.

I couldn't ask him outright who had borrowed the book before me. Such interest could be dangerous. I wasn't supposed to be curious about what was happening in the Gray Mountains because I wasn't supposed to know about it. I clamped my mouth shut and only gave him an answering nod.

I stopped to stand in front of Lord Ruben's door for a moment to gather my thoughts. The guards on either side of the corridor merely glanced at me with a kind of haughty unconcern, accustomed to my occasional presence. With a deep breath, I raised my hand to knock on the door, which Felton had left slightly ajar.

What stopped me from knocking was the sound of Lord Ruben's voice, raised in irritation, as he none-too-gently berated someone.

'We are not going to have another Lydia of Carron. That uprising was put down, and there is no one fool enough now to try starting another one like it. The Lady Lydia, as you call her, is leading no armies and starting no revolutions. Fear of her influence is like fear of a shadow. Less than a shadow,' He added with a dry laugh.

'I do not doubt you are correct,' a calm, level voice

replied. I leaned closer to the door, surprised. It took me only a moment to recognise the voice as belonging to King Stephen.

Just the other side of this door, my uncle was shouting at the king.

To his credit, King Stephen did not reply with any irritation. 'The difficulty is that the Lady's legend lives on. I fear there will be others who wish to carry on her work. Especially given the circumstances.'

'Your Highness,' Lord Ruben's own voice fell back to the gentle murmur he was known for, 'There is nothing to fear. This venture can hardly fail on its own, and I can think of no being in this world who is prepared to fall in the way Lydia of Carron fell.'

My cheeks began to burn as they spoke. This was not a conversation that was meant to be overheard, least of all by me. Someone else clearly realised this, because I heard a gentle cough beside me. I looked up to see one of the guards watching me with an impatient look on his face. I lowered my head to acknowledge my embarrassment at being caught eavesdropping and knocked on the door without further hesitation.

A moment later the door swung wide, and from the calm look on my uncle's face I never would have guessed he had been shouting moments earlier. Lord Ruben looked completely in control of himself as he gestured for me to enter, and he even offered me a smile.

'Lady Tara,' Lord Ruben announced with a glance at the king, who gave an almost imperceptible nod. 'Do come in.'

It was thus with great surprise that I found myself seated across from both my uncle and the king.

In spite of having lived in Gydrocc castle for half a dozen years I had never spoken directly with the king before. Even with my having been recently named as Lord Ruben's heir, I hadn't been formally introduced at court.

The king smiled at me past his immaculately kept moustache, the expression on his face much more gentle than the one on Lord Ruben's. The king was handsome in a way that my uncle wasn't. There was always a kindness behind the regal, masterly gestures, and when he smiled, it was easier to imagine that he was a cheerful minstrel out to entertain the children than ruler of all Clovia.

For comparison, my uncle often looked more like a strict dictator and had an air of slight menace hanging around him that may or may not have only been my imagination.

'I'm glad you're here,' Lord Ruben said, drawing my startled gaze away from the king. 'Please, tell us the purpose for your visit.'

It was almost impossible to believe that only moments ago he had been so outraged about Lydia of Carron. Lord Ruben's features, so similar to mine, looked firm, composed, and serious, but not at all angry. Somewhat menacing, perhaps, but not angry. I swallowed and tried to put my thoughts in order. There was at least something I could tell Lord Ruben that he would expect to hear from me.

'I…I wanted to report that Princess Amanthea is settling in well, and that all is well after sending away her guards and maids.' The words tumbled out of my mouth almost without thought.

I couldn't ask about the book, or what was happening in the woods, as I wasn't supposed to know about it, and I was extremely hesitant now to ask if I could go visit mother. It may have been my express purpose in coming here, but she had been more than right in her letter to imply that Lord Ruben would want me by his side, not hers.

'Good, good.' The king blew out through his moustache in a gentle laugh and looked at Lord Ruben. 'At least we won't have her weeping through dinner this evening,'

Lord Ruben looked at the king, then back at me. I shrugged, feeling suddenly shy. 'I don't think she's the weeping type.'

'No indeed!' The king laughed. Lord Ruben smirked at that. Their meaning wasn't obvious, but I felt it might not be the right time to ask for clarification.

'Tara,' Lord Ruben said, looking at me again, 'I wonder if you might do us a favour?'

'Of course,' I said automatically, aware of the king's gaze.

'We worry about the princess.'

I looked from him to the king and back again. Both were wearing similar impenetrable gazes that hid well whatever it was they were thinking. The best I could do was to tread carefully.

'I'm not certain what there is to worry about,' I replied slowly. 'She seems to be adjusting well, and has become used to the workings of Gydrocc.'

'That isn't what I mean.' Lord Ruben waved a hand dismissively and leaned forward, his elbows on the arms of his chair. 'We've heard stories from reliable sources that indicate the princess is something of a troublemaker.' He paused, as if considering his words. 'That she does not necessarily respect authority as she should.'

The words washed over me first without penetrating my understanding. Doesn't respect authority? What, because she kept trying to make conversation with people while they were busy? As far as I had seen, the princess was as obedient as could be expected, if sometimes surprising.

Although, as the comment sank in, I remembered the morning she had followed me all the way to the 'yellow tapestry' without my knowing. I frowned.

Lord Ruben laughed. 'I see you begin to understand. You will certainly agree that a face is not to be trusted just because it is pretty.'

'No indeed.' He didn't need to tell that to me. I was more likely to resent beauty than to fall prey to it.

Lord Ruben leaned back, and reached for a goblet on the table between him and the king. 'Tara, we would like you to keep an eye on her.'

'I thought I was already doing that.'

'Yes, quite,' he agreed calmly. 'But you have been doing so as a confidante, as a lady-in-waiting. Helping her from her perspective. What we would like you to do is keep an eye on things from our perspective.'

As he spoke, the meaning became clear. A strange mixture of emotions crowded for attention—guilt that Lord Ruben appeared to trust me in spite of everything he knew and didn't know I was getting up to, nervousness about performing the task, worry that he might find out I wasn't as trustworthy as he thought, and a greater guilt at what was certainly a betrayal of the princess' trust.

'You want me to spy on her. To let you know her comings and goings.'

'Not to spy, precisely, but to watch her. Let us know if she does anything suspicious, or if she wanders where she should not go.'

I thought about the morning she had followed me to Philip's tower, but mentioning that would have incriminated me as much as it would her, possibly more so. Philip was a friend, but Lord Ruben didn't need to know about my visiting him at odd hours and in secret. Anyway, it felt like betrayal to even think of mentioning Sid following me then. She was not a bad girl, after all, not as far as I could see of her.

Besides, if I was going to trust Lord Ruben even the smallest amount, there were others who deserved that amount of trust as well.

'I will,' I said finally, pushing the incident with the yellow tapestry to the back of my mind. 'Is that all?'

Lord Ruben shook his head and rose. I did as well, and bowed slightly to the king. As I turned to leave, Lord Ruben stopped me with an upraised hand, his gaze on my hands.

'What book do you have there?'

I looked down, almost surprised to see that I still held the book Amelie had procured so easily from the depths of the library. The way Lord Ruben asked the question was strange, as if he already knew the answer. The tide of worry rose higher in my chest.

'History of the Dark Woods,' I said, and bowed my head slightly as I held it up for inspection. Lord Ruben looked at me in silence, and I shrugged, unable to keep his gaze. 'I thought I might enjoy reading about the forest.'

The weight of the book left my hands, and I saw the back of Lord Ruben as he turned to the king. He placed the book on the table behind him with his other papers.

In airy tones he said, 'Unfortunately I rather destroyed the binding when I borrowed it for my own reading not long ago. It will have to go back for Felton for mending before anyone else reads it. I fear more permanent damage.'

Lord Ruben did not look at me as he said this, but I could hear a frown, and see it reflected on the face of the king.

I might have averted one difficulty by having avoided mention of my mother, but I could not have been more foolish to bring the book she recommended about the forest right into the hands of my uncle. Why had I assumed he would not know about the Gray Mountains? Why hadn't I realised that nothing happened in this kingdom that Lord Ruben didn't know about?

King Stephen took one last, lingering look at the book, then stood. 'You may go, Lady Tara. And I shall go as well.'

I bowed again and left the room as quickly as I could, my footfalls heavy on the stone floors as I practically ran back to my tower.

I scanned my recollection, confused about Lord Ruben's words. Amelie had handed that book to me and mentioned that someone had recently been reading it, so I had opened it, admired the frontispiece, and closed it again. Memory told me that the binding had been undamaged when I took it from the library.

Lord Ruben had lied to me.

TWELVE

I didn't go back directly to Sid's room. Instead I went to my own, found the letter from mother, and read over it quickly one last time. It wasn't safe to keep now; there had been times before when servants had come to clean my room and disappeared with letters, undoubtedly on the orders of my uncle.

Now was not the time to take a chance. Especially considering the conversation I had just overheard, if Lord Ruben read this latest missive it would be enough to send me from being my uncle's current favourite to sharing the same fate as my mother.

The letter safely in hand, I began pacing the room. Whatever was in that book was important in some way to what was happening in the forest. Mother's letter suggested as much, but Lord Ruben's confiscation of it was, to me at least, a confirmation.

It confirmed something else as well: that Lord Ruben, and very probably the king, were well aware of what was going on in the forest. Perhaps they even had something to do with it.

The thought made me stop, and I stared out the window. Why would they? There were mines closer to Gydrocc with high quality iron ore, so it did not make sense to mine as far away as the Gray Mountains. Were the Clovian mines not producing enough? Such a thing had not been mentioned in any of the court meetings, of that much I was certain. It was not the type of thing that would be ignored by Clovian tradesmen.

So the answer must have been in the book. I resumed pacing with a curse at myself. The book was confiscated because I had walked into a trap, and to make things worse it was a trap set by my own foolishness.

And what about the king and Lord Ruben wanting me to spy on Princess Amanthea? Sid had proved herself nothing if not friendly in her time here, though of course that could have been an act for the benefit of the maids that had escorted her. It felt like a betrayal to spy on her. She was not unkind, and I thought that given enough time we could become friends.

I was not left long to my thoughts; a knock at the door came as I stared at the folded letter again, and the door immediately opened to admit Sid. 'May I come in?' she asked as she peered around the door.

'Of course.' I sighed and dropped into the nearest chair, feeling more exhausted than the events of the day merited. Sid closed the door behind her. She had thankfully not brought her maid along, so I had one less person to worry about lying to. Sid walked over to the bed and sat down facing me.

'Did things not go well with your uncle?' she asked. Her eyes were kind, and though she looked rather like a finely painted doll, she did look genuinely worried.

There wasn't much I could really say, unless I wanted to explain everything. I shrugged and went for a non-answer.

'As well as they could be expected to.'

'Does this have something to do with your letter? Did you receive bad news?'

'No…yes,' I said, annoyance at my own foolishness in carrying the book to Lord Ruben overpowering my desire for secrecy. 'My mother wanted me to read a particular book, as she thought it would be enjoyable, but when I went to see my uncle he took it from me and said it was damaged.'

The princess only continued to watch me with those luminous blue eyes, apparently unsure how these things related or why they were important.

'I suppose it wasn't?' Sid said after a moment.

'Not that I could see.'

Again, there were a few moments of silence. 'So he

didn't want you to read it,' Sid said finally.

For a moment, I could see why Lord Ruben thought she might make trouble. Her eyes narrowed as she thought, and I could almost see the cogs working in her head. She was thinking something through, and there was a determination in her gaze that worried me.

'Never mind,' I said, suddenly hoping she would stay out of trouble so I wouldn't feel obligated to report anything to my uncle. 'I'm sure it wasn't terribly important.'

'What book was it?'

'History of the Dark Woods. It's about the Gray Mountains.'

Sid gave me a strange look, and again I got the sense that she knew something I didn't.

'Never mind,' I said again, unnerved by her silence. 'Let's get back to your embroidery. I'm sure Alois doesn't want to be left the entire afternoon.'

Back in Sid's room, I moved toward the fire and leaned down to warm my hands. As nonchalantly as I could, I threw my mother's letter into the flames. It would be safer there.

THIRTEEN

The morning of the half moon, with no new information and a growing fear at the thought of going to the mines unarmed, I made my way to the castle armoury, Philip's arrow charm tucked into a pocket on my dress. The armoury stood next to the barracks, a solid little building where any number of weapons could be found, including the crossbows Philip had recommended for my use.

The impressively wide captain of the guard, Hawkins, stood outside the armoury with his eyes on the soldiers, who were currently busy kicking a ball across the lawns. Hawkins was a large man, more muscle than fat, with a thinning crop of reddish hair and fists that could crack walnuts. In spite of his appearance he could be surprisingly gentle and was a good friend to many of the courtiers. He smiled a fat, gap-toothed smile when he saw me, and I returned the favour.

'Good morning, Lady,' Hawkins said as he bowed low over my hand. 'You look much improved.'

The bruises on my face were still noticeably yellow, though the worst had now faded. Soon enough they would be gone and I could hold a conversation with someone without my face being the first issue on the table.

'Thank you,' I said as graciously as I could. 'Hopefully in future I can avoid such obvious clumsiness.'

Hawkins grinned. 'How can I help you today?'

I peered around him toward the armoury. 'Philip wanted me to test a new charm. Apparently he can enchant arrows to never miss their target.' Not strictly true, but it would do under the circumstances. Hawkins was not a suspicious sort, so was not the kind to wonder exactly why Philip would ask me to test such a charm rather than a soldier.

Hawkins laughed, which brought my attention back to him. 'Has he changed it since last it was tested? I tell you truly, Lady, that charm was never a very good one.'

My smile faltered. Philip didn't usually exaggerate the usefulness of his work, but he did on occasion produce dud charms. 'This one?' I asked, and pulled out the coin with the bullseye. 'He seemed to think it worked well enough.'

The big man shook his head and turned to the armoury door. 'I can show you, if you like.' He ducked inside.

'A crossbow, please,' I said, poking my head into the dusty room that housed many of the castle's weapons.

'Have you ever used a crossbow before, Lady?' Hawkins looked up from where he stood in front of the projectile weapons, surprised. There were a few of the female courtiers who practiced archery, but they primarily used the stock of rather dainty training bows that Hawkins kept for the younger soldiers.

'No,' I said without hesitation, 'but I thought the best test of a weapons charm would be to see how it fares in the hands of an untrained lady.'

Hawkins threw back his head and laughed. 'Well, right you are. If a fine lady such as yourself can get a weapon to be deadly accurate with one of his charms, surely it would work for anyone.'

I wasn't sure whether to be flattered that he called me fine or offended at the parting jab, but accepted the small crossbow without complaint. It took only a moment to wedge the charm into a groove in the wood before I followed Hawkins across to the archery field.

'This way, lady,' Hawkins said as he set down the quiver of crossbow bolts and held up the long metal hook he carried. 'This is for loading the bow.'

He took the crossbow from me again and demonstrated how to place my foot in the stirrup at the front of the crossbow and draw the string back using the metal hook. The string clipped in place, Hawkins unhooked the metal implement and handed me the crossbow. He then unlaced the top of the leather quiver to produce a single crossbow bolt.

'Place it on the top there,' he said as he handed both implements to me. 'In the groove.'

I did so, and Hawkins corrected my placement without comment. After a long look, I thought I would be able to load it correctly on my own, and Hawkins showed me the trigger.

'Just aim and squeeze. Much easier than a longbow.' He stood back and took hold of my shoulders to aim me at the targets on the other side of the field. 'Give it a try.'

I glanced at the charm as I took aim at the target, and concentrated the best I could on hitting the target squarely in the middle. From what Philip had said, a bit of concentration would be good enough to direct the arrow to its target. Hawkins apparently didn't agree, as he gently guided my elbow so I was aiming more or less at the target.

With a not-too-gentle squeeze and a twang of metal, the bolt was gone. I heard it sink into the target with a satisfying thud. I smiled brightly, then looked for the bolt. It was in the large target, yes, but only barely. It had missed all of the painted lines and struck the very edge of the hay bale. An inch further to the left and it would have gone out into the field.

'Were you concentrating?' Hawkins demanded in a fairly good impression of Philip. 'I don't think you were concentrating enough.'

I laughed. It took several attempts before I managed to reload the crossbow and took aim again. 'Don't help me this time,' I said over my shoulder as Hawkins went to reach for my elbow. 'If you help me aim I'll hit the target regardless.'

'I don't think you're in any danger of that right now,' he replied, but withdrew his hand.

I squeezed again, and again there was that satisfying thump. Again, I had struck the target, though this time right at the very base, far below the painted bullseye.

Hawkins and I looked at it for a long moment before he made a knowing noise. 'It's an accuracy charm, and not a very good one. It hardly does a man any good to aim for the enemy and hit the ground instead.'

There was no good response for that. Though I trusted Philip and thought he wouldn't give me a bad charm, it was possible he was becoming a little oblivious as he aged. 'One more, then. We'll see if I can concentrate any better.'

Hawkins smiled at that as I reloaded the crossbow.

This time, I concentrated very hard, not on the target, but on the bullseye right in the centre. I thought of that red spot no bigger than my fist, and of the bolt going straight through the centre of it. And when I squeezed, I closed my eyes.

There was another thump, and no sound from Hawkins. I opened my eyes to glance at him first, only to see him scratching his head.

'Were you aiming for that one?' He asked, pointing to the target three hay bales down from mine. I looked over to it, surprised, and shook my head.

The bolt had sunk right into the centre of the bullseye.

Hawkins and I stared at it for a while, then I looked at the charm again. Concentration, yes, but apparently it needed extreme specificity as well.

'Can I take these?' I asked, and held up the crossbow and remaining bolts. 'I want to show Philip later.'

Hawkins shrugged, still staring at the target with a crossbow bolt in the dead centre.

When night fell I crept out of the castle with almost excessive caution. Every few steps I looked back over my shoulder, convinced someone was following me. Between the very real danger that Lord Ruben's newfound suspicion brought down on me and the possibility of a sneaking princess, I had good reason to worry.

Niggle was saddled in record time and I was gone. My caution crossing the plain just outside the castle wall dissolved the moment I had cover from the trees and I rode with excessive haste in an attempt to lose anyone that might be tailing me.

Gradually, my terror at being discovered by someone from Gydrocc subsided and was replaced by the sense that I was letting the dragons down by coming tonight without anything more that could be useful. I slowed our pace and tried to think of something—anything—that I could contribute tonight aside from just being there.

Perhaps it wasn't surprising that my thoughts went to the soldiers guarding the mines. The thought of danger made me think of the pearl as more than just a piece of jewellery for the first time in days.

It was, as Bryn had said, the symbol of the bond we now shared, and it would provide me with some basic protection, but exactly what that entailed I wasn't sure.

I pulled the pearl out from under my tunic as I rode and held it up to the sky. Even the dim light from the moon was enough to make the pearl reflect a shimmering milky glow. If I covered the half-dark moon with the full circle of the pearl and squinted I could almost believe that I held the moon between my fingers.

At the base of the cliff I tied Niggle and began to climb, worries about Lord Ruben forgotten temporarily as my concentration was absorbed in finding my footing. The path up the cliff side was not easy but it was at least familiar. My hands quickly grew cold with the wet rocks and mud that were the only grip on the initial ascent.

When I reached the hairpin path, I brushed myself off and climbed with slightly wobbly knees. The pearl swung heavily on its chain, a reminder that whatever else happened tonight, I wasn't going to become dragon feed.

Near the top of the climb I paused to catch my breath. My hands were nearly frozen so I cupped them together and blew some warmth into the cavity. Preoccupied with getting myself a little warmer and a little calmer before meeting Bryn, I almost missed seeing a flash of white on the path below.

I froze.

Someone had followed me.

FOURTEEN

Scenarios flashed through my mind more quickly than I could fully process them. Was it a spy of Lord Ruben's sent to follow me? Bandits? An enemy of Bryn's? There could hardly be an easier target for foul play than someone climbing a cliff face–one tug on an ankle could spell a precipitous fall and an agonising death in the lake below. That I wasn't dead already said that either they hadn't been able to keep up with me or that they didn't mean me harm; I wasn't going to bet on the latter of the two.

In less time than it takes to pull on a pair of boots, I was turned around with my back against the cold rocks that formed the edge of the cliff with my feet planted firmly on the rocks in front of me and I was preparing the crossbow. The string caught the trigger with a gentle click and I loaded a bolt as I scanned the path below.

Where was it? The little flash of white had been gone almost before I saw it. My eyes were open so wide in the darkness that it almost hurt to keep looking, but between a long hard look and a long hard fall, I'd rather take the look.

A bush on the path below rustled. I swivelled with the crossbow tight against my shoulder and squeezed the trigger. The bolt whistled in the cold air, slapping away leaves on its way through the thick undergrowth. The bolt hadn't gone where I meant it to, but it didn't seem to matter. There was a gasp from one of the bushes.

I grabbed at the hook used for resetting the crossbow string and hoped for time to get another arrow loaded before my stalker showed himself, but took note of the position of my knife in the event I was attacked.

Just as I laid the second bolt on the crossbow, a figure all in blue and white tumbled out of the bushes onto the path below to lay flat on the steep ground, face buried in the mud.

'Please don't kill me!'

This time it wasn't fear that froze me, but mortification.

'Sid?'

The figure below me raised up slightly from the

ground, enough that I could see the familiar face of the princess. Sid's golden hair was full of leaves and twigs, and there was a large smudge of mud on her chin. Her face was transformed by terror, and she looked for once like a normal, not-excessively-beautiful human being.

'What are you doing out here?' I demanded as I lowered the crossbow, my face heating up.

'Yes, because I'm the only one who sneaked out of the castle headed off to who knows where,' Sid shot back sarcastically as she pulled herself up onto her knees very slowly, obviously mistrustful of the steep, muddy ground beneath her.

'Well.' I released the crossbow to let it swing once more from the strap around my shoulder and carefully came down the path to lend a hand. 'Well obviously neither of us should be out here,' I said as I took Sid by the arm and helped her to stand, 'But at least I know what I'm doing. And I'm dressed for the occasion.'

Sid shot me an annoyed look as she shook out her now horribly stained skirts. 'How was I to know you were going climbing, especially on a path this treacherous? It's not exactly the cleverest thing to be doing in the middle of the night.'

I held up one hand to silence her. 'This isn't worth arguing about. Go back to the castle.'

The princess folded her arms tightly and shot me a withering look. It was so different to what I'd been seeing from her at the castle for the last few weeks that I gaped. She gave a calculating look around at where we were, then straight at me.

'Lord Ruben doesn't know you're out here, does he?'

'No. And I have no intention of him finding out.' I gave her a meaningful look.

She shook her head. 'I won't tell him. I won't tell anyone. But I do want to know what's going on.' Her voice turned pleading. 'What's here that you keep sneaking off to do?'

So she knew I'd done this before. Perhaps that wasn't too surprising. I knew that she was good at following silently, I just hadn't expected that she could follow me for miles without my noticing. It was a mistake on my part, and if it had been anyone else behind me it could have been a fatal error.

'How did you even get out of the castle?' I demanded. I knew I had locked the guard gate door behind me; there was no way she'd come out that way unless he had a copy of the key.

'The front door,' she said in haughty tones.

If it was true, it was miraculous. If it was a lie, her face said there wasn't any way I was getting the truth out of her.

There wasn't time to worry about it now either way. I looked up the cliff, then at the sky.

It was getting late; Bryn might already be waiting for me, and it wasn't wise to test a dragon's patience. If she wasn't going to go back to the castle now, perhaps I could take her the short distance to the top of the cliff? It would be faster than persuading her to do anything else.

A part of me hesitated to trust Sid. As friendly as she had been since her arrival, it hardly seemed prudent to let her in on a secret that could result in my exile or death. On the other hand, there was a dragon waiting at the top of the cliff, and if anything could intimidate someone into silence, it was a dragon.

'Come on then,' I said finally as I motioned for her to follow me up to the clearing. 'I'm late.'

'Late?'

I ignored her and began the last part of the climb. Apparently Sid thought it was worth following me the rest of the way, because I could hear her footsteps close behind me.

As I clambered over the edge of the cliff and reached back to help Sid up the last bit of the climb, she gave me a look of awe. 'How do you do this at night and still manage to get through the day?'

'I don't sneak out every night,' I replied shortly as I turned away from her to look across the clearing. I was late and could only hope that Bryn wasn't angry about it. 'Usually just a couple of times a month.'

Across the clearing from where Sid and I stood, bright and grey-gold in the moonlight, was Bryn. He was all dragon, scales and wings and claws the size of my arms, drinking from the pool. Steam rolled off him in waves as cold droplets of water touched his warm scales.

'It's impressive regardless,' Sid said as she straightened up and examined her dress with a critical eye, checking for irreparable damage. It seemed only natural that her first concern was toward her appearance rather than any concern that we weren't alone.

Our voices must have carried over to Bryn, because he turned his great face toward us. I glanced at Sid, but she hadn't yet seen the massive, serpentine dragon at the other end of the clearing. How she managed to overlook that fact for so long was a mystery. Bryn began his approach with that strange, ungainly gait of a dragon on flat ground, awkward but almost entirely silent.

'Sid,' I said gently as I took her arm and guided her away from the edge of the cliff, 'There's someone you should meet.'

Sid turned just as Bryn loomed enormously over us, head held high, wings half spread. His mouth opened a little, in that reptilian way that showed an array of teeth the size of daggers, and a hiss emanated from the depths of his chest.

Only one of us fainted and it wasn't me, but I couldn't blame Sid. She fell slowly thanks to my hand on her arm, but it was still close enough to the cliff I had to scramble to see that she didn't go over the edge.

'Bryn!' I gasped as I grabbed at Sid's arms and guided her body away from the cliff edge. 'What was that for?'

He let out a huff of hot air like a warning and gave his neck a great shake.

With a shake of my own head and what I hoped was sufficiently threatening look, I said, 'Go over there,' and pointed to the other side of the clearing. 'I need her to be awake to tell her we'll be back.'

Draconic facial expressions aren't exactly the easiest thing to read, but if I was to guess, Bryn was making the petulant look of someone who knows they've done something wrong but doesn't want to admit it.

I couldn't imagine why he had taken such an instant dislike to Sid; she was a lowly human woman with no experience when it came to dragons. Somehow this didn't seem like simple offence at the fact that I had brought someone with me.

Bryn did as I asked, though with no small amount of noisy wing-shaking, so I turned my attention to Sid. In a typically ideal ladylike faint, all it took to wake Sid was a quick slap on each cheek. Her eyes fluttered open and focused on me, her mouth soundless as it made the shape of the word 'dragon'.

'Yes, dragon.' I grimaced. Even on the verge of unconsciousness she was dainty and perfect. 'Nothing to worry about. I'll be back soon. You should get some rest now.'

Sid didn't take any more persuading in her half-delirious state of shock. She curled up into a little ball on the grass and watched Bryn on the other side of the clearing with wide eyes.

I returned to Bryn, who was perched on the edge of the cliff ready to go. He glared at Sid momentarily, then grumbled and shook himself as if he had seen an apparition.

'Calm down,' I said as I climbed onto his shoulders. 'Really, she's nothing to worry about.'

His angry snort was not reassuring.

FIFTEEN

We arrived at the forest near to where we had come the first time. It was easily recognisable from the one tall tree stripped of branches at the top, deep claw marks around the trunk where Bryn had landed before. This time, Bryn found a small clearing nearby that was barely large enough to land in. His claws scraped the treetops as we came down and he nearly ran into the trees at the other end.

The moment we were on the ground, Bryn shrugged those massive scaly shoulders so suddenly that I almost fell off.

His obvious irritation made me slide down so quickly my knees buckled and it was all I could do to stay on my feet. In my surprise, I staggered and it took a few moments to regain a sense of which way was down—same as last time.

It did not take Bryn any time at all to recover his bearings. He had, immediately upon landing, begun to shift from dragon to human, and when I looked back toward him it was to see scales, wings and a tail retracting into bare human flesh. I turned away abruptly and wished dragons had a more strict sense of modesty.

'What is she and what are you doing with the likes of her?' The barked question came from behind my back moments later, once Bryn had a human tongue back in his head. I glanced back to see that he was fastening red and gold robes around him, the pack he kept around his neck in dragon form lying on the ground. I was so stunned at the fact that he had managed to dress so quickly that a reply didn't come.

Bryn gave up on the buttons at the front of his robes halfway and left the collar flapping. Irritation lent a growl to his voice. 'Have you any idea what she is? What sort of a creature that thing is?'

'She's a princess,' I said, pulling myself up to height in an attempt to look haughty. 'Engaged to Prince Caleb, to be married at the winter solstice.'

'She's a princess alright,' Bryn said as he threw his hands into the air. 'What else would she be with heritage like that? You humans,' he said in disgust, 'Always attracted to the shiny things. You welcome evil creatures into your homes just because they are beautiful.'

As the jittery feelings in my legs and arms died down, my senses gathered themselves back into my head. He wasn't talking about her personally, he was talking about her relatives.

'She's beautiful because she's descended from fairies.' I put my hands to my hips. 'And I resent the implication that humans only care about loo—'

'That's what I mean!' Bryn practically exploded with the force of his reply, ignoring my offended riposte. 'Troublemakers! Spellcasters! Thieves! The worst kind of deceivers that any dragon has ever come across!' Bryn shouted. Echoes carried through the trees in the moment after, and an owl hooted in response.

This was not something mother had ever warned me about in all the lore she had taught me as a child, and she would have been the one to know. There were no tales I knew of about a mutual enmity between the dragons and fairies.

Bryn lowered his voice with a glance at the trees and stepped closer to me, close enough I could see his eyes burning as if he still held dragon form. 'The fairies have been betrayers of the forest for as long as the dragons keep a history, and we have kept a history far longer than your kind have been walking this earth. The fairies are the worst kind of trouble, and not in any way the kind of people that anyone should be making deals with.'

There wasn't really any response I could think of that wouldn't just escalate the situation, so I clasped my hands in front of me like a reprimanded child.

'I will keep that in mind. Unfortunately I have to live with her and can't do anything about it. Now, can we please get on with what we came here to do?'

Bryn stared at me for several moments, his breath still uneven both from the exertion of the flight and his anger. Thankfully it wasn't long before he calmed, and even his eyes seemed to dim. Though still the same glowing red, they seemed considerably less fiery. He stepped back, turned, and took several deep breaths. 'There have been some changes since last we were here.'

The response was brusque, but this was apparently Bryn's way of showing that he could put his anger aside in favour of more important things. I moved to follow him out of the clearing, but stopped again almost immediately.

There had been something, a noise in the trees to our left.

'Did you hear that?'

'What?' Bryn asked, distracted. He was fumbling with the undone buttons of his robe again now that he was calmer and did not spare a glance at the trees.

'It sounded like…'

Embarrassed, I couldn't finish the sentence. Giggles, I thought, but that was preposterous. Part of me wondered if Sid had somehow managed to follow me even here, but that seemed like a very bad thing to mention right at the moment.

'Never mind.'

Bryn glanced at me but was content to leave it be. He led the way through the forest, much easier to keep up with as a human than he had been as a dragon.

'I've been speaking with whomever I could since last we met,' Bryn said quietly as we walked, 'but no one seems to know any more about the mining. There have been a number of creatures driven out of their normal ranges; a few have come to us seeking redress. They want us to attack, to destroy the humans and to see that they never come back.'

I tried to imagine displaced bunnies approaching a dragon's lair to plead for vengeance and couldn't quite manage it. The thing I could envision from his words was a pack of dragons torching the mountainside and everyone on it. I glanced at Bryn, but he gave no indication of any desire to put the whole thing to flame. Not yet, anyway.

'This isn't your usual flying range,' I said. 'Surely whoever is directing the mining chose this part of the mountains because there aren't usually any dragons that might be disturbed.'

'Indeed. It has been a long time since dragons and men were at war, and I'm sure neither side wants to see a return to that. But if these people don't take care, they'll anger other creatures enough that they'll have a fight on their hands regardless.'

That wasn't a pleasant thought either. The last fighting between humans and the creatures of the forest had occurred a decade ago, and had been at least one contributing factor to my mother's exile.

'My mother sent a letter,' I remembered suddenly, thinking of the small turmoil it had caused when I attempted to carry out her wishes. 'She wants me to read History of the Dark Woods. Have you heard of it?'

'No,' Bryn said as he ducked under a low tree branch. 'What does it say?'

'I don't know,' I admitted, stooping to avoid the same branch. 'I went to see my uncle to ask permission to visit mother but I never got a chance to ask. He was making a complaint to the king about the "infamous Lady Lydia of Carron" so I didn't think it would be an appropriate time.'

Bryn snorted. 'I should say not.' His pace slowed and he looked at me for a moment. 'Why was he complaining about your Lady mother?'

Lady mother. The last time someone had addressed my mother so formally—and kindly—had been when I was a child, well before her exile. I knew the dragons held my mother in esteem, but it still came as a surprise that the form of address would be so kind. She was something of a legend to many outside of Gydrocc, but it was always a surprise when I heard anything other than hellfire and damnation for her. Touched in spite of myself, I had to clear my throat before speaking again.

'Something about not wanting his latest venture to

fail, that there would be no rebellion, and that there would be no one else like her to come put a stop to things.'

As I spoke, the words took on a meaning to me that they hadn't before when I first heard my uncle say them. I stopped short. Apparently Bryn wasn't as thick as I was, because it looked like he put two and two together immediately. He stopped to stare, surprise written all over his features.

Of course Lord Ruben didn't just know about what was happening in the Gray Mountains.

Lord Ruben was in charge of what was happening.

SIXTEEN

'My father has never trusted that man,' Bryn hissed, and his hatred at the thought of my uncle was like poison in my blood. I couldn't help thinking that Bryn and his father were right not to trust Lord Ruben; after all, my own mother didn't trust him, and he was her brother.

Without another word, we turned and continued on through the woods.

The possibility that my uncle was the mastermind behind destroying part of the forest and starting a mining operation that was getting on the nerves of every magical creature for miles, dragons included, was not something I had considered before. It was an immense risk for him to take.

But Lord Ruben was not the type to do this sort of thing out of spite, or without a firm plan. He wouldn't do something like this for revenge. This would be about profit, and no doubt his plan went beyond simply angering a load of creatures he believed were barely sentient.

Hmhmhmhmhm.

The sound stopped me dead in my tracks and I grabbed Bryn's arm. He made an annoyed noise as my fingers bit into his skin, but I wasn't watching him. Something was in the trees, watching us. Until a moment ago I wouldn't have said for sure, but now I knew.

It was an unnerving sound, a little giggle that sounded like it might have issued from a child. Given that no decent child would be wandering around in these woods in the middle of the night, it was almost certainly something more sinister. My grip on Bryn's arm tightened further.

'Something is following us,' I said firmly as I scanned the trees. 'I don't know what it is and I don't like it.'

Bryn turned to look around. 'I didn't hear anything,' he said calmly, then shrugged. 'Whether or not something is following us hardly matters. I can tell you it isn't human, and there isn't anything else in this forest that wouldn't recognise me for what I am.'

His nonchalance was enviable.

'And what about me?' I asked, nearly tripping over

my own feet to keep up with him as he continued walking. 'They can tell I'm human.'

'You walk with a dragon,' He said simply. 'Take comfort in that fact.'

My method of taking comfort in that fact primarily meant that I stuck as close to Bryn as I could for the rest of the short journey. A deep sense of foreboding seeped under my skin and lit every part of my mind with worry at what we might find behind any one of the trees.

It was with some relief that we reached the edge of the clearing, where light from the fires in the camps lent a sense of security in spite of their distance. Bryn crouched at the edge of the trees to look across at the encampment and I did the same.

Campfires were spread along the side of the mountain like a string of beads, all of them tended by one or more sentries who looked bored but not entirely relaxed. Each sentry held tightly to wooden staves or the hilts of their swords as if ready to be attacked any moment.

'Have any of the creatures in the woods attacked the miners?' I asked in a whisper.

'No.' Bryn shook his head. 'The animals complained to us, but none have taken matters onto themselves. Not yet, anyway.'

'Then the sentries are being awfully cautious for no good reason,' I pointed out. A normal night sentry could hardly be expected to be as alert as this group seemed to be, especially when guarding a mine that produced something as common as iron ore. Bryn nodded, still watching the guards.

'Father wants us to have a look inside the mines.' Bryn pointed to the entry to one of the mineshafts. 'He worries that they may have disturbed something inside the mountain that they didn't mean to.'

I looked sharply at Bryn. 'And what exactly might they have disturbed instead of a bunch of rocks?'

Bryn grimaced. 'There's a reason the dragons avoid this part of the mountains.' His voice had gone so quiet I could hardly hear him. 'Our tunnels extend only so far before they end, and none of our tunnels come here.'

I wasn't certain, but there might have been a touch of fear in Bryn's voice as he spoke. Fear, perhaps, and awe. Something about this place made him nervous, though he tried not to show it.

'So you want to explore these tunnels?' I asked doubtfully. 'These tunnels that even the dragons avoid?' Suddenly I wished I had stayed home. 'Why is this a good idea for two nearly unarmed people, one of whom can't turn into a fire-breathing dragon at will?'

Bryn looked at me and grinned. 'Being with a dragon is as good as being armed.'

'That's comforting.' The sarcasm in my voice was unmissable. Dragon or no dragon, these tunnels looked like a very good way to be crushed by tons of falling rocks, lost forever in a maze of tunnels, or to fall down a vertical mineshaft. That was if we even made it past the armed sentries.

'Come on,' Bryn said, grabbing my hand. 'We don't have all night.'

And he pulled me abruptly into the firelight.

Bryn either timed our appearance very well or was the recipient of extreme good fortune, because the nearest sentry was turned away toward another part of the forest as Bryn and I ran past the nearest fire and up the side of the mountain.

It was a good thing Bryn seemed to know what he was doing, because I could hardly tell what was happening as he pulled me first one direction then another across fresh mud and clumps of grass. My feet slid on the damp earth as we ducked out of sight behind a pile of logs just outside the nearest tunnel.

I glanced out at the sentries and was relieved to see that none of them were looking toward us or the tunnels. It was something close to miraculous that Bryn managed to guide us past them without being noticed. The sentries still had all of their attention focused on the treeline, so we had a good chance of going unnoticed.

Bryn gripped my hand again and pulled me toward the nearest tunnel, just a few steps from our cover behind the felled trees.

It seemed darker here, though it was closer to the fires, but it only took a brief glance to see that this tunnel was completely blocked. Wooden planks had been nailed over the frame from top to bottom.

Bryn frowned and looked over it thoroughly in the dim moonlight as I scanned the area behind us for sentries. 'Why would they have closed this one?'

'Perhaps it's not stable,' I said absently. My heart leapt as one of the sentries at the other side of the line of fires turned, but he didn't sound the alarm; we must have gone unnoticed. This was far more treacherous than simply avoiding the guards to escape Gydrocc for the night, and it had an obvious effect on my heart rate. The soldiers in my own castle weren't likely to try to kill me on sight, for one.

I scanned the hillside below us for any other sentries that might have noticed intruders in their midst, but there was still no sign of commotion.

'Maybe it didn't lead to any iron ore,' I said a little absently, 'or they tapped out the seam, though it seems quite early to have done that.'

Bryn frowned, and pulled me on to the next tunnel entrance, not far from the first. This one he looked into and dismissed immediately as well. 'It doesn't go very deep. They must have decided it was too close to the other one.'

We continued along the side of the mountain for what seemed like an eternity, though that could have been because at every step I was worried we might be spotted. Finally Bryn stopped at another tunnel with a satisfied look on his face. When we stepped up to it,

Bryn peered inside and nodded.

'Come,' he said, beckoning to me. 'Let's see how far they've gotten.'

SEVENTEEN

Bryn stepped inside the mine shaft, his head ducked so as not to scrape the low ceiling. I looked after him with no small amount of trepidation, the soldiers behind forgotten momentarily as the tunnel absorbed my concentration. I had been in smaller spaces than this, but not small spaces that might collapse at any moment, with the weight of a mountain over my head.

Bryn was, contrary to my expectations, impressively patient as I hesitated at the door. His calm form standing ahead of me in the tunnel was enough to help me swallow my fears, and I stepped into the dark tunnel behind him.

We only managed a few steps forward before Bryn stopped abruptly with a muttered oath. Unable to see in the almost complete darkness, I ran into the back of him.

'The ceiling is low,' He hissed as he snatched my hand once more in some agitation. 'And there are side tunnels. Hold on or you'll get lost.'

'I hope you'll remember where we're going and how to get out,' I said, terror rising up at the mention of side tunnels. It was far too easy to envision wandering through these tunnels until we starved, unable to find the way back out.

'Don't worry,' Bryn said, his voice dripping with venom. 'A dragon's sense of direction is almost as good as a fairy's.'

It was only fear of distracting Bryn from his navigating that kept me from giving a sharp retort. Yes, there were rivalries among some of the older magical cultures, but Bryn could have at least given Sid as an individual the benefit of the doubt.

Annoyance at his attitude took the edge off my fear of the tunnels. It was temporary, but made the long walk seem more bearable. The darkness became complete before we had gone very far at all, and only pressed more heavily on us every step we took deeper into the mines.

I don't know how long we continued to walk, and in the complete darkness I had no way of gauging the distance, but it was always downward. Eventually, Bryn's pace slowed until we stopped completely. 'We're in a cavern,' he said, and immediately I could hear echoes from all directions in what must have been a very large space. A gentle, rhythmic tinkling noise punctuated the silent darkness, an undercurrent to the echoes of our voices.

'Natural or manmade?' I asked quietly, unnerved as my question bounced back at me.

'Natural, I think.' Bryn crouched low, pulling me down with him. There was for a moment the sound of small rocks clicking together before Bryn said, 'I smell water.'

I did too, now that he pointed it out. It was like a clean breath of surface air after the cold dustiness of the tunnels. The rhythmic tinkling was probably a drip somewhere. 'Does that mean something?'

Bryn didn't answer, but pressed a small sack into my hand. 'Here, take this.'

'What is it?' I accepted the bag a little awkwardly in the darkness.

'Some of the rocks from the floor,' Bryn said. 'Take them back to your alchemist for examination. Surely with more of them he can tell us if there's anything unusual about them.' He stood, pulling on my hand again.

'Wait,' I hissed. I pulled Bryn to a stop for long enough to thread the bag onto my belt, then fumbled for his hand again in the darkness.

He took hold of me immediately and we were off, the fist-sized rocks in the bag drumming against my thigh.

Bryn seemed sure of the direction we were moving in, and I followed bent over slightly to avoid any low-hanging rocks. The darkness that had been pressing down for so long already was becoming more and more oppressive, and I wanted nothing more than to be out of this mine. At the sight of a dim light ahead, I breathed a sigh of relief.

'Thank the gods.'

But Bryn suddenly lunged to one side, and I could do nothing but stumble after him down what must have been a side passage, away from the glorious, freeing light.

'That's not daylight,' he hissed as we came to a halt. He pushed me roughly against the wall and settled himself in beside me. It was obvious from the curve of the stone behind us that we were now hidden in a claustrophobically small crevice in one of the walls.

Pressed up against the cold wall of the mine, I was grateful for Bryn's warm proximity. All of the stone around us, both pressing into my back and hanging overhead, was cold enough that it seemed to steal the life out of me. It felt as if the longer we stayed the more likely it was we would simply be subsumed into the cold rock, to become nothing more than human-shaped outcroppings of stone.

The light we had seen gradually grew brighter until the tunnel we had just dodged out of was lit with the yellow light of a mining lamp. We were not far from the main tunnel, which Bryn watched with intense concentration, pressed as far back as he could into the small space that hid us.

Eventually, the first of the miners passed with a yellow lamp in hand. He looked tired and very thin, as did the five others who followed directly behind, each carrying a small lamp and heavy pack. Three small boys with far more muscle and less fat than was natural took up the rear, pushing low carts along the bumpy tunnel floor.

They did not see us hiding in the little offshoot tunnel and continued on their way completely unworried. The lamp light receded with the echoes of their boots, which left Bryn and I in complete darkness once again. Now that the light come and gone, the darkness seemed far more heavy, almost like a physical presence on my skin that left my scalp tingling and my fingers itching for some kind of action.

'Let's go.' I couldn't control the shiver of fear in my voice. I pulled Bryn out of the alcove in the direction the miners had come from, which must have led to the surface.

'No,' Bryn replied immediately, and I could feel him turn back toward the cavern we had just come from. 'They brought light with them, and I want to see what's in that cavern properly.'

'If you can see well enough to navigate the tunnels why couldn't you see the cavern?' I moaned quietly as we headed down the tunnel once more, aware of the noisy echoes the words made even in my terror.

Bryn didn't reply. He only kept us moving in the direction of the cavern. The smell of water rose up around us again, more noticeable now that I was looking for it, and as we rounded a last curve I could see lantern light ahead of us.

It took exactly half a moment to decide that it was worse to see the tunnel around me than it had been to walk in the dark. The walls were so close on both sides that it wouldn't have taken reaching very far to touch them. The ceiling was low enough I was afraid to stand up straight. I hadn't noticed in the alcove because we weren't moving, but it was certainly obvious now as we walked back to the cavern.

Fear that the walls would collapse on us gnawed at my insides. It was so consuming that I almost didn't realise when we reached the cavern, but once my eyes were drawn to the large, open space, I was unable to look away.

The cavern was not just large, it was enormous. Gydrocc Castle would have easily fit inside the space, excepting maybe the tallest of the towers. The miners were setting up on the far side of the cavern, across a makeshift bridge spanning a stream that bisected the space. They looked like ants crawling up the other wall of the cavern as they prepared to work.

I was surprised at the amount of light in the cavern, given that the only source of light was the line of lamps set up on the other side of the stream. That is, until Bryn silently pointed out the massive crystalline stalactites hanging from the ceiling.

The stalactites were like strange chandeliers of glass and stone, not pure crystal, but with significant chunks of crystal sticking out of them. Water dripped constantly from the crystalline masses onto the floor, the small, musical noises magnified by the size of the space.

Between the crystals in the stalactites and the water reflecting the light around the room, the small light of the lamps was magnified to give an eerie bluish glow to the entire place. Bryn seemed unfazed by the strangeness of it all and led me away from the entry to the cavern along one wall a few steps so we would not be seen if anyone else came in. He pulled me down to crouch behind a large stalagmite and peered out around the side.

As it turned out, he was right to see that we were hidden. Not five minutes after we stepped out of the way, more miners came into the room, this time a group of ten with a further five young boys following. The first boys on the other side of the room began gathering up the few rocks that had been broken from the face of wall, ready to make their way back to the surface.

I glanced at Bryn, wondering how we were possibly going to make our escape now. Surely there would be a near constant flow of people in and out soon. Though it was still very early in the morning work had apparently started in earnest and it was not likely to stop soon.

Bryn frowned as he looked out, perhaps thinking the same thing. As the second set of miners crossed to start work, the first boys came back, each hefting a sack on their back. Only one of them carried a lamp, leading the way for the others.

Bryn tapped my shoulder and mouthed 'Follow them.'

I nodded, and we waited as the boys came across the bridge. They were already working up a sweat. As they approached I could see that they could not have been more than ten years old or so, but the lines of dust and tiredness on their faces made them look like old men ready to lay down their tools and take to a sick bed. It was the way of the mines and always had been, but the thought that they would spend the whole of their short lives in mines like this made me feel physically ill.

The boys did not notice us near the tunnel entrance, they were too busy trying to keep from tripping on the uneven ground. As they reached the tunnel entry a loud creak and something like a moan echoed around the cave.

The boys froze, and so did the miners. The sound of chiselling ceased abruptly and the miners seemed to collectively hold their breath, eyes on the ceiling.

The wall behind me was vibrating. Confused, I looked back and put a hand to the stone. It was just the most minor of vibrations, but it lasted through three of my stalled heartbeats. My fear that the entire weight of the mountain would come down on us renewed itself.

The shaking slowed in the silence, then stopped, and the moan settled into a ghostly echo. The miners and boys looked around briefly, and the chiselling began again. The boys picked up the handles of their carts and made their way out of the cavern as if nothing had happened.

Bryn could have led me anywhere at that moment and I likely wouldn't have noticed. I only wanted to be out of that mountain and out of it now.

If we hadn't had to follow the boys on the walk back to the surface I'm certain I could have covered the distance in half the time. We trailed along behind them at a good distance, just close enough that we never quite lost sight of the light from their lantern.

Finally it started to get lighter in the tunnels. The dim lantern light was overtaken by natural, real light, light that seemed to me the greatest salvation I could ever have hoped for. Bryn held us back after the boys disappeared from view out of the mine, and it was only then that I realised that something was wrong.

The light from outside was very strong after the darkness in the mines, far stronger than it would have been if it was still night.

We had gone into the mines in darkness, but we were coming out in the light. Bryn grimaced and I stifled a moan. We had missed the sunrise; the whole camp would be awake, and we would have to get out of here in broad daylight.

EIGHTEEN

Well, broad daylight was perhaps an exaggeration, but not much of one. After the darkness of the mines even to the thin rays of early dawn were like a beacon in my eyes. We lingered at the entry to the mine while our eyes adjusted to the brightness, just deep enough inside that we could disappear again if someone came inside.

My eyes were still dazzled by the light when Bryn squeezed my hand and pulled. One of our hands—probably mine—was so slick with sweat I had no idea how he held onto me as he pulled me out of the mineshaft at a run.

Almost the instant we emerged, I heard shouts. My eyes had not yet adjusted to the brightness, so I could only see a few feet in front of me through squinted eyelids. Bryn, on the other hand, seemed to have suffered no ill effects from the sudden change in light levels, and led the way with a fleetness of foot that told me we were in trouble.

'Duck!' He hissed, and I felt an arrow fly past the back of my head to a chorus of annoyed voices. I ducked and heard another thump as one embedded itself in something to my left.

I blinked rapidly until I could see what kind of trouble we were in. A quick look behind showed two sentries with swords aloft trying to catch up with us. Below us on the mountainside standing by the campfires were several bowmen, all of them either ready to fire or nearly so.

'Do you have any weapons?' I shouted at Bryn as we abruptly changed direction to go uphill.

'Just myself,' He panted. 'But it takes time to shift, and I can't do it at a run!'

I looked behind us at the guards, who were catching up, and the bowmen, who would fortunately soon be out of range.

'Find a place to change and do it! I'll try to give you cover!' I shouted.

We passed the first of the mineshafts, running up the mountainside instead of down, where we had come from during the night.

There would be plenty of space for Bryn to take flight here, where the trees had all been cut down, while there wouldn't be if we went into the forest.

We ran past several piles of logs and scattered tarp-covered wagons half full of rocks from the mines. Bryn chose one of those piles of logs, clambered up it, and began to shift forms without taking time to loose so much as a single button on his robes.

I climbed up after him as quickly as I could, the trees rough under my hands, and pulled the crossbow forward from where it hung around my shoulders. The sentries were not far behind; they would be on us in moments.

There was just enough time for me to load the crossbow and fire one bolt, which I aimed very roughly at the soldier who led the charge against us. I pleaded silently with any deity that would listen that the bolt would fire true and tried to concentrate so Philip's charm would have the best chance of working.

I squeezed the trigger, and the moment the bolt was away dropped the crossbow back to its strap. The bolt missed its mark badly but landed between the feet of the sentry in the lead, which fortunately startled him so much he tripped.

I yanked my dagger out of its scabbard and began to pray with a fervency that would have made a believer blush. In all of my lessons as a lady in court, sparring was not something that had been covered. If it came down to dagger against sword I would be dead in an instant.

There was the sound of fabric tearing behind me,

which I took as a good sign. Surely Bryn would be finished shifting before the sentries reached us and we would be off safely. Balanced astride two logs, I tried to strike a menacing pose and brandished my dagger.

The sentries slowed, horror-struck, their eyes on what was happening behind me. The image of a dragon bursting out of a man's skin was not something I had seen before but I could imagine the effect, especially when it happened unexpectedly like this.

Unfortunately the bowmen standing below were not as terrified, as they were farther away from the emerging dragon. They had run up the mountainside to get back in firing range and were now ready to rain death on both of us, dragon or no.

The first arrow struck one of the logs I was standing on, and the second flew past less than a hand span from my face. I turned around and ran for Bryn in hopes he was ready.

He was, although only barely. The scales on his back seemed to harden under my hands as I dived for his shoulder. As I passed his head he let out a stream of fire that caught the front end of the logs and must have singed the eyebrows off the sentries. I grabbed his neck, as his pack was not strapped in its usual place there, and swung myself on awkwardly as Bryn's wings unfurled.

Bryn lunged forward to take flight. I dropped my dagger and nearly unseated myself trying to grab for it as we took off. His wings laboured heavily to catch the air, which was very still, and he had to take several lumbering leaps down the mountainside, over the heads of the terrified sentries, before he could get enough lift to clear the ground. We barely managed to avoid scraping the treetops as we went, arrows still whizzing past.

I couldn't so much as think of moving, or holding onto anything other than Bryn's neck. His scales seemed extremely slick under my still-wet palms, and I feared with every downstroke of his wings that I was going to lose my grip.

To keep my head down as arrows flew past was terrifying, as I couldn't see where we were going or whether Bryn might need to make a sudden manoeuvre in the air, but if I lifted my head it would sacrifice my grip. I chose a tight grip and no view.

We left behind the arrows and swords so quickly it was hard to believe they had really been there at all.

The sun rose behind us to light up the countryside below and gradually warmed my back through my coat though my face froze in the wind.

Tired, shaking, and glad of my life, my mind wandered. Wouldn't it be ironic if I survived the night and all of the terror of the mines only to fall off the dragon when all was otherwise safe? I almost laughed through chattering teeth. It would be just my luck.

But Bryn flew more slowly than usual, for which I was very grateful even though it made the journey longer. The steadiness was reassuring, especially given that I had nothing but smooth scales to hold onto.

It was midmorning by the time Gydrocc Lake came into view. My absence had certainly been noted by now, to say nothing of when I got back to the castle sometime around midday. As we approached the cliff-side I remembered Sid; had she stayed at the clearing the whole night, or had she done the sensible thing and gone back to the castle when it got near sunrise?

Bryn circled a couple of times before coming in to land quite gently in the clearing. It would have been a perfect landing except that he closed his wings quite suddenly before his front legs touched the ground, which made his body to drop very suddenly. I couldn't help a shriek when his feet came into abrupt contact with the ground. Unable to keep my grip I slid from his neck and tumbled to the ground ungracefully.

'Ow,' I managed, as I fought my way back onto hands and knees, the crossbow wedged uncomfortably under me. 'You could have been a little gentler.'

Bryn snorted as I regained my feet and I felt a pull on my coat. I turned to see Bryn had caught the hem between his teeth, luminous red eyes directed at me with a doleful expression.

'What?' I asked, tired and more irritable with every moment that passed. The thought of what might happen when I returned to the castle was more than a small worry now that all was said and done.

Bryn whimpered.

I didn't know dragons could whimper.

I frowned and looked into those big eyes, which seemed to be pleading. Bryn jerked his head toward his right side, my coat still in his mouth. I had no choice but to follow as he pulled me with him.

As he led me around to his other side, I looked across to see the rest of him and gasped. Streaming from the golden scales high on his foreleg was a stream of coppery dragon's blood. It seeped down like thick tar to cover most of his leg and claws.

Halfway down Bryn's leg an arrow stuck out from between his scales. The end of the shaft had been broken off somewhere on the journey, leaving a stump six inches long. I rested a hand on Bryn's broad snout and he released my coat.

'How did that happen?' I breathed, overawed at the idea of something as simple as an arrow piercing the thick hide of a dragon. Then I realized—of course, he hadn't been a dragon the whole time. At some point, whether while we were running or while he shifted from one form to another, an arrow had struck him in the arm.

The only thing I could think of that would help was to remove the arrow. With a glance at the pool of cold water where the upper waterfall landed, I took hold of the side of Bryn's face and led him over to the water. I knelt and motioned him toward the pond.

Of the properties of dragon's blood, one stood out to me in particular, and that was that it could burn through most things given enough time. I couldn't just stick my hand over the wound and pull the arrow out without getting blood on me, which could leave me as badly injured as he was. His leg would need to be mostly clean before I attempted anything.

I nodded my head at the water. 'You'll have to dip your leg in, I'm afraid.'

He glared at me. I made a helpless motion in the direction of the water. Bryn lifted his massive chin, closed those big red eyes, and plunged his leg in with a splash. He immediately gave what sounded like a belch behind closed lips and smoke poured out from the gaps between his teeth.

The worst of the thick, sticky blood rinsed free after a few minutes so I could see the wound. It was impossible to tell just how deeply embedded the arrow was, but it hardly mattered. It would still have to come out past dragon scales, which was not going to be an easy task.

With a deep breath, I reached forward into the water.

The water was absolutely frigid. I gasped and made a face that was apparently amusing enough to Bryn that he grinned with all of his teeth, which let out the last of the smoke from his little belch. I grimaced at him and stuck the rest of my arm in. It started to shiver almost immediately.

It only took moments to lose most of the feeling in my hands from the cold as I explored the stump of the arrow with my fingers. Bryn bore this well enough, though it must have hurt as I touched the arrow, which did not move under my fingertips. It was well enough into the muscle that it wasn't going to go anywhere without considerable force.

I gritted my teeth, looked at Bryn, and said, 'Don't move.'

With one quick movement, I grabbed the arrow and pulled. It didn't come out right away, but slowly slid toward me. Bryn keened as the arrow moved, a strange high-pitched sound that made my eardrums throb.

I didn't have enough leverage to get it out quickly. My hand slid back on the arrow and I had to readjust my grip several times, sloshing cold water over the rest of my arm. With a grunt, I gripped the arrow one last time and pulled with all my might.

The arrow came free so suddenly I almost landed in the pool. A gush of blood followed, lost quickly in the moving water. Bryn didn't flinch, but let out a kind of relieved sigh.

I released the arrow into the pool and pulled my hand out of the water to pat Bryn's shoulder, my fingers shaking with the cold. 'Any chance you could warm me up?' I asked, holding up my freezing hands.

Bryn snorted and rolled away from the water onto his side. He tucked his cold, injured leg in close to his chest and motioned with his head for me to come closer. I followed, and at Bryn's continuing gesticulations placed my hands on his barrel chest.

The broad expanse of golden scales was warm to the touch. Bryn breathed in deeply and let out a kind of purr. Almost immediately his scales warmed further until it was almost unbearable to keep my hands on him. It was almost as if he was stoking an internal furnace with those regular, deep breaths.

It was so warm and pleasant standing next to him that I was almost lulled to sleep standing up. Only the hesitant sound of a very human throat being cleared jerked me back to consciousness.

'Tara?'

Sid's voice was trembling as she approached from the other side of the clearing. Still shaky from both fleeing and flying, I turned to see her wrapped tightly in her cloak looking cold and tired. She eyed Bryn's prone form with a kind of suspicious fear.

'Oh, Sid,' I said with a tired sigh. 'I forgot you were here. We need to go.' I looked at the sun, high in the sky now, and tried to think of some excuse for our absence.

'What are we going to tell them back at the castle?'

'I have no idea.' I was so tired now I almost didn't care. I turned back to Bryn and directed a motherly look at him. 'You should rest here until that stops bleeding. No one will disturb you.'

Bryn nodded once, closed his eyes, and curled up more tightly now that I was standing well enough away from him. He didn't seem to have even noticed Sid, or remembered who or what she was. That was a small blessing of both of us being so exhausted. There was no way I could have handled another confrontation right at that moment.

'Come on,' I said as I walked over to Sid. 'Let's get home.'

NINETEEN

Sid's voice was dreamy as she rode back to the castle beside me on her borrowed horse.

'You're the maiden sacrifice.' She rolled the words over her tongue as if savouring them. 'You,' she said slowly, 'are the sacrifice to the dragons.'

'You've said it enough times now, you know,' I said coolly. 'We could just ride the rest of the way in amiable silence.'

Sid looked across at me, still beautiful in spite of the rat's nest of hair on her head and a muddy dress. I could see at a glance that the refrain was still playing in her mind; she was looking at me, but the distraction on her face was obvious.

I sighed. This was not unexpected, but it was annoying. She'd said the same thing about a dozen times in different ways since we reached the bottom of the cliff to make our way back to the castle.

'So,' Sid said conversationally, 'how did it happen?'

I made an impatient noise. 'We can talk about that later. For instance, if we manage to get back into the castle without being caught, interrogated, and punished.' I shook my head. 'Now is the time to figure out how to stay out of trouble, not to linger on the cause of it.'

'We could tell them we went out early berry-picking,' Sid suggested.

'It's too early in the season for berries.'

I led us into a thicket that stood off the main road where we hopefully wouldn't be stumbled upon by patrols. The castle was just visible through the thick brush that lent us camouflage.

I dismounted and handed Sid Niggle's reins so I could peer through the undergrowth at the castle to get some idea of what might be happening. If there was very much activity outside or atop the castle walls it would be far more difficult to make our way inside quietly.

'You say you managed to sneak out through the main gate last night,' I said thoughtfully. 'Any chance we could do the same today?'

'Not really.' Sid frowned. 'The guards were inside the gatehouse with some of the maids last night, it wasn't exactly the height of stealth to get past them.'

The guards of Gydrocc. Regular lions, them. Heaven forbid we have to defend ourselves against actual enemies.

'Do you think we could get as far as the stables?' I asked as I watched a patrol go out from the main gates toward the town at the other side of the castle from us. 'We could unsaddle the horses, hide these things—' I held up the crossbow meaningfully, '—and make our way across to Philip's tower.'

'If anyone sees you, though…' Sid trailed off. I looked back to see her eye my clothing meaningfully and immediately took her meaning. There was no way I could convince anyone that I wasn't up to something when I was wearing a very muddy set of man's clothing.

'Maybe they won't recognise me,' I said with a dry laugh.

Sid straightened suddenly and snapped her fingers. 'I have it!' She said, and started tying the reins of both horses to a tree, her face radiant. 'You'll wear my dress, and we'll say we went out for an early ride but you fell off your horse.'

I looked at her, dumbfounded, as she turned back to me, already undoing the laces at the side of her dress. It was very simple but there were at least two flaws readily apparent. To me, at least.

'Won't it be a bit obvious if I'm wearing your dress and you're wearing your underclothes?'

Sid waved a hand dismissively. 'A Marchant

underdress looks like a Clovian outer dress. With my cloak over the top no one will notice. All you have to do is put on my dress and leave your other things here. We can get them later.'

She was right that no one would notice the difference between her underdress and overdress. I had seen both and frequently wondered why she bothered wearing such a fine dress underneath an even finer dress every single day.

'Only one problem,' I said, turning to face her.

'What?'

'I'm almost twice your size.'

Sid opened her mouth to protest, looked at me more closely, and closed her mouth again. She looked down at herself, looked at me again, and squinted.

'This dress has laces. We can make it work.'

Half an hour later I was uncomfortably perched on my horse trying not to move my arms much. It felt as though any gestures larger than a gentle flick of the wrist would have the stitching on Sid's dress release its now tenuous grip on the fabric.

The laces had helped make up for the difference in our sizes, especially on the arms, but the final result left me with the back laces almost completely undone. My regular tunic, muddy as it was, had to go over the top to hide the makeshift work. It would never do for an audience with the queen, but to get past the guards it could just be enough.

We rode sedately out of the treeline toward the castle, our pace meant to inspire the idea that we had not been the victims of an unfortunate accident. Sid didn't speak, but held her head up high as if she had done nothing wrong. At her example, I did the same. It wouldn't hurt to look confident in the face of the unknown.

It was only when we reached the gate that it became obvious we had been missed.

There was only one guard standing at the main gate as we approached. He snapped to attention at the sight of us, his eyes wide, and called to someone inside the castle walls.

'They are safe! They are safe!'

Sid and I exchanged a worried look. Though we expected this reaction, it didn't make it any less nerve-wracking to see the scenario played out in front of us. The alibi we had come up with was about to be put to the test and we could only hope it was sufficient.

We entered at the main gate to see Hawkins running toward us, his round face shining with sweat. 'You're safe!' he cried, and went down on one knee between the two of us with a salute, which forced us to pull our horses to a halt just inside the gate. 'The king was going to have my head for not sending someone with you when you went out this morning. Next time you must let someone know when you go out riding!'

I smiled at Hawkins, and breathed an exaggerated

sigh of relief at Sid, who giggled. If they had only assumed we had gone out for a ride and were very, very late returning, it was far better than I could have hoped.

'We left so early I didn't want to disturb anyone. Accept my profound apologies for causing you difficulty,' I pleaded a little mechanically. Exhaustion was catching up with me, moreso today than on other mornings I had sneaked out before, given the way the night had gone. I dismounted stiffly, all of my limbs crying for rest.

Hawkins was too relieved to ask any further questions, but all thought of appeasing him disappeared at the sight of Lord Ruben standing beside Queen Isabelle at the main doors of the castle.

Lord Ruben looked furious, and while the queen was not generally one to make a fuss, her stony demeanour expressed quite clearly that we were in trouble. Lord Ruben made an unmistakeable motion for us to come here now.

With a quick glance at Sid, I started off across the courtyard, hoping that my strange manner of dress would go unnoticed. Sid caught up with me after a moment and threaded her arm through mine.

I glanced at her, but she only continued to look forward at the queen. Her closeness was comforting; the fact that I wasn't going alone to my fate today was a reassurance that I'd never had the pleasure of experiencing before.

Sid and I were swept through the main doors between Lord Ruben and the queen without ceremony and ushered into the nearest reception room. It was a small room with only three chairs and a table, and a small window high in the wall that let in the meanest amount of light or air.

Queen Isabelle sank into the central of the three chairs without taking her eyes from us and waved off one of her ladies in waiting who made an attempt to fan her moist brow.

'Where have you been?' The queen demanded without introduction. Her face was stern, unforgiving; I knew her better than I knew the king, but I had never seen her in such a forbidding mood. There was as much fire in her eyes as there had been in Bryn's last night.

'Why was your maid not informed that you were going out?' Queen Isabelle did not wait for an answer to either of her questions. 'You had the entire castle in an uproar. And what on earth have you done to your dress?'

The last question was aimed at me with a disgusted gesture. The dress I now wore—Sid's—was covered in mud from her fall at the cliff during the night, and undoubtedly looked worse in the tidy surroundings of the castle than it had out in the wilderness.

The story we concocted earlier came easily to my lips. 'I fell from my horse, my lady, but I am unhurt.' I bowed my head and dropped a small curtsey.

'We only wanted to go out early to watch the sunrise from the cliffs, Lady,' Sid said meekly. Her expression was innocent as she spoke, her eyes downcast as if she was embarrassed to have caused so much trouble. Perhaps she was. Either way she was sufficiently convincing as she continued in smooth, humble tones. 'Lady Tara has been telling me that sunrise over the mountains from the top of the cliffs is a phenomenon unmatched anywhere in the world and I wanted to see it for myself.'

'That is not a safe ride,' Lord Ruben said immediately, unfazed by Sid's complimentary tone. His eyes cut to me. 'Why were you riding so far, without an escort and without leaving a message for us? We are informed you did not even visit the kitchens for breakfast.'

I looked to Lord Ruben, answers forming on my tongue swiftly. This was not, after all, the first time I'd had to dig myself out of a hole when it came to not being where I was supposed to. As I looked at him, though, the memory of my conversation with Bryn stopped my tongue and my thoughts. This was the same man who decided to dig up a mountainside and anger a whole host of creatures so he could have some mining done; what qualms would he have about betraying me if I slipped now?

'I was convinced we would make it back in time for an early luncheon,' I said as calmly as I could, 'and Princess Amanthea expressed that she did not wish to eat so early in the morning, for fear of upsetting her stomach on the ride.'

'So you were simply held up?' Lord Ruben's eyes narrowed. 'By a fall from your horse?'

'Yes, milord.' I bowed my head meekly for good measure. The same gesture had made Sid look humbled and sorrowful, so perhaps it would do the same for me, as I couldn't easily muster the energy now to continue facing my accusers.

Queen Isabelle slapped the arm of her chair suddenly, which made Sid and I jump. Her tones were cutting, sharper than I'd heard before. 'It was foolhardy. Extremely foolhardy. There are patrols out looking for you now, and you've caused such a commotion that I can hardly speak.' I glanced up to see her eyes flashing with anger. 'Princess, you should know better.'

I looked across at Sid, who looked up at the queen in surprise. The queen was angry, but above that she looked magisterial, wise, and very powerful as she drew herself up to rebuke Sid. Queen Isabelle's dark eyes flashed and the red flush of anger climbed her tanned cheeks as she spoke.

'You have been brought to this kingdom to wed a prince, not to go gallivanting across the countryside with no chaperone and no care for those who would worry at your disappearance. You are destined to someday be queen of this kingdom and I cannot see how you are ever going to be prepared for that if you insist on denying yourself blame in a situation where you have caused this amount of disruption. You will go to your chambers and you will make yourselves presentable. I will decide your punishment and send for you.'

Sid sat in stunned silence, her cheeks turning red as the queen's words sunk in. If the queen had directed that angry tirade at me it might just have reduced me to tears, especially given how tired I was. Seeing Sid berated like that was almost enough to set me off. Sid couldn't possibly have had a restful night either, but she still looked quietly composed and only nodded as she murmured an apology.

The queen did not acknowledge Sid's words with as much as a nod. She looked to the door, which was immediately opened, and Sid stood to leave. I followed her lead with a last glance at Lord Ruben, and the two of us backed out the door.

We slowly made our way back to our tower, events of the night and morning obviously catching up to both of us. Sid leaned close to me as we turned the corner into the wide corridor leading past the main hall.

'Lord Ruben is a sharp sort. I think he noticed that the stain on your dress doesn't have a match on your tunic.'

I looked down and immediately realised she was right about the mismatched stain. I hadn't thought of that when we were changing but it seemed very obvious now. Anyone who thought about me taking a fall from my horse would figure out fairly quickly that it was impossible to stain my underdress like that without a matching stain on my tunic.

'Hopefully it won't matter,' I said without much heart. 'There isn't a lot of reason for them not to believe us.'

Sid cleared her throat, her eyes red. She seemed to have some difficulty as she turned to me and said, 'I'll change into something clean and come up to your room. You should change as well.' She cleared her throat again and looked away as we turned to our tower. 'Then you're going to tell me what's going on.'

She mounted the tower steps with ease, and did not turn to face me again. She disappeared behind a flurry of golden hair and a heavy oak door. As I climbed the stairs past her door, the sound of muffled sobs slipped out the cracks in the wood.

TWENTY

I was still struggling to get out of Sid's dress when she came into my room a few minutes later. Her eyes were still shining, but she had regained her composure fairly swiftly and her expression said that she didn't want to talk about what had happened downstairs. Seeing that, I turned my attention to the dress again.

Two of the seams had popped in my fight with the embroidered silk, but that had only made it more difficult to get things undone so I could get it off. With Sid's help I managed to get it off over my head, and I threw it on the floor in frustration. Sid sat down on the bed as I washed my hands and face and wrapped myself in a robe.

'You want to know what's going on,' I said as I tied

the robe shut and crossed to sit down on the end of the bed next to her.

'I think that's only fair,' Sid said seriously. 'It's not every day someone sneaks out of the castle and I find them conversing with a dragon in the middle of the night.' She settled herself more comfortably and gave me a pointed look.

I drummed my fingers on the nearest bedpost as I thought of the best way to introduce the story. Sid already knew the kingdom's history with dragons, so I didn't need to get into that. I only needed to explain why I was the one that had been chosen.

'First of all, you need to know that my mother is a little strange.'

This was an understatement, but a good enough place to start. Sid nodded, watching me with those big, bright eyes. I suppose that to a fairy descended princess, no parentage seems too strange.

I sighed. 'Have you heard of Lydia of Carron?'

'The champion of good causes, the defender of righteousness, the feeder of unicorns?' Sid laughed as if I had asked her whether the sky was blue. 'Of course I have! Who hasn't?'

Feeder of unicorns. Wonderful. Even people who admired her couldn't think of anything less ridiculous than feeder of unicorns. I couldn't help another sigh.

'That's my mother.'

Sid's jaw dropped open. 'Your mother is Lydia of Carron?' She bounced onto her knees and leaned forward anxiously. 'You mean your mother is the woman who led the fairies to victory against the marauding armies of the Grens? The same who bartered with destiny and saved the were-folk of Dunelm?'

'I wouldn't say bartered,' I protested weakly. 'She only met destiny the once and she said it was more of a friendly conversation over a cup of tea than actual bartering.'

'I've heard stories about her since I was a tiny child!' Sid was practically bouncing up and down with excitement. 'My favourite was always the story of how she rode a unicorn through the lines of battle at Snowsdown with an enchanted harp that made the soldiers forget all about fighting. Did she actually do that or have the stories been exaggerated?'

'Yes,' I said shortly, holding a hand up for silence. 'That Lydia of Carron. That's my mother. You may have heard the story of how she walked into a dragon's lair and got him to stop marauding?'

Sid nodded. I grimaced. 'The dragon from last night is…' I trailed off. I hadn't actually thought about what my relationship to Bryn was called now, and the usual words seemed somehow inadequate. 'I have a contract with the dragon from last night. To marry him. Eventually. The dragon my mother negotiated with in that cave is my future father-in-law.'

If Sid had looked stunned before it was nothing compared to the expression on her face now. 'You're engaged to a dragon?'

'Yes,' I said shortly. 'It's a way of keeping the dragons from seeking maiden sacrifices. The reason I met up with him last night is because there's something going on in the forest and he wanted my help.'

'Why your help, and not someone else's?' Sid looked confused for a moment, then gave a sly smile and leaned toward me with mischief written all over her face. 'Are you sure he just wanted your help?'

'Yes. Er, no. Not like that. We needed to meet to make the contract binding.' Her questions–spoken and unspoken –were difficult to answer all at once. 'He came to me for help because of my mother. He figured if I was anything like her, I'd be willing to help find out what was going on.'

Sid straightened and snapped her fingers with understanding. 'Were you actually meeting up with him the night you got those bruises?' She suddenly looked worried, and perhaps a little disgusted.

'He took me flying,' I said defensively, not wanting her to think ill of Bryn even if he thought ill of her. 'I wasn't expecting how rough the ride would be. It's quite a bit trickier than riding a horse.'

'I can imagine,' Sid said, her eyebrows raised. She leaned back against the bedpost and stared at me, and I could see that she was trying to rein in all the questions that no doubt wanted to tumble out.

She was as much an ally as I was ever going to have

under the circumstances, and while she wasn't the person I would have chosen, something made me think she would be more helpful than anyone else I might have chosen. I leaned forward, quite serious. 'Sid, I'll tell you what's going on, but you have to swear to me that you won't tell anyone else. I don't know what Lord Ruben would do if he knew I was defying him like this, but I can tell you it wouldn't be pretty.'

Sid looked surprised, but nodded. 'Of course.' She held up one hand as if making an oath. 'I'll keep your secrets just as I know I can trust you to keep mine.'

I had one guilty thought about the fact that I'd agreed to spy on her for Lord Ruben, but pushed that away. There were other things to deal with now.

I took a deep breath and explained as briefly as possible about what Bryn and I had found in the forest at the foot of the Gray Mountains. When I mentioned where this was all taking place, Sid's face darkened, but she said nothing.

At my description of the mines, she shook her head, confused. I finished by telling her about the letter from mother and my suspicion that Lord Ruben was the orchestrator of the whole event.

Sid said nothing for a long moment, then gave me a thoughtful look. 'I know the place you're talking about.' She leaned back on her heels on the bed. 'But I'm not certain why anyone would be mining there. That part of the forest is right on the border of Marchant and is famed for being cursed.'

That was the same thing Bryn had said when he mentioned the forest initially, though he hadn't been able to give any more information. I perked up at the possibility of finding out something new. 'Do you know what kind of curse?'

'No,' Sid said apologetically. 'Only that the patrols don't go there and no one has lived in that part of the forest for decades.'

My mind went back to the strange childish laughter in the forest the night before and I shuddered. 'That forest is something strange, that much I can tell you for sure. If I never had to go back there again I'd be more than happy.'

I looked across the room to the bag of rocks Bryn had handed me so many hours ago. Exhaustion struck me again as I thought of going to Philip's tower to ask him for help in identifying any strangeness about the product of the mines. This whole thing was turning into a never-ending list of tasks that were difficult if not impossible to accomplish.

'Why would anyone want to disturb a cursed forest?' Sid leaned back, looking more confused by the moment. 'I can see why your fiancé wanted help.'

'He's not my fiancé,' I protested flatly. Both of us must have known I didn't mean it, because Sid didn't respond to that. Instead, she flopped back onto my bed.

Sid stared at the ceiling and said, 'Well if there's something Lord Ruben wants in the forest that at least explains my betrothal.'

I straightened up, stunned. 'What are you talking about?'

Sid turned bright red. 'Oh. Um. It's nothing.'

'Tell me,' I said seriously, 'or I will summon a dragon to carry you off right this minute.'

Sid was so startled she coughed, then let out a great peal of laughter.

'Fine, you win.' She rolled onto her side to face me. 'I'm not exactly well-liked at home.'

She must have seen the disbelief on my face because she shook her head and continued. 'No, really, they don't like me. I'm a troublemaker. I sneak off and steal things and I have a tendency to say things I shouldn't in court. They've tried getting me married off to someone for years but no one would take the offer until Prince Caleb, and that was something of a miracle.'

The words poured out of Sid like they'd been waiting inside for a long time to come out. When she finished, she took a deep shuddering breath like she wanted to say more but had found her restraint again. There was certainly more, but whether she wanted to talk about it was not up to me.

'Oh,' was all I could say.

Sid stared hard at her fingernails and continued carefully. 'My family won't have minded giving up something they desperately want rid of—me—with the understanding that someone else will use something that they don't need—which is whatever your uncle is looking for in those mines. My family got what they wanted without having to give up anything they think is important.'

I sat in stunned silence for several moments as we both considered this. I thought of my agreement to spy on Sid, and wondered what Lord Ruben was up to; was he suspicious as to why the royal family of Marchant had been so quick to give up a prized daughter in exchange for those 'trade connections' he was so eager for? Perhaps he already knew that Sid was considered a troublemaker back home, and assigning me as spy was simply a logical response to the situation.

'Lord Ruben asked me to spy on you,' I said abruptly. Sid's head snapped up. I shrugged. 'I'm not sure what his motivation is, but he wants to know your movements, specifically whether or not you do anything suspicious.'

'Well if he wants to find out about suspicious movements it isn't me he should be watching,' Sid said with a pointed look at me.

'I know.' I shrugged. 'You can imagine why I was so worried about showing up so late this morning.' I yawned broadly, unable to help myself. We had spent so long sitting on a soft surface that my tenuous hold on consciousness was slipping away. All I wanted to do was sleep the rest of the day away.

I hid another yawn behind one hand and said, 'Is

there any chance you could make excuses for me if anyone comes around today?'

'Of course,' Sid said, standing. 'Get some sleep, you must be exhausted.'

She slipped out the door quietly, and I sank into the bed, overwhelmed at everything that had happened, but so tired that sleep took me just moments later.

When I woke to the last fading rays of daylight, it was to find a bowl of soup and a slab of bread on the table in my room. The soup was stone cold, but I ate it anyway, my stomach rumbling for anything remotely edible. I picked up the bowl to get the last of the bits from the bottom and saw that something else had been brought put on the table while I was asleep–Fionnuel's History of the Dark Wood.

Confused, I opened the front cover and found a note from Sid.

I thought I might help. It was hidden in another stack of books and the librarian said it wasn't available, but I went back later and found it. No damage that I can see! Don't read it in public, I don't think we want to advertise that I sneaked in and took it.

I actually laughed out loud. To think I had been so ready to hate her when she arrived, and here she was being genuinely useful. I never would have had the nerve to actually steal a book from under Felton or Amelie's nose, though I might pretend that I did. The fact that Sid had remembered the title of the book from only a brief mention several days ago was more than a little impressive. This princess was far cleverer than she let on.

For a few minutes I searched for a suitable place to hide the book before I tucked it under my mattress with my other papers. It wasn't the safest place to hide something, but I couldn't think of anywhere else.

I climbed back into bed, mind and stomach satisfied, and closed my eyes again. It didn't take long before I was lost in sleep.

TWENTY-ONE

The following morning when it was time for Sid and me to get on with our morning tasks, I brought the History down to her room and began to read while Sid and Alois got on with their sewing. Sid was attempting to fix the seams on the dress I had torn so badly the day before without very much success. I felt guilty about that, but not enough that I tried to help; my sewing skills were limited by my patience, which was never exceptional.

As was expected from a book of history, Fionnuel's book didn't make for very interesting reading. It was certainly not the type of thing I was accustomed to reading in large chunks. After less than half an hour Sid had to nudge me awake.

'Sorry,' I muttered as I stretched out sore muscles. The chair was hardly comfortable, and my neck already had a crick in it from my long sleep the night before. The fact I managed to fall asleep now in such uncomfortable circumstances said a lot about my interest levels in the apparently important book.

Sid scoffed, shoved the dress she was working on into Alois' lap, and snatched the book out of my limp hands. 'I'll do the reading, you get on with something else. You're getting nowhere with this.'

I rubbed my eyes with one hand and reached for the book with the other. 'No, I couldn't make you do that. It's extremely boring, I promise, you won't make any better progress than I will.'

'Yes I will,' Sid said stubbornly. She put the book on her chair and sat down on it, arms folded across her chest. 'You're no use to anyone falling asleep, you might as well be doing something useful right now, like heading off to say hello to Philip.'

The meaning of her words was not lost on me. I stood stiffly and excused myself.

It took me longer to navigate the stairs than it would have normally. My legs ached both from riding a dragon and from running so much, and the rest of me felt simultaneously wobbly and stiff as I first went upstairs to collect the bag of rocks from my room then down toward the rest of the castle.

At the main corridor I struck off at a slow walk for Philip's tower.

Along the hallways I nodded and bade polite greetings to courtiers that passed until an excited voice called out behind me and brought me to a halt.

'Lady Tara!'

This was a voice I knew, but not one I was accustomed to having address me in the hallways. This was the voice of the one person in the castle I found most difficult to talk to, because every time we held a conversation I tended to blush and stammer.

'Prince Caleb.' I dropped a painful curtsey as he drew up beside me, all long limbs, strong arms, and dark olive skin with a face that could melt the snow in winter. He was smiling just a little, just enough that I felt my face redden with the thought that the smile was for me.

'I'm glad you and the princess made it back safely this morning,' he said, and motioned for me to continue walking. 'We were all very worried at your disappearance.'

'It wasn't wise of us to leave without telling anyone,' I said honestly as we struck out at a meandering sort of walk in the direction of the alchemist's tower. I didn't really want the prince coming along to Philip's tower, it would only make things difficult to explain in his presence, but at the same time I didn't particularly want him to leave. It was unusual for him to seek out my company and I didn't want to discourage him from doing so in the future.

CHAPTER TWENTY-ONE

'You went to show her the sunrise?'

I looked at Prince Caleb, uncertain what he meant asking that. He wasn't looking at me, he just continued walking with his face forward, hands behind his back.

It could be that he doubted whether we actually went to see the sunrise, or that he wished he'd thought of taking Sid himself. Or, perhaps, the king and Lord Ruben were using him as a way to get additional information from me.

'Yes,' I replied with as much ease as I could. 'It is beautiful from the cliffs. Have you ever been?'

Caleb shook his head. 'Somehow I've never found the time.' There was regret in his voice, and I knew why. It was no secret that the crown prince didn't get time to enjoy himself exploring or viewing the simple beauties of Clovia. His time was spent training, learning, and visiting foreign kingdoms. No doubt he wished he had that kind of opportunity for leisure.

We walked on in silence until the yellow tapestry, where I hesitated. Prince Caleb noticed the pause and looked around. 'Where are you walking to? I'll escort you.'

'Oh, that's not necessary,' I said as kindly as possible. 'I don't mind walking alone.'

The prince looked at me for a moment, then seemed to make a decision.

'Your uncle does.'

My heart stopped for a moment and I looked at Prince Caleb, my eyes wide. For a moment everything seemed frozen in time, his wide green eyes watching me completely without guile. Lord Ruben had sent him. This wasn't just a chance meeting in a corridor. My uncle was suspicious of me.

'What do you mean?' I asked flatly, and held Prince Caleb's gaze. He looked back at me, his expression becoming curious the longer I stared.

'He worries that you're going to do something foolish and asked me to keep an eye out for you and the princess,' Caleb looked me up and down, as if checking to see whether I was preparing to run away. 'After what happened this morning I can't say I blame him.'

I felt my face growing hot once again. Foolish. We had been foolish, that's what everyone thought. Regardless of the reason I had gone out, I would be thought foolish as long as that reason was kept a secret. If the story was that we had run away from the castle and left no word just to watch a sunrise, of course we were going to be called foolish.

The word still stung.

'Well,' I said, striving to keep my tones even, 'I'll just be on my way. Philip is expecting me.' I turned and started toward the alchemist's corridor with a calm demeanour though inwardly I wished nothing more than to set the record straight and not be called 'foolish' one more time.

'Philip?' Caleb sounded intrigued, and his footsteps were quick as he caught up with me. I couldn't blame him. Few people were allowed in the alchemist's workshop, and the prince was not one of them. 'You're going to the alchemist?'

'Yes,' I said shortly. 'We keep a good friendship.'

'I'll escort you there, then. It sounds suspicious enough to warrant an escort.'

I directed a sharp look at the prince, who offered me an unexpected smile and a wink. My stomach gave a great flop as if I'd just leapt of a cliff with a dragon again, and my lips formed a shaky smile without consent from my brain.

We walked the rest of the distance in silence that might have been companionable if I hadn't been so taken off-guard by Prince Caleb's friendliness. When we arrived at Philip's tower we were let in without a word, but Rue gave the prince a curious look as we walked in the door.

Philip stood just inside the door of the living area fiddling with some candles. He smiled at the sight of me, but sobered when he saw Prince Caleb. At my pleading look, he offered a bow.

'Lady Tara,' he said as he took my hand. 'I was expecting you.'

It was unusual that Philip didn't ask questions or make any comment about why I was there. It was for the best, as it gave Prince Caleb nothing to ask uncomfortable questions about, but I was nonetheless surprised to be led directly up to the workshop. Philip wasn't normally happy to let new people in unannounced.

Philip led the way into the crowded workshop and headed immediately for a cleared space on one of the benches. He motioned me forward and I took great care not to bump into any of the many boxes and bags on the floor as I made my way across to him with my bag of rocks. Caleb hovered near the door looking around in awe. He had certainly never seen anything quite like this room, full of colourful potions, magical artefacts, and an assortment of items that were best undescribed.

'What are you working on?' Caleb asked as he stepped toward the end of the long table where Philip usually performed his strange experiments. A collection of what looked like colourful twigs and small stones was spread out across the work surface, which gleamed brightly in the sunlight streaming through the window. A pair of potions on small fires boiled away cheerfully a few feet away on the stone table top.

Philip smiled at the open curiosity in Caleb's voice. 'Pixie bones,' Philip walked over and picked up what I suddenly recognised to be a bright blue femur, miniature size. Caleb recoiled, and Philip smiled more brightly. If there was anything he enjoyed more than genuine curiosity, it was giving people a shock. 'I'm testing their viability as a replacement for unicorn. Much easier to come by pixie.'

'I have something for you,' I said in a bid to change

the subject. Caleb already looked more than ready to be on his way, and perhaps like he wasn't going to be in the mood for lunch. I offered the bag of rocks to Philip. 'Here.'

Philip returned to my side, took the bag and looked confused as he hefted the weight of it. I nodded subtly toward Prince Caleb. 'I thought I'd bring them back to you today so you could do the examination you wanted. I'm sorry to have borrowed them when I went out for my ride.' I stressed the last few words, and Philip made a knowing sound.

'Of course, of course!' He said, clapping himself on the forehead as if he'd forgotten, this bit of playacting for Caleb's sake. 'Well, let's have a look at them now and see if you can point anything out to me.'

Philip cleared a place on the table next to his collection of pixie bones, careful to move the bones in Caleb's direction, and emptied the bag out onto the table top as the prince backed away in disgust.

The rocks that tumbled out of the sack ranged in size from bits of gravel up to a couple of pieces almost as big as my fist. It looked as though Bryn had simply collected a double handful from the floor of the cavern. All of the stones were grey under a layer of brown dirt and very dull looking, though it was obvious that they were indeed iron ore.

'Hm.' Philip leaned close and spread the stones out with one crooked finger. 'They look just the same as the other one.' he looked at me curiously, obviously wondering why I had bothered to bring more of the same from the caves. I could only shrug. I knew no more about the stones than Philip did at this point and given the company we had at the moment I couldn't mention that Bryn just wanted a closer inspection.

'Lady Tara, we should go,' Caleb said with a nod to Philip and a wary glance at the full room. 'I'm glad that we could bring back your...rocks.'

Philip nodded and waved a dismissive hand at Caleb as he leaned down closer to the pile of rubble, squinting. I smiled briefly at him. 'Thank you for letting us visit,' I said politely to Philip. 'I hope to see you again soon.'

Caleb was already holding the door open for me when I turned to leave. The prince was more than a little eager to go, and that eagerness could have spelled the end of Philip if the old alchemist hadn't gasped just as I stepped toward the exit.

I turned back at the sudden intake of breath to see Philip gazing at the rocks with a strange expression on his face. I followed his gaze to the table, and immediately understood the reason for his shock.

The rocks from the bag had begun to vibrate. The solid stone of the table underneath them was still as the stones began to bounce all in a rhythm with each other, each striking the table at the same time to create a synchronous *tap tap tap tap* that became faster with each passing moment.

The three of us stood silent and surprised as the

tapping increased in frequency. The tapping became so fast that within a minute it was impossible to distinguish one tap from the next. Gradually the stones drew together to make a little mound, tapping now against each other as well as the table.

What happened next I would not have believed if I hadn't seen it myself. The mound grew tall and narrow, rocks shifting against each other by some unseen force until they stood in a column nearly as long as my forearm, the tapping now a high-pitched hum. The stones continued to move against each other, shifting to make a form that was familiar and yet strangely misshapen.

Within three minutes of being dumped on the table, the little handful of stones had made the shape of a small man.

The hum of stones moving against each other tapered away and left the little stone man standing still on the table, a little statue formed by something other than human hands. It was not perfectly formed; one arm was longer than the other and the body lopsided. As one, Philip, Caleb and I leaned closer to get a better look.

Little stone arms lifted themselves in something like a yawn. The quiet grating of stones sliding against each other accompanied the gesture, the sound magnified in the otherwise silent room.

The little stone man took one wobbly step forward and made a movement almost as if it were looking down at itself, though it had no eyes to see with, nor even much of a head other than a poorly-balanced and rather small piece of gravel.

Philip exhaled finally, and a single word escaped his lips. 'Amazing.'

The stone man froze the moment Philip's breath hit him, and for a long moment no one moved. Slowly, little stone legs bent until the thing was crouched, cautious, like a cat frightened by a larger creature.

And it attacked.

TWENTY-TWO

It leapt from the table top onto Philip's face, which sent the old man stumbling back in shock into another table. Glass vials and charms spilled from the surface onto the floor and shattered, sending strange liquids flooding across the floor.

I gasped and stepped over the broken glass to Philip's side before he had even found his feet again. I grabbed the homunculus around the middle with one hand and pulled. It came off Philip's face only very reluctantly, leaving a long scrape down each of the alchemist's cheeks where the thing's 'hands' had been.

The thing turned in my hand before I had a chance to react. The two arms clamped down on the fleshy base of my thumb in a blindingly painful grip.

'Gah!' I shouted, and reflexively shook my hand violently. With my other hand I shoved until it fell off toward the floor, then yanked my skirt up and aimed a forceful and thankfully accurate kick at it. My foot connected rather painfully with the stone centre of the homunculus and sent it flying across the room into the fireplace, where it struck the stone hard enough I was certain the homunculus would shatter.

It didn't. Instead, it rose up, grabbed a burning stick as long as it was from the fireplace, and charged across the room towards me with the flaming pike lowered like a lance ready to stab.

'Stand aside!' Prince Caleb shouted.

I was suddenly glad the prince was there. He shoved at my shoulder and sent me sprawling into the table next to Philip. Chivalry demanded he protect the elderly and feminine, even against the strangest of foes. If ever Caleb had seen a stranger foe I couldn't imagine what it was.

Beside me Philip was scrambling for anything that might help. Uncertain what any of us could do to destroy a creature made of stone, I only watched, feeling very helpless.

Caleb seemed to think the best course of action was to use the ornamental sword that hung from his waist. He had it unsheathed and pointed at the little creature as it came running. What good a sword would do I couldn't tell; what I could tell was that Philip and I were in danger of accidental dismemberment if the sword swung wide. I stumbled out of the way and pulled Philip along with me.

The homunculus took a running leap from the floor, waving the flaming stick in front of it as it flew directly toward Caleb's face. Caleb drew his sword back, and for one long moment I thought that the flaming stick would end up directly through one of those princely eyes.

At the last moment, Caleb swung with the flat side of his sword, which connected with the little creature with an almighty clang. A second later, there was the sound of glass shattering, and a deathly silence.

Philip and I looked at Prince Caleb, then at the window.

The window had shattered and the leading between the panes was now bent and broken. A large hole now graced it directly in the centre where the homunculus had struck it. I hurried around the table toward the window, threw it open, and looked down to see where the thing had gone.

We were high enough from here, and close enough to the outside wall, that I could see exactly where the thing landed.

There was a section of moat on this side of the castle, from a previous king's aborted attempt at making the castle more highly guarded, which had been abandoned halfway through digging and was now full of mucky water and pondweed. There was also now a large circle of clear water where something had splashed down with great speed, and a large number of ripples radiating out from it.

I was so relieved I laughed. 'It's gone in the moat,' I explained as I carefully drew my hand back from the shattered window.

Philip and Caleb came to the window as well to see. The ripples in the moat disappeared swiftly, along with the cleared spot in the water.

'Is it dead?' Caleb asked bluntly.

'One doesn't kill rocks by drowning,' Philip said. 'Nor by hitting them hard with a sword.'

Even as he spoke, we could see a disturbance on the edge of the pond. A green lump crawled out of the water, then rose to its 'feet'. It gave something of a look around, then wobbled off toward the trees, a little drunk man in a green moss tunic.

'I'll go find it,' Caleb said seriously, pulling away from the window and sheathing his sword. 'I'll take a search party and we'll find that thing.' He looked seriously at Philip. 'We'll bring it back so you can kill it good and proper.'

'I hardly think that's necessary,' I said with a nervous laugh.

'It might go out and reproduce in the forest!' Caleb waved a hand in agitation. The thought of the creature surviving out in the woods obviously unsettled him, and it was easy to see why. If it could reproduce, it would mean dozens of those things out in the forest, ready to attack whoever passed by.

'It won't reproduce,' Philip said seriously. 'But please do bring it back. Not yet,' he added as Caleb went to salute. 'I need to find something to put it in before you'll be able to catch it. Now that it's awake I somehow doubt it would go quietly into that little bag again.'

Caleb nodded sharply, his soldiering sensibilities overriding everything else, including his worries about escorting me. 'I'll come to you in the morning and we'll go out straightaway tomorrow.'

Philip nodded, and Caleb went to leave. 'Wait,' I said, suddenly frantic. Caleb and Philip both turned to me. I looked from one to the other, my mind in turmoil.

If Prince Caleb took a patrol out to find the stone man, Hawkins, as his captain, would ask questions, and Hawkins reported directly to Lord Ruben and the king. There was no way I wanted them knowing that someone had brought stones from the mines into the castle, especially when it could be so easily traced back to me.

'How will we explain this to Hawkins?'

There was a pause. After a thoughtful moment, Philip shrugged and looked at Prince Caleb. 'Hawkins will understand that it's simply one of my experiments gone wrong. Word hardly needs to go as far as the king, or even Lord Ruben.' Philip laid a crooked hand on Caleb's shoulder. 'I'd rather you not tell Hawkins the details—it could potentially be rather embarrassing for me word gets around that this experiment went so badly.'

Caleb gave the sharp nod of someone who knew his duty even if he didn't know the whole of what was going on. With a final salute, he took my arm and escorted me from the room.

I breathed a silent sigh of relief. If I knew him at all, Caleb wasn't going to mention anything dangerous to Hawkins. Not after Philip's explanation.

All the same, this was becoming far more complicated than I had ever imagined.

TWENTY-THREE

I was with Sid in the tower when the messenger came. Alois, who had gone down into the main hall to retrieve food for the three of us while Sid read Fionnuel's History, fetched us the moment the commotion started. I was sorting through a recent list of exports with an eye out for any iron ore leaving the country when we heard her quick staccato footsteps coming up the tower stairs.

Alois slammed the door of Sid's room open and leaned inside, breathless. Without apology or explanation, she forced the words out past gasps for air. 'There's a messenger here babbling about dragons!'

Both Sid and I scrambled to our feet from the chairs in front of the fire. Books and papers dropped to the floor in a forgotten heap. Together the three of us flew down the stairs, and at Alois' indication, toward the great hall.

We found a crowd packed into the large room. Whispers flew around the room like nasty little biting bugs, quiet and constantly moving, all of them with the sharpness of terror and morbid speculation.

'The last time a dragon was spotted three people died!'

'Not to mention the fire damage!'

'—homes burned, villages ravaged—'

'It's the old days all over again, we'll have to find a sacrifice—'

I shoved my way through the crowd to get to the centre of the room from whence the commotion had obviously sprung. As I approached the first thing that came into view was the tall feathered cap of the messenger. The feather shook violently as he spoke quietly but enthusiastically to Lord Ruben, who, I could see as I squeezed through the crowd, had the messenger by both arms and looked ready to explode with anger, his face pale.

By the time I was close enough to hear what was going on Lord Ruben had come to himself and realised he didn't want these details shouted out in front of the whole court. He released one of the messenger's arms and dragged the poor man out toward the halls, where they could make their way to the king's quarters. The crowd parted swiftly for them, and they were gone in a heartbeat. The moment the messenger was out of sight around the corner, all of the whispers broke into full volume questions.

Mine was just another voice lost in a sea of terrified speculation as I tried to find someone who heard what had happened. I grabbed the lad next to me, one of the younger guardsmen, frantic as anyone else for news.

'What happened? What was the messenger talking about? Dragons?' I added, horrified and fascinated all at once. Had there been some sort of upheaval among Bryn's family and friends since I had seen him last? Were they out marauding in spite of our agreement?

The guard looked at me with wide eyes. 'A dragon attacked a group of foresters a couple of days ago on the border of Marchant, in the Gray Mountains.' He shook his head, stunned. 'Apparently there was a human with the dragon, as well, a warrior of some sort. The two of them caused all sorts of destruction and burned half of the camp. Those woods are cursed, I tell you. Everyone says so.'

The blood drained out of my face as he spoke. Without a word, I turned away, feeling sick. He didn't notice; there were too many other people vying for his attention in hopes of hearing more.

Of course we'd been noticed. There was no way we wouldn't have been. And of course someone had reported what happened. The fact that news had travelled to my uncle only confirmed my suspicions that he was behind the whole thing, but it was hardly any comfort to know that I was right in this instance.

Sid stood near the back of the crowd, unwilling or unable to get through the mass of people. I drifted past, caught her hand and led the way out of the room. She furrowed her brow as I pulled her along, but didn't say anything until we were well on our way back to the tower.

'Tara, what's going on? You look like you've seen a ghost.'

I looked back to see Alois walking not far behind looking was pale and terrified at the thought of a dragon. I stopped and beckoned to her.

'Alois, in all the commotion we forgot to get anything to eat. Could you please head to the kitchens and see if they have something for us? I didn't see anything left in the great hall.'

Alois looked from me to Sid, her mouth hanging slightly open. It took her a moment to focus, but she finally said, 'I'll bring it to the princess' room,' and dropped a curtsey.

I pulled at Sid's hand again, worry lending me speed that my sore muscles didn't want to allow. Once in Sid's room, I closed the door tightly behind her and said, 'That messenger was telling my uncle all about what Bryn and I got up to at the mines.'

Silence hung thick and heavy for several moments as we both thought. Sid lowered herself thoughtfully into the chair by the fire that she had vacated not long ago and picked up History of the Dark Woods from the floor where she had dropped it, fingering the spine. Her calm expression surprised me; I had expected obvious terror or worry, not composed thoughtfulness.

'What does this mean for you?' She asked, looking at the book.

'I don't know for sure,' I said, walking to my own chair slowly. I couldn't bring myself to sit down, so rested my arms on the back of the chair. 'Hopefully he won't make a connection between our absence—yours and mine—and what happened at the mines.'

The conversation I had overheard between Lord Ruben and the king a week ago echoed in my ears again, with their mention of Lydia of Carron. They had disagreed as to whether anyone would take up her old standard, or make any fuss about what was happening at the mines; they had their answer now. I just hadn't expected to be the one providing it. Apparently following in my mother's footsteps was as inevitable as the passage of time.

At least now I had proof that Lord Ruben was the one behind the mines in the forest. The knowledge settled around me with a strange sort of comfort. It was as if by knowing that he was the antagonist in this issue, it clarified the course of action I needed to take. I knew he was my foe, but he didn't know I was his. I intended to keep it that way, if such a thing was possible.

'The question is,' I said, as much to myself as to Sid, 'are they going to make a connection between Lady Lydia's legacy and me?'

'You are her daughter,' Sid said carefully. Her thoughts ran along the same lines as mine in spite of our mutual silence. 'They would be foolish not to make the connection.'

Our eyes met and my mind flooded with all of my previous infractions against Lord Ruben's wishes. The contract with the dragons was not the first time I had disobeyed him in secret. I had no illusions about whether my behaviour was known to people in the castle; careful interviews with servants, Hawkins, and Philip would show a pattern of night-time jaunts outside the castle wall and contradictions between what I said I did and what I actually did with my spare time.

It was really only a matter of time before Lord Ruben found out. He was remarkably clever, and the only reason he hadn't noticed my behaviour was because he hadn't thought me a threat. Now, however, my actions were in direct opposition to his wishes. It seemed unlikely that he would remain ignorant of my opposition to his will.

'Let's try to keep me from getting exiled,' I said less than humorously, thinking of my mother. 'If he asks we stick with our story that we went out to see the sunrise. And don't let him see that book,' I said, re-membering how he had taken it from me.

Sid gave the cover of the book one last look, then stood and went to hide it. By the time she had it tucked into her trunk between the folds of a dress near the bottom, Alois had returned with bread and cheese.

'I hope you don't mind, it was all they had,' Alois said as she brought the tray over to the fire.

Sid closed her trunk and returned to her chair with a wary smile. 'We don't mind. Actually I suddenly don't feel hungry.'

I couldn't have agreed more.

TWENTY-FOUR

For all of my worries that Lord Ruben was going to make a connection between the mine attack and my absence on the day in question, there were no immediate outpourings of anger or punishment from my sometimes mercurial uncle.

Gradually, the talk of dragons died down as there were no further sightings, and within a week the court jester was using the idea of dragons as part of his routine, earning himself gales of rather relieved laughter.

It was several more days before a request came that I attend Lord Ruben in his offices. This was a normal enough event, given that I was heir to my uncle's fortunes, but when the message was delivered by one of the guards my heart gave a flop and sank down to my stomach.

The message was delivered before I went down to meet Sid in the morning, for which I was glad; my hands were cold and shaking as I left my room to walk across to Lord Ruben's offices, and I didn't want her to see my nervousness.

The halls were practically abandoned as I walked, the guard who delivered the message two steps behind me. It would be all too easy to see me out of the castle and into exile without making a fuss if he sent me off now before most of the castle had risen for the morning. The halls seemed colder than usual and I hid a shiver as I turned to climb the stairs to Lord Ruben's apartments.

I hid my shaking hands in the folds of my skirt as I drew up to Lord Ruben's door, and only took one hand out long enough to knock before burying it again. If he saw my nervousness, he would wonder at it, and if he hadn't already put things together about me, I didn't want to give him another reason to suspect me.

Lord Ruben pulled the door open the moment I knocked, an open smile written across his face. My heart leapt out of my stomach back to its rightful place in my chest and suddenly I could breathe again.

'Good morning, Tara, come right in.'

He wasn't angry. He couldn't have found me out yet. This was simply one of the usual monthly interviews he kept with me. Relief allowed me to smile back at him as I entered the room and took a seat across from him at his desk.

'How is the new portrait?' He asked as he seated himself, reaching for a quill with one hand and parchment with the other.

I grimaced, surprised, as I thought of the painting. 'It will look much like the others.'

Lord Ruben glanced up at me, quill halfway into the inkpot.

'So we must continue to hope your intellect makes up for any lack of looks.'

On any other day this kind of comment would have bothered me. Today I could shrug and grin in response. 'Apparently.'

He nodded, unsurprised. I wondered why he bothered commissioning new portraits of me if we both knew it would never do any good.

'I hope things have been going well with Princess Amanthea,' he said as he scratched out figures on the parchment.

'Yes.' I suddenly remembered that I was supposed to be his spy. 'She has learned her way around very well by now and is becoming fully accustomed to our ways of living.'

Lord Ruben nodded and looked across at some of the other papers spread across his desk. 'Has she said anything about her home?'

'Her home?' I repeated dumbly. Had Sid ever even

mentioned home other than to say that she hadn't been well liked there? I could answer that question very honestly. 'She doesn't speak of it much.'

'Is there anything you recall that she has said specifically?' He leaned forward, his attention sudden and intense. 'Anything that you've spoken of?'

His interest surprised me. What could he possibly be looking for? Perhaps this went back to the dragon sighting at the mine, as it was on Marchantian land.

My mind turned back to conversations Sid and I shared over the last weeks. The best I could recall, Sid had only mentioned home a couple of times, and the only one I could imagine being of interest to Lord Ruben was her comment about the woods being cursed.

'After…the messenger came—' I said slowly as I rearranged the timeline to be something more convincing than the truth, '—the messenger who spoke of the dragon on the border of Marchant—the princess mentioned how the forest there has always been thought to be cursed. She was surprised that any Clovian foresters would want to try their hand at making a living there, due to the strange nature of the forest.'

Lord Ruben watched me closely, unblinking. His continued silence spurred me on with my partially fabricated version of events.

'She wondered if there was some reason Clovians would want to be in the forest. She thought that the possibility of...foresting...there was part of the reason for her betrothal to Prince Caleb.'

'She is surprisingly astute for someone whose primary appeal is her face. Go on. Did she say anything else?'

I grimaced at the implication that Sid's beauty was her only asset. Then I remembered that I had thought the same thing at first.

'Only that she didn't think herself the greatest prize as a wife. She thought there must have been some other reason for the betrothal.'

Lord Ruben leaned back in his chair. 'Interesting indeed,' he said as he steepled his fingers and looked at me over the top of them. 'She thinks of things that I did not expect her to.'

The answer was unsettling, and for the first time I thought that Sid might be right that there was another reason for her betrothal than simply the fact that she was not well-liked at home. I decided it was worth the risk to push the issue a little farther.

'Is there a reason for the betrothal, then? Aside from Prince Caleb needing a bride? A reason that there are Clovians cutting out that forest when it is thought to be cursed?'

If I thought Lord Ruben would be pleased with me for apparently taking an interest in the politics of the situation, I was mistaken.

He smiled, but it was the kind of smile that reminded me he was capable of exiling his own flesh and blood because he disagreed with their politics.

'Perhaps that is something we can discuss in due time. Right now there are other things to concern yourself with.'

He reached over and picked up a scroll, looking over the contents as he spoke. 'The Spring Festival is opening a fortnight from now. I expect you to be in attendance at all of the festivities.'

Lord Ruben said it blandly, because of course it was a given that I would be in attendance. All the ladies of court would be.

He continued. 'Lady Ainsley has requested that you attend her for the course of the evening, and I have agreed, under the circumstance that she spend the next two weeks teaching you how to dance. Last year you were a disgrace to our house.'

My cheeks suffused with colour and my heart dropped right back into the pit of my stomach. He was right, I was a terrible dancer, and I had made a complete fool of myself the previous year. I didn't like Lady Ainsley, but she was a fine example of what was expected of a woman of the court and so was a natural choice for this task.

She was also one of the people I liked least in the castle, and the feeling was mutual.

My lips stretched into a thin grimace. 'Of course,' I said through gritted teeth. 'When would she like to begin her instruction?'

'Tomorrow,' Lord Ruben said as he rose from his

chair to signal the end of our meeting. 'She and I have agreed that you will spend the next two weeks entirely in her company and stay in her rooms, as, in her words, "Grace is not something that can be taught overnight".'

My heart, currently residing in the depths of my stomach, skipped a beat. Staying with Lady Ainsley? Not only would that mean I would have very little time to spend with Sid discussing the book, as I would be expected to dance attendance on Lady Ainsley, but there would be no way I could get out of the castle to see Bryn if anything happened.

I stood and bowed a little, feeling too clumsy with irritation to curtsey, and let myself out. As I walked down the hall back toward my own rooms, my feelings about Lord Ruben hardened into a heavy premonition of danger.

He was putting me with Lady Ainsley for more reason than just to improve my dancing. It was possible—no, probable—that he had more evidence against me than I thought.

Perhaps he had indeed spoken to the servants and put together some idea of what I was getting up to at night. Even if he had no suspicions of me whatever at this time, he couldn't have countered my desire to leave the castle more thoroughly. For the next fortnight, I was a prisoner as surely as if I had been put in chains.

The thought chilled me, but I couldn't help

thinking that whatever happened, I wasn't in a position to stop my search for answers. Someone had asked me for help, and I wasn't going to let them down, reptilian or not.

Though I loved Gydrocc, living within its walls meant that opportunities to see the world and make changes in it were very few and far between. Lord Ruben was going to disown me eventually, as surely as the sun rises in the morning, and I didn't want to be left with nothing when he did.

My life was my own, and I had no intention of throwing it away in an attempt to please someone I could never fully satisfy nor even trust.

Head held high, I began to climb the tower toward Sid's room. We had to talk.

TWENTY-FIVE

My move to Lady Ainsley's rooms was not a welcome thing from anyone's perspective. Sid gave me a look of utter betrayal when I said I would be with Lady Ainsley for two entire weeks. It took several minutes of explaining that it wasn't my choice before Sid calmed down and helped me get things ready.

'I still don't know exactly what was so important in that book your mother mentioned,' Sid said to me quietly as we gathered up a few of my things for my stay on the other side of the castle. 'It tells all the legends I'm familiar with about the forest, of tree spirits and talking ravens and will-o-the-wisps, but it doesn't speak of the little stone men like you brought back and I don't know how a decent history could have overlooked something like that.'

'Wonderful,' I whispered back as I picked up my hairbrush and shoved it into my bag rather violently. 'There could be hundreds of those little stone men who could come alive at any moment to start destroying things and we don't even know why.'

Alois followed three paces behind Sid and me with my bedding as we walked to Lady Ainsley's rooms. I carried my bag and Sid, of course, carried nothing. Lady Ainsley lived near the front of the castle, unusually on the ground floor in one of the more out-of-the-way passages. She had not been long in the castle, and I remembered the stink about the rooming situation that had been raised when she arrived.

Lady Ainsley insisted on having a place on the ground floor, for reasons she didn't care to make public. There were not many ground floor rooms in the castle, and the ones she insisted on commandeering were usually reserved for some of the more elderly visitors to Gydrocc.

Most people had not been on her side in this particular battle, with one notable exception: Lord Ruben. He insisted that she have her way, referencing some old scar that had wounded the 'dear Lady' that could not be ignored. Eventually, most had come to terms with their irritation by assuming that Lady Ainsley had some sort of hidden disability.

I was not one of that group. To me, Lady Ainsley gave the air of one who was spoiled, not wounded.

Wounded or not, she was beautiful, and a political schemer to rival my uncle. She believed in her own best interests and little else; rumour had it that her husband had died under suspicious circumstances many years before, leaving her a wealthy young widow with no children to think about. Money passed through her fingers like water, but she always seemed to have more, and no one knew quite where it came from.

It didn't take long to walk down to Lady Ainsley's room from the tower. Her rooms were not far off the main corridor that led into the castle, which meant that she could easily spy on everyone that entered and left the castle. In my mind this was why Lord Ruben allowed her to stay in those rooms, and why he tried to stay on her good side. She was a more effective and willing spy than I could ever be.

I stopped in front of her door, inhaled deeply as I raised my hand to knock, and welcomed myself to a fortnight in hell.

My quick knock was answered by a rapidly swinging door that revealed a sneering woman twice my age who I later learned was Lady Ainsley's maid Ivanna. She let us in and directed Alois and me to put my things down just inside the door without a word.

Lady Ainsley swept into the room as we straightened from arranging my things, radiating an air of colour and expense. A petite, slender woman, Lady Ainsley was nonetheless impressive. Atop her head sat an exotic contraption somewhere between a hat and a veil that covered her hair completely and added four or five inches to her not very significant height. It trailed three veils of different colours in a silk so fine it was nearly transparent. Dressed in green, blue, and gold silk imported from the south at her own expense, it looked as if her clothing alone could have been sold to purchase a large farm and manor outside the castle.

'Welcome,' she said, spreading her arms wide, trailing veils as she did so. Two of the veils from her hat on this occasion were attached to the wrists of her dress, which I thought made her look a bit like a large beetle with wings half-spread. 'I do hope you'll enjoy your time here with me, Lady Tara.'

'I am certain I shall,' I lied easily, and dropped a curtsey bad enough that Ivanna grimaced and Lady Ainsley's lips very nearly twisted into a frown.

Sid stepped forward, a small, unsettling smile on her face. 'I hope you will treat my Lady Tara well while she is here,' she said in icy tones.

I glanced over at Sid, surprised. There was a steeliness underlying her voice. It was the first time I had seen her greet an older woman without at least some show of politeness in the form of a curtsey. She was a princess and could get away with it, but it still surprised me.

Sid continued coolly. 'I do not know how I shall get by without her.'

'Yes,' Lady Ainsley said coolly, looking Sid up and

down with visible distaste, 'I've heard the two of you have become rather inseparable.'

It sounded like an insult. Lady Ainsley waved a hand dismissively. 'Do not worry, I shall return her hale and whole. And considerably improved, if I have my way,' she added. 'I have seen you dance, dear, and you always look as if you're wearing stone blocks instead of shoes the way you galumph around the floor.'

'Thank you for your kind offer to assist me with my dancing, Lady Ainsley,' I said with a bow of my head as my cheeks reddened.

Sid turned to me, took my by both arms, and kissed my cheeks. 'You will still come to me in the morning, before luncheon. I would be bereft completely shorn of your company.'

Over her shoulder I could see Lady Ainsley's eyebrows raise. Obviously that hadn't been part of her plan, and Sid hadn't mentioned it before now. But when Lady Ainsley didn't disagree, I felt my heart lift. At least I could spend part of the day in the company of someone who actually liked me.

Sid released me with a final smile and headed for the door without any farewell to Lady Ainsley. The older woman pursed her lips as Alois closed the door behind the two of them. I expected some kind of rebuke for myself or for Sid, but Lady Ainsley turned her attention to business.

'Your new routine will be as follows,' she said

without preamble as Ivanna gathered up my things and moved them into the next room. 'We breakfast with the castle, then we return here for studies. Out of respect to the princess, you will be allowed to go to her for half an hour before luncheon. We eat luncheon with the castle, then we turn to your dance instruction, which will take place in the second hall. You will dance until dinner, which we will eat with the castle, then we will return here and you will read to me until sundown, at which point we will sleep. There will be no variation to this schedule and there will be no mutinies from you. Understood?'

'Understood,' I mumbled, aiming my face at the floor but watching Lady Ainsley.

'Good. We start now.'

That first week with Lady Ainsley passed in a blur of elocution, manners, and dancing instruction. The dance instruction was painful, especially given that my muscles were still sore from the night at the mines, but it was nothing I couldn't manage. In fairness, it was hardly any worse than the time I had spent with governesses when I was younger.

It was at the end of that week that Sid finished reading Fionnuel's History. I found her sitting in her room before luncheon looking thoughtfully at the closed book on her lap.

'There doesn't seem to be anything of any real interest,' Sid said to me as I walked in. 'Did your mother give any hint as to why she wanted you to read it?'

'Not that I can recall,' I replied with a shake of my head as I crossed to the other chair by the fire. 'And I don't have that letter anymore to check. It went in the fire after I spoke with my uncle.'

'That's probably a good thing,' Sid said darkly.

'What do you mean?'

She hesitated. 'There have been people in and out of your room all the time since you went to stay with Lady Ainsley.' Sid stared at her hands as she spoke. 'I don't recognise them, but they're not the usual servants and they're certainly not people I would think have any business in there.'

'Have they taken anything?' I asked, my mind racing. There was a good chance that someone could find something incriminating amongst my belongings if they were really looking for it, and I couldn't think of anyone that would send someone to rifle through my room aside from Lord Ruben.

'I don't know.'

'Come on. Let's find out.'

I led the way out of Sid's room and up the tower stairs to my own. The door was tightly shut, just as I had left it, and there was no obvious sign that anyone had been inside. I pushed the door open and my first thought was that everything looked just as I had left it; even the mattress on the bed was slightly askew, as we had left it when we stripped the bed for my move down to Lady Ainsley's apartments.

'Is anything missing?' Sid asked as she crept into the room behind me.

'I don't know,' I said, wishing there was some other response I could give, wishing that I had some idea what was going on. I looked to the small basket on the edge of the dressing table that held my trinkets. That was the only thing that had been visibly disturbed; it looked bare, even taking into account that I had already removed my hairbrush and a few veil clips for my stay with Lady Ainsley.

It took a moment, but I finally remembered what it was that I kept in that basket.

'All of my charms are gone.' I picked up the basket and rifled through it. 'All of them. Every charm that Philip has ever given me.'

I set down the basket suddenly and turned. Someone had definitely been in here, and they had taken the few bits of magic I kept around.

There was only one other thing that Lord Ruben would be interested in, and that would be anything to do with my mother.

My trunk stood on the other side of the room, and with a glance at the front I realised that someone had been through it. I crossed the room and crouched in front of the chest. The clasp on the front was not securely shut. The lid lifted easily in my hand to reveal the folded clothing, apparently undisturbed, setting on the top.

It took no time at all to dig past the dresses and tunics to the bottom of the chest where I kept my few treasures, but when the cotton and silk was pushed aside, all that was there was the wooden chest.

'Everything of my mother's is gone,' I said finally, resting my hands on the smooth bottom of the trunk. 'This is Lord Ruben's doing. He took everything of my mother's and everything with a hint of magic.' I shook my head, frustrated, but also surprised at myself. What did I really expect? It was only logical that he would take these things away at some point.

'What did you have of your mother's?' Sid asked, kneeling next to me to look inside the trunk.

'One of her books,' I said, thinking of the small package I had been given when mother was exiled. 'She'd written some notes in the margin. A pair of gloves, a dress for my wedding, and a little box with some jewellery.'

'It doesn't sound like anything unusual to me.' Sid stood. 'Maybe by the time you aren't staying with Lady Ainsley anymore all of it will be back. Perhaps he just took it because he wanted to see what all you had from your mother.'

Sid's words were somewhat reassuring, but all I could think was that Lord Ruben had suspicions of me, suspicions that I had probably only managed to strengthen in the last few weeks with my occasional disappearances at night and the things he had found in my room. There was hardly any reason for a lady of the court to be keeping charms that had more to do with war than with housekeeping.

But the question of why Lord Ruben had done this now echoed in my head. It was only when I stood and felt the smooth surface of Bryn's pearl fall back against my chest that I realised what my uncle must have been looking for.

Did he know about the agreement mother made with the dragons? I put one hand over the pearl that lay hidden under my dress. A report came to him about a dragon and a rider at the mines, and a few days later I was put under constant surveillance by one of his more trusted spies in the castle. He had gone through my things and taken everything that even smacked of magic, or of my mother and her potentially toxic influence.

Even if he didn't know he certainly suspected. The path of secrecy I walked was swiftly becoming a narrow, high wall; the slightest slip and there would be no return.

'Well done, Tara,' I said quietly to myself, 'You've done a very fine job of arousing absolutely everyone's suspicions.'

TWENTY-SIX

I had nearly forgotten about the little misadventure with Prince Caleb, Philip, and the little stone man by the time I heard anything more about it. I was in a dance lesson when the message came.

A small liveried servant entered and bowed to Lady Ainsley as I attempted to avoid stepping on the toes of the dance instructor. He grimaced and cleared his throat to regain my attention as my eyes wandered. I turned back to him but strained to hear what was being said at the edge of the room.

'A message for Lady Tara,' the servant said quietly as he bowed to Lady Ainsley and presented the note. Lady Ainsley accepted it without comment and waved the servant away. When the door closed behind him I heard the crackle of parchment. The sound made me falter; she was opening the note without even notifying me of its arrival.

The dance instructor stepped painfully on my foot and I yelped. He stepped back, offended either at my exclamation or the fact that I wasn't paying attention, and it was all I could do to mutter 'sorry,' and keep dancing.

Lady Ainsley didn't even mention the note until lessons were finished for the day and we were walking back to her apartments after dinner.

'You received a message today from the court alchemist,' she said as we turned the corner to her rooms. 'He would like you to visit at your earliest convenience.'

It took all of my willpower not to glare at Lady Ainsley. She wasn't even going to offer me the note to read for myself.

'Thank you for informing me. Would you be able to spare me now for any length of time?'

I tried to be polite but she could certainly hear the undertones of mutiny in my voice because she turned back to me at the doors to her room and said with a sneer, 'If you wish to see him you may go tomorrow before luncheon instead of seeing to that empty-headed princess. I'm sure she won't mind a day without your charming company.'

Her sarcastic tone was met with a glare from me that I didn't even try to hide. I said nothing as she let us into her rooms for the night, and hurried to get ready for bed. The sooner I slept, the sooner it would be morning and the sooner I could see Sid and Philip.

The next day when I was given my free time I hurried to find Sid, who usually waited for me in her rooms. I charged inside, grabbed her hand, and dragged her down the stairs toward Philip's tower with only a hurried apology to Alois, who looked on with confusion at the rush.

'Philip asked me to visit yesterday but Lady Ainsley wouldn't let me go,' I whispered to her as we hurried down the halls. 'We don't have much time before I have to be back and Philip may have something useful.'

Sid nodded but pulled at me to slow down. I gave her a confused look, to which she shook her head. 'We may be in a hurry, but we don't need to look like it. We don't need to raise any suspicions.'

Annoying as it was, Sid was right. I slowed my pace and we walked arm in arm as if we had nothing more in mind than a stroll around the castle. When we arrived at the alchemist's tower what seemed like an eternity later, Rue did not hesitate to lead us to the workshop, where I could see Philip was pleased to see us.

'I suppose the princess knows what's going on?' he said cheerfully as we walked in the door. He clasped my hands and placed a kiss on both cheeks, which I gladly returned with a nod. Philip smiled at Sid. 'When both of you disappeared that morning it did become rather obvious.'

'Not to everyone, I hope,' I said, worried at how easily Philip put the pieces together.

'No indeed,' Philip said as he led us to the back of the room, where we could hear the grating sound of stone against metal. 'I only guessed because I knew where you were going.'

As we approached the back wall, the grating became more pronounced. Philip didn't seem to notice. 'Prince Caleb has been surprisingly good company, by the way. He found me the perfect thing to contain the little stone man, and even suggested a few things I might try on it. Not that they were very helpful things,' Philip admitted, 'but at least he gave it some thought.'

He directed our attention to a metal chest at the end of one of his stone benches and it became obvious what the source of the noise was. The chest was not much taller than the little stone man, slightly longer than it was tall, and shook violently at intervals where it rested. Occasionally it would stop shaking and there was a terrible grating sound of stone on metal.

'He found the stone man, then?' I asked as I stared at the little chest, which was bound in thick cast iron that must have made for a weighty cage.

'They put it in there when they found it out in the forest and it seems to have done the job of keeping it in.' Philip patted the top of the chest. The stone man jumped inside and crashed against the lid with enough force that the chest jerked madly. Philip snatched his hand away as if burned.

'It hasn't gotten any less aggressive,' He pointed out needlessly.

'May I see it?' Sid asked, leaning forward to look at the chest more closely, as if by moving closer she could see through the thick metal sides.

'I'm afraid I'm not going to open the top unless there's quite a good reason. And a level-headed soldier or two standing ready,' He added. He turned to the books and scrolls spread out across the top of the bench. 'Unfortunately nothing I've read has proved helpful in finding a way to make the creature calm down. Though I think I know now why it woke.'

That caught my attention. I straightened.

'What do you mean?'

'These things don't animate themselves, there has to be some input from something. A bit of a push, if you will.' Philip picked up one of the books on the table and motioned to a diagram on facing pages. 'It is an elemental creature, so naturally there will be some elemental weaknesses to stop it, and an elemental input that will make it wake up. Theoretically if you knew the right elemental input you could create any kind of elemental creature.'

The thought of a little man of fire made me grimace, then I thought of Bryn; perhaps that's where dragons came from originally?' Philip continued. 'I think that in this case, our little stone man was wakened by the sun.'

'The sun?' The memory of pouring the little bag of rocks out onto the sunlit table unfolded in my mind. 'You mean just by putting those rocks in the sun we accidentally gave it the right—what did you call it? Elemental input?'

'It seems so,' Philip said mildly. 'I don't suppose they're leaving those rocks out in the sun there at the mine or else their camp would have been destroyed long ago.'

In my mind's eye a detail about the mining camp that hadn't been clear before suddenly came into sharp focus. All of the carts of rocks they had pulled from the mine were covered with thick tarps. They obviously knew the consequences of letting those rocks sit in the sun, so had taken every precaution.

'I suppose one rock by itself isn't going to animate,' I said, thinking of the first stone Bryn had given me and how it had not reacted at all to the sun. 'What can your books tell us about what things might make a little stone man...' I searched for the right words. '...go back to sleep?'

Philip made a disapproving noise. 'The books are quite clear that the elemental weakness of stone is always ultimately going to be water, but our particular stone man appeared unaffected by his dousing in the moat. The other possible weakness I've found is fire, though it would have to be extremely hot and burn for quite a long time to truly disassociate the thing, and as this one is made of iron ore fire may only make it stronger.'

He was right; a long, hot exposure to fire would, for something made of iron ore, only burn away impurities and could potentially turn it to steel, which was hardly going to be any easier to combat.

'However,' Philip said, setting down the book and reaching for a different scroll, which he unrolled halfway to look at while he spoke, 'I think that a truly scorching heat for a short period of time would be enough to disassociate some of the parts of the creature, which might be sufficient to stop it; you would have to eat away at it piece by piece, but I think it's doable.'

'Fair enough,' Sid said. 'And I think if it came down to it Tara could find a source of very hot, quick fire.' She looked at me pointedly and I knew we were all thinking of Bryn. 'But what on earth sort of reason would anyone have for digging up a bunch of rocks that they know are going to turn into violent stone creatures the moment they're exposed to the sun?'

That stopped us all for a moment. It was Philip who answered first, and he said what all of us were coming around to thinking.

'Those rocks look just like iron ore. Valuable iron ore. They could be sold to anyone, anywhere, and destroy an entire town before anyone even realised there was something to worry about.'

'It's a weapon,' I said. 'A very devious weapon. You could sell it to your enemy and their whole country could be ravaged by the time they came up with a way to destroy the creatures. You could declare a very secret war on a place just by giving them those stones, and never have to send even a single one of your own troops.'

The awful silence that followed was long, punctuated only by the sound of stone grating against steel. Enough stones had come out of those mines already to create two dozen man-sized stone golems, which would be an army unto itself. Gydrocc itself would easily fall if attacked by a group of creatures like that.

'I guess this means that King Stephen has made an enemy that he wants to get rid of,' Sid said quietly.

Philip looked up at the two of us. 'Or he found an old one.'

TWENTY-SEVEN

Afterward, I would be very grateful for the fact that Lady Ainsley let me sleep longer than usual the morning of the spring festival.

She herself didn't wake until mid-morning, and unusually didn't insist that I get out of bed immediately upon her waking. It was nearly the time she usually let me go see Sid when she finally rose and commanded me to do the same.

Lady Ainsley must have seen the confusion and wonderment in my expression that morning, because as she removed herself from bed in a quite leisurely manner she said, 'If we intend to dance all night, we need to be prepared. A well-rested lady is a far more attractive prospect than one who looks like she has been working all day.'

Food was delivered to Lady Ainsley's room at midday and I was not allowed out to go see Sid. Instead, I was drafted to assist in drawing up a hip bath full of hot water for Lady Ainsley. She watched us work with a look of scorn, regal in spite of completely loose hair and a rough cotton robe.

When the bath was ready, she stood and looked at me. 'After I bathe, you will bathe and Ivanna will dress you.'

With no other option given, I sat in the next room while Lady Ainsley washed. When I was called in, much to my irritation, Lady Ainsley did not leave, and Ivanna demanded I strip down without any ceremony.

I undressed almost defiantly until I got to my underdress, under which I remembered there was the pearl from Bryn. While Lady Ainsley and Ivanna were unlikely to recognise that it was magical, they were likely to question where it came from and why I didn't wear such a valuable piece of jewellery openly.

My hesitation did not go unnoticed. Ivanna grabbed my underdress and whipped it off over my head roughly. Standing naked aside from the pearl, I shivered.

Lady Ainsley glanced up at me and did a double take.

'Where did you get that necklace?'

What was I supposed to say? I didn't have a ready lie prepared in this kind of event, so I only stood in stony silence, arms folded across my chest. When she continued to watch me, looking more irritated by the moment, I finally conceded with, 'It was a gift.'

'From whom?' She looked from the pearl to me and back again, as if wondering exactly what sort of person thought me valuable enough to give me such a precious item.

'Sid. Er, Princess Amanthea,' I corrected myself. 'A thank you for my help as her lady-in-waiting.'

'A fine lady-in-waiting you make, you desolate creature,' Lady Ainsley said dismissively. Satisfied that she had resolved the issue, she returned her attention to brushing her hair out. 'Fine. You will set it aside for tonight. Your uncle has sent the jewellery that you are to wear.'

I stood in stunned silence. If Lord Ruben was looking for confirmation of whether I had kept the contract with the dragons, this was the best way to do it. If he knew anything about the dragons he would know about the kind of enchantment that would be on the dragon's treasure. All he had to do was make sure I didn't have anything on me that *could* be dragon treasure, then sit and wait for a dragon to arrive.

Ivanna may have had no compunctions about removing my clothing, but when I did not give her the pearl immediately, she made no move to take it. Reaching out to take expensive jewellery without the wearer's permission was a good way for a servant to lose a hand or their job. Possibly both.

Instead Ivanna stood with hands outstretched to take it from me.

I cast around furiously for any excuse that would keep the necklace on my person longer. To take off the necklace would signal to Bryn that I was in distress, and I had no idea how long it would take him to decide he needed to 'rescue' me if I took the necklace off now.

'I would rather wear it tonight,' I said in my proudest tones. This was no time to sound worried and pleading. 'I like it, and it brings me luck.'

Or, rather, it brought me the reassurance that Bryn wasn't going to show up and start torching the castle, which amounted to the same thing.

'No amount of luck is going to help you tonight,' Lady Ainsley said without looking at me. 'Give it to Ivanna, she'll put it with my jewellery and we'll lock it up safely. You may have it back tomorrow.'

At my best guess, it would take Bryn roughly two hours after the pearl was removed to show up, taking into account that he wouldn't come if the pearl was off me for less than half an hour. So if I removed the pearl now, just after midday, there would be a dragon flying around the castle by mid-afternoon looking for me. There was no way that would go unnoticed.

The only thing I could think to do was to try to keep the pearl on me for as long as possible in the afternoon and only take it off finally just before the beginning of the ball; then, while Lady Ainsley and

Ivanna were distracted, I could sneak back in here with Sid and we could get the pearl back out. Hopefully Bryn would realise I was safe halfway here and turn around to go home.

In a moment of decision, I removed the pearl, but instead of handing it to Ivanna, I set it on the floor next to the bath as I climbed in.

'We'll put it away later,' I said to Ivanna in reassuring tones that must certainly have come off as condescending in spite of my best intentions. If Lady Ainsley had been paying attention she would have scoffed and objected, but her full efforts were now thankfully concentrated on styling her hair.

I bathed quickly and replaced the pearl once I was dry. There was nothing else for it now but to finish getting ready and do my best to keep Lady Ainsley's attention from the pearl that I tucked into my clean underdress.

I needn't have worried about Lady Ainsley's attention being directed at me for most of the remainder of the afternoon. The amount of time and effort it took to get her dressed for the party was immense, and made Sid's often long and involved preparations look measly by comparison.

It was mid-afternoon by the time Lady Ainsley inspected herself in the mirror and pronounced herself 'finished.' She looked beautiful but painfully done up: her face had been completely repainted to hide imperfections; her hair, so long in preparation, was completely hidden under an intricately constructed ensemble of veils and jewels; and the dress she wore was so stiff with beads, pearls, and embroidery that it would be difficult to sit without damaging it.

'Come, then,' Lady Ainsley snapped at me as she moved to sit down on a backless chair that wouldn't wrinkle her dress. 'Fetch your dress. Lord Ruben sent it along earlier.'

With some trepidation I fetched the dress from the front room and brought it to Ivanna to put on me. I recognised it immediately. It was not one of my favourites, as when laced up fully it was difficult to walk, let alone dance or eat dinner.

'Isn't this going to be hard to dance in?' I gasped as Ivanna pulled it over my head and tugged at the laces. She was not gentle and kept jerking me in different directions in an attempt to get the laces as tight as possible.

'Not if you move slowly and gracefully.' Lady Ainsley smirked. 'So for you, yes, it probably will be.'

I bristled but said nothing. It wasn't worth it to start an argument with her now. There were other things to worry about, especially as I was forced to pull the pearl out from under the tight dress and off over my head. Resting in the palm of my hand it felt strangely heavy, and my chest very light without the weight of it.

Lady Ainsley picked up a small chest from the table and waved it in my direction. It was full to brimming with other jewellery wrapped in silk. I could just see the glint of emeralds and rubies between the folds of the fabric.

I placed the pearl into the chest gently, and as my hand moved away I felt a pang of guilt that I was parting with it so easily, especially given the dire warnings Bryn had told me.

Sid and I would just have to do our best to get the pearl back before anything happened.

'Now, Lord Ruben sent jewellery for you as well,' Lady Ainsley said in business-like tones. She picked up a silk-wrapped parcel from the table and opened it very professionally for me to see. 'They aren't pieces I would have chosen for an event like this, but he is a man. He wouldn't know about things like this.'

As the wrappings fell open, I gasped in surprise. I recognised the jewellery that had been sent. Until a week ago, it had been resting at the bottom of the chest in my room.

'Oh,' I breathed, and my heart swelled.

Lord Ruben had taken mother's jewellery so he could send it down for me to wear tonight. I found my eyes growing misty as Ivanna latched two necklaces around my neck, one of them so short it barely circled my throat and the other so long that the heavy black pendant on the end reached my navel.

There was also a thick bracelet I had long admired, made of twining gold vines and leaves that circled tightly around my right wrist. I couldn't help a smile as

I slid it past my hand to rest atop the sleeve of the dress.

I had not ever worn any of this jewellery. In one respect, I thought it would be painful for me to wear something of my mother's in public, and in another, I thought Lord Ruben would not like seeing the reminders of his faithless sister. The fact that Lord Ruben sent them specifically for me to wear tonight caught me completely off-guard.

'What do you think?' Lady Ainsley said grandly, with a gesture to the mirror. I stepped forward to look at myself. Even with my hair still unbound, I looked and felt like something greater than I had been before. I felt like an adult, like my mother rejuvenated. It lifted my spirits more than I cared to admit.

The moment was rather rudely interrupted when Ivanna suddenly attacked my hair again, apparently having deemed my attempts to brush it insufficient. I actually found I didn't mind, I was so preoccupied with the thought of wearing my mother's things.

Lady Ainsley made a great show of locking away my pearl in the little chest. She then placed the small chest in the larger chest at the end of her bed and locked it as well. With a rather grand gesture, she tucked the keys into a pocket in her right sleeve.

All I could think was that there was no chance of getting the keys out of her sleeve over the course of the night. I hoped Sid was decent at picking locks, because I certainly wasn't.

Jewellery safely put away, Lady Ainsley handed Ivanna a veil for my hair and I was forced to sit down for another quarter of an hour while my appearance was finished off. Ivanna was not gentle as she plaited and arranged my hair, then pinned the veil on. I winced more than once as she tugged my hair so tight that my face felt stretched back.

Finally finished, Lady Ainsley stood and motioned for me to follow. I glanced once more at the mirror to see that I did indeed look presentable, and followed her out of the room. At the door into the corridor, Lady Ainsley waved a dismissive hand at me and turned away.

I sighed with relief as Lady Ainsley walked away from me down the hall. Music and conversation echoed along the corridors, which were rapidly filling with revellers.

Finally free from Lady Ainsley's company, I made a beeline for the second hall through crowds of people both from town and farther afield, all come to enjoy the king's hospitality.

It was a tight squeeze to get through the more crowded parts of the corridors. People had been arriving in town for the last few days, many of them guests of the king with invitations to stay at the castle or one of the manors in the surrounding area. The castle would be full to bursting all night and tomorrow morning it would be a struggle to find any bit of floor empty of sleeping revellers.

This was fairly typical for the spring celebrations; Gydrocc Castle's spring festival was one of the best known festivals for miles, and people were keen to enjoy the hospitality of a wealthy country that didn't bother to keep tabs on exactly how much beer and wine was drunk in a single night.

I pushed through the sweaty crowd into the second hall and found Sid standing near one of the fires surrounded by young ladies and gentlemen that I didn't know, expertly fielding their questions about Marchant as if she simply didn't know what to do with all of that attention.

Sid spotted me and took my arm as I squeezed past one of her admirers. 'If you'll please excuse me,' she said to the crowd. 'I'm needed elsewhere.' And with a brilliant smile, Sid led the way through the crowd with considerably less trouble than I'd had.

We fought our way to a bench in a less crowded corner, where Sid sat us both down and smiled at me. 'You look wonderful, Tara.'

'Thank you,' I said, feeling considerably lighter than I had earlier, in spite of the difficulty we still needed to face in getting the pearl back before Bryn arrived. I held out my right wrist with the bracelet on for her inspection. 'Lord Ruben didn't take my mother's jewellery for sinister purposes. He wanted to send it for me to wear tonight.'

'This is your mother's?' Sid asked in awe, fingering the bracelet. 'It's beautiful. All of it. And you do look lovely,' she added, 'but I still don't think he needed to steal it.'

'He didn't steal it,' I said rather more defensively than I intended. 'It made for a nice surprise. I would never have thought to wear it.' I leaned close. 'In spite of everything my uncle can be nice on occasion. Untrustworthy, but occasionally nice.'

Sid made a noncommittal noise. I motioned her closer. 'There is an unfortunate downside to this,' I said, and explained about the enchanted pearl, now locked away in Lady Ainsley's room, presumably calling down an enraged dragon as we spoke.

'That's no good,' Sid pointed out unhelpfully. She leaned back against the wall and scanned the room. 'What should we do?'

'Are you any good with locks?'

'I think you can guess the answer to that,' Sid said quietly with a glance along toward a nearby duke. 'It's not like the library was open to the public when I got that book out.'

'If you can manage the locks we can get it out, hopefully before anything happens.'

'Lady Ainsley is already here.' Sid pointed reservedly across the room to where Lady Ainsley's tall feathered hat was visible. 'Does that mean her rooms are empty?'

'Ivanna—her maid—she'll still be in the rooms getting things sorted. We just need to make sure she's out here and not in the hallways, then we can go back into the room.'

Such was far easier said than done. We made our way to the hallway that connected to the corridor where Lady Ainsley's room was and lingered as unobtrusively as possible. In the crowds of guests all we could do was to keep an eye out for Ivanna and hope that we would see her leave.

The longer we stood faking conversations in the hallway the more I worried. I had managed to go the last hour without thinking about what would happen if Bryn made it all the way to the castle. Now nightmare scenarios consumed my conscious thoughts.

Maybe Bryn would be sensible and fly in from very high, where he would only look to be a bird.

Then he could…well, he could dive-bomb the castle. That wouldn't attract attention, I thought sarcastically.

The sensible thing would be for him to come in human form, on a horse or in a carriage. He could easily get through the front gate without suspicion if he looked like he had when I first met him. Just the attractiveness of his face would be entry fee enough on a night like tonight.

Not that he would necessarily plan on doing the sensible thing. If he was worried enough, he might do something brash. Like dive-bomb the castle.

I cast a worried glance at Sid, who saw my expression and could only shrug. All we could do now was wait for Ivanna to leave.

Eventually, after what seemed an eternity, a well-coifed woman in bright blue came down the hallway. It took me exactly three separate looks at her to understand that it was Ivanna. In the time between Lady Ainsley and I leaving and now, she had transformed completely from a bog-standard maid into a lovely woman with a considerable amount of life and energy in her.

I nudged Sid and gestured. Sid spotted her, eyebrows raised, and nodded to me. Arms linked together, we headed down the hall for Lady Ainsley's rooms.

The door to Lady Ainsley's rooms was just like all the others in the castle, made of dark wood with heavy cast-iron bands across it and a lock of the same material. Sid immediately lowered herself until her eye was level with the lock while I watched to ensure that we were alone in the corridor.

'Easy,' Sid said sweetly, smiling up at me as she pulled one of her long hairpins out from her careful coif. A few golden curls bounced down to rest on her shoulder as she inserted the straight pin into the lock and began to work. I almost laughed at the contrast of dainty femininity and outright scoundrel-ism.

Within a minute there was a heavy scraping and Sid pushed the door open. She rose to her feet gracefully. 'Welcome home,' She joked, and motioned me inside.

TWENTY-EIGHT

We closed the door behind us, and I slid the bolt to. I didn't want anyone walking in to find us breaking into Lady Ainsley's jewellery chest. It was only unfortunate that driving the bolt home was an imperfect solution. The perfect solution would have been to have a key to the rooms so we could lock it the usual way.

I led Sid through to the next room, opening one of the shuttered windows to let in some light as we went. Sid went immediately to the chest at the foot of the bed and went to work with her pin.

My other things were already gone from the room; I would be going back to my own tower room tonight and would have had to speak with Lady Ainsley in the morning to get my jewellery back.

Unable to help Sid, I leaned out the window to look at the sky. The sun was nearly set and darkness was closing in fast. At least an hour and a half had passed since I'd taken the necklace off. We were rapidly running out of time to get it back around my neck so that Bryn wouldn't worry.

'How's it coming?' I asked, pulling my head back inside the window.

Sid grunted and pulled away from the lock. 'This pin is too large,' she said as she twisted stray strands of hair back up into her coif and pinned them with her tool of theft. 'Where are Lady Ainsley's?'

There was quite the collection on the table, but when I showed them to Sid she made a dissatisfied noise. 'This is a very fine lock,' she said, picking up one pin and then another, judging them for size. 'I don't know that any of these are small enough.'

A loud boom echoed around the room. Sid and I jumped, and there was the clatter of pins on stone as the basket in my hands overturned. 'What was that?' I hissed, visions of angry dragons dancing through my head.

Both of us hurried to the window and looked out across the small private courtyard and craned our necks to see above, wondering if Bryn had crashed into one of the towers.

What met our gaze instead made us both breathe a sigh of relief.

'Fireworks,' Sid breathed as there was another boom and sparkling flames descend over the castle. 'Just fireworks.'

If I had been less terrified that something terrible was going to happen any moment, I might have laughed. As it was, I turned my back on the darkening sky outside and hurried to pick up the scattered pins.

'Will any of these work?' I held up a handful. 'Are they really too big?'

'I'll have another go,' Sid said with a shrug. 'But I'm going to need a light in a minute. It's getting too dark to even see the keyhole.'

There was a lamp on the desk, which I took upon myself to try lighting. Unfortunately it was something Ivanna had brought from her home kingdom, and I was unable to figure out how to get the cover off in the dark to light it.

'Do you really need a light?' I asked as I wiped lamp oil from my hand onto my skirt. Very ladylike, I thought. Lady Ainsley would berate me to no end when she saw the stain. 'I can't get the lamp to work and I don't think I can find the tinder. If we were in my rooms, I could…' I added by way of justification.

'Almost,' Sid said, her voice thick with concentration. I could hear scraping, like the door but smaller. There was a tell-tale click, and Sid released a pent-up breath. 'Got it.'

'Good,' I said, moving to her side and as she threw open the top of the chest. I pulled the second, smaller chest out and placed it on the floor. 'Do you think you can get this one?'

Sid blew out a massive puff of air. 'Merciful heavens, this woman keeps her jewellery well protected.'

Not that well protected if a rogue princess could break into it, I thought. My next thought pertained to why Sid could make that judgment and exactly how many times she had stolen jewellery in her life.

The loud booms of fireworks continued intermittently outside, a flash of coloured light accompanying every one. The sun had now slipped behind the last of the mountains, leaving the room in almost complete darkness.

Sid made a frustrated noise as she worked the lock. 'I don't know that I can do this,' she said, and I heard the clicking of metal pins against each other. 'This lock is smaller than the one before, I can barely even get this pin in.'

'Keep trying,' I said, heading for the window again. 'Anything is better than a massive dragon showing up in the middle of the spring festival.'

Or at least, that's what I would have said if I had managed to finish my sentence, because at that moment a massive shape dropped out of the sky directly into the courtyard outside of Lady Ainsley's rooms.

I choked on the words before they could climb out of my throat and coughed madly.

CHAPTER TWENTY-EIGHT

'What?' Behind me, the scraping of picks stopped abruptly.

'It's Bryn,' I managed. At least on the plus side, there weren't any screams from alarmed partygoers, so he must have managed to drop in unnoticed.

But the thing about dragons is that they don't tend to blend into the background, even in the most pitch black of nights, even if they're surrounded by something of exactly the same colour, even if they aren't smoking angry. It wasn't pitch black outside, Bryn didn't exactly match the décor, and he wasn't happy.

Currently, Bryn was glowing. All of the smooth edges of his scales seemed to be lit by the same internal fire that roared in both of his glass-smooth eyes. His face was pointed directly at the window, his eyes locked on me with a deadly sort of gleam.

'Hello, Bryn,' I managed.

Bryn snorted and lit an azalea bush directly in front of him on fire. I gasped, Sid made a satisfied sound at having some light, and Bryn stepped on the bush with one massive forefoot, putting out the flames immediately. Sid moaned.

'Sid, there's no point anymore,' I said over my shoulder, deflated. 'Bryn's already here, getting the necklace won't help anymore.'

'That's a shame,' Sid replied, 'Because I've scratched this lock enough that someone's bound to notice our little break-in now even if I can get everything locked up again.' She pulled the pins out of the lock and hefted the chest of jewellery back into the larger chest.

I turned my attention back to the courtyard to offer some kind of excuse, gasped, and turned to face Sid again. She looked up, startled, from where she was attempting now to re-lock the larger chest. 'What's wrong?'

'Nothing,' I said breathlessly and shook my head, my arms spread to clutch the sides of the window frame. The image of Bryn halfway through changing from dragon to human form burned the back of my eyes. 'Just worry about getting that chest back in there and making it look like this never happened.'

'Working on it. What's wrong?' She asked.

'What?'

Sid stood and put her hands on her hips. 'What on earth has gotten into you?'

'Nothing,' I blurted. 'Just worry about the chest.'

From behind me, I could hear Bryn's irritated voice. 'Where exactly is the necklace I gave you?'

'Are you dressed yet?' I asked sheepishly, refusing to turn my head one iota.

'Yes,' He replied, seething.

Slowly, I turned to face him.

He was indeed wearing clothes, similar robes to the ones he had been wearing when we visited the mines, though those ones had been ruined with his unexpected transformation to dragon form. His eyes still glowed an unnatural red in his bronzed face.

I swallowed, my hands clasped in front of me in something like a plea for amnesty. 'Lord Ruben made some demands of me and said I couldn't wear it tonight.'

Bryn sized me up, or at least what of me he could see through the window. His eyes lingered on the jewellery I was wearing. 'You couldn't have persuaded him to let you exchange one of those worthless pieces of jewellery for the one thing that actually matters when you wear it?'

I blinked, surprised at his choice of words, then bristled. 'These were my mother's.'

'And they don't tell me anything about whether or not you've been captured or are being tortured or anything else!' Bryn slammed a fist into the window frame, seething. 'On tonight of all nights you had to go and do something stupid.'

'I didn't ask you to come, thank you very much, and I was doing my best to get the blasted necklace back on me before you arrived,' I said as calmly as I could. 'If you were so busy you should have stayed where you were.'

Bryn frowned tellingly. After a moment he shook his long blonde hair out of his eyes and gave a great huff. In the silence that followed, I heard the rustle of Sid's skirts.

'So are you going to introduce me?' She asked from behind. There was something strange about the way she asked the question.

'Sid, this is Bryn. Bryn, Sid.' As I spoke I turned to look at Sid and suddenly I realised what it was that sounded odd.

Sid was staring at Bryn like a girl who had sighted her true love for the first time. She batted her eyelashes in a way that was almost comical and tucked her chin down demurely. The little smile that she directed at him, even in the near total darkness, could have stopped a rampaging bull.

Bryn was not a rampaging bull, and wasn't fazed by the attentions of a fairy-descended princess. He did no more than glance at her briefly before returning his attentions to me.

'Do you have any idea how dangerous it was for me to come here tonight?' He shook his head angrily, though his voice was quieter now and his eyes were cooling to a warm burgundy that might have been mistaken for brown. I took this as a sign that his rage had abated at least partway and nodded at him in acknowledgement of his point.

He pointed to the sky above the courtyard. 'There are hundreds of people out there, I had to wait for darkness and try to pinpoint where the necklace was from the sky without getting hit by any of those fireworks. That's not easy, I'll have you know.'

'I'm sorry.' I shrugged, more irritated than apologetic. 'There wasn't anything I could do about it without tipping someone off to the fact that the necklace is dragon treasure.'

Bryn frowned, as if there was a lot more he wanted to say, but contented himself with, 'Dragon treasure is not something to be ashamed of.'

An awkward silence followed during which I hoped Bryn was finished being angry, Bryn continued to glower, and Sid waited in the silence like a puppy dog wanting to be noticed.

'Are you going to let me in?' Bryn asked moodily after a few minutes.

'Oh. Oh!' I stepped back from the window. 'Sorry! But you don't have to stay. Certainly it would be better for you to leave now that you know I'm safe? Especially if you were busy with something,' I offered, hoping that it would be some consolation for the wasted trip.

'I don't see how I can leave.' Bryn lifted one leg easily to the height of the window and levered himself inside, where he dropped barefooted to the floor without a sound. 'Not without being seen. You would need to help me get outside of the castle gates.'

'Right,' I said, immediately calculating in my mind the fastest route to the front gate. 'I'll take you there now.'

'You could at least offer him a drink,' Sid said from behind me, a little too eagerly.

'I wouldn't mind a drink,' Bryn agreed, though with a suspicious look at Sid. 'But there's something going on. I was going to have to get in contact with you tonight one way or another.'

The thought of Bryn trying to get in contact with me under the nose of Lord Ruben was more than a little worrying at this point. At least right now he would be able to hide in the mass of other people that had come to the castle from surrounding villages.

'Fine. One drink and you tell me what's going on. Then you'll have to go.' I ushered him toward the door.

'And you come with me,' he said without moving.

I stopped my rather frantic gesticulations and turned to face him. 'What are you talking about?'

'There's something going on at the mines. That's where I've just come from.' Bryn stepped close to me and lowered his voice. 'It looks like they've stopped bringing out ore. For whatever reason, they've started closing the tunnels. I can only guess they have enough now and need to get the stones moved away from there.'

Things began to add up in my mind. Lord Ruben had me almost completely confined to the castle for two weeks under the watchful eye of Lady Ainsley, with freedom only available after the night of the spring festival, which was also the time that they were stopping work in the mines.

Everything was far too neat for it to be coincidence. Lord Ruben must have well and truly suspected me of something to have organised things this way.

I took a deep breath and briefly explained this to Bryn and Sid. Bryn frowned, and Sid nodded.

'He's been suspicious of you, and you have every reason to be suspicious of him.' Sid shook her head knowingly. 'It was Lord Ruben that sent Tara this jewellery to wear, after he'd stolen it from her,' Sid said to Bryn, motioning to the necklaces and bracelet.

'What?' Bryn looked at me sharply. 'You mean they were in his possession before he asked you to wear them?'

'Yes,' I said, looking from Bryn to Sid and back again. 'Is that significant?'

Bryn snorted impatiently. 'He may have had a spell laid on them.'

'A spell?' My mind went blank and I suddenly felt very young and very foolish. 'What kind of spell?'

'Perhaps to track your location.' Bryn shrugged. 'Perhaps something more sinister. It could be anything.'

'Can you tell?' I said, looking down at the pendant I had only been too pleased to put on earlier with a sinking feeling in my stomach. In my eagerness to wear mother's things, I had not considered that Lord Ruben could have had a motive other than my happiness.

'No,' Bryn admitted. 'It's not really my forte. But I would be highly suspicious of anything your uncle gave you, even if it was supposedly out of the goodness of his heart.'

'Fine,' I said brusquely in an attempt to mask my

embarrassment. 'Setting that aside, what if something really is happening at the mines? What if they're done getting the ore out and they're going to start taking it away now?'

'Have they taken any of it away from the mines yet?' Sid asked.

'No.' Bryn shook his head. 'We've been watching, waiting for it, but I suppose they wanted to move all of it at the same time so none of it gets misplaced anywhere that it could do some damage.'

'So all of the carts are still there,' I said, grateful to turn my attention to the problem at the mines instead of my own problems with Lord Ruben. 'That means we could do something about them if we got to the mines tonight.'

'Precisely.' Bryn gave a wicked little smile. 'If we did it right, we could make sure none of those rocks leave that mine anytime soon.'

'Good.' I thought of the little stone man that had wakened in the sunlight. 'Bryn, do you know why they're collecting those rocks?'

'No,' He said with a shake of his head. 'You were supposed to look into that, as you recall.'

I flushed red and took a moment to tell the story of how the little stone man had formed in sunlight and begun attacking everything that moved.

'Philip has been working on finding a way to at least immobilise the thing, but I don't know that he's found anything. We should ask him before we leave. I don't want to be left to battle one of those things, even with dragon flame as a weapon.'

'Good,' Sid said, clapping her hands together. 'So we'll get a drink and then we'll go see Philip, yes? Then you two will go have your adventure?'

TWENTY-NINE

As quietly and as quickly as we could manage, the three of us left Lady Ainsley's rooms. Sid managed to work the lock on the door back into position so it would look undisturbed, though I could only hope that they wouldn't notice that the lock on the chest at the foot of the bed was now scratched.

Once we were in the halls, with light from the occasional torch, Sid's worshipful expression renewed itself upon looking again at Bryn.

I couldn't blame her; it was the first time I had seen him in the light and he was, if possible, more handsome than I had imagined. He looked like a gleaming bronze statue of a great hero come to life.

Bryn ignored Sid for the most part as we walked to

the great hall, but occasionally cast disgusted glances in her direction. She didn't seem to notice and continued to watch him with great fascination.

The great hall was packed with people around the edges of the room, though there was at least some space in the centre where the dances were taking place. We wound our way through the room to one of the tables, where a massive cask of ale was set up.

'Allow me,' Bryn said roughly, as he pushed through the last of the crowd toward the cask, leaving Sid and I standing where we were.

'How chivalrous,' Sid said, watching Bryn's retreating back.

'You know he doesn't like you,' I warned.

Sid shrugged. 'Perhaps he'll change his mind when he gets to know me.'

I rolled my eyes and refrained from reminding her that he was a dragon: he had different taste in women, and a definite dislike for anything fairy.

It didn't take long for Bryn to make that clear in his own way–he returned moments later with only two mugs of ale. He handed one to me and began drinking from the other immediately, refusing to so much as look at Sid. She pouted, distinctly put out.

'We can share,' I laughed, and offered her my drink.

Together the three of us gradually migrated toward a bench, where Sid and I sat down at Bryn stood behind us to lean against the wall with his drink.

'We can't stay too long,' Bryn said quietly. 'It will

take time to get to the mines and I don't want to risk seeing another sunrise there, especially considering what you said about your little stone man.'

I agreed with him, but for entirely different reasons. In the past several weeks I had become used to attracting a lot of attention when I was with Sid, but being with Sid and Bryn turned the interested audience from an all-male one to a crowd of pretty much everyone. What gazes weren't drawn to Sid's fair countenance were drawn to Bryn's brooding one, and it made good sense to get out of here before people began asking where this handsome stranger had come from and how he knew myself and the princess.

It didn't take long for Prince Caleb to appear in front of us. 'Good evening, ladies,' he said, though his gaze was for the most part directed at Bryn. 'I'm pleased that you made it tonight. I was watching for you and worried you might not be feeling well.'

'We appreciate your concern,' Sid replied courteously. She gave him a smile, but Caleb's attention was still on Bryn, whom he regarded with cool disdain.

'Prince Caleb, this is...Bryn. He hails from the mountains and has come to sample the ales.' I managed a brief smile as I introduced the two of them. 'Bryn, this is Crown Prince Caleb, heir to the throne in Gydrocc after his father.'

'Nice to meet you,' Bryn said flatly. Caleb grimaced.

There was the immediate sensation that there was about to be some sort of masculine war of gazes embarked upon at any moment. Sid obviously noticed it just as much as I did, because she turned to Bryn. 'Do you dance?'

'No,' Bryn said shortly. 'Tara, you should have something to eat.'

Before I could make any kind of response, Bryn stepped over the bench next to me and pulled me to my feet. We weren't three steps away when he asked none too quietly, 'Who is that? I don't like him.'

I glanced back at Prince Caleb, who looked rather dazed at Bryn's rudeness. 'He's the crown prince of Clovia,' I whispered back, a little horrified and more than a little amused. Apparently Bryn was able to overlook the cloth-of-gold waistcoat and fine silks that marked Prince Caleb as different from the average man.

Or perhaps to a dragon, all men were average men.

Without a word, Bryn steered me toward the food table, where he grabbed a large piece of bread and a larger chunk of meat. Thinking of what Bryn had said about going to mines, I did the same, though in smaller portions and with a side of cheese.

We were halfway through eating when Sid appeared at my side. 'I have an idea,' she said excitedly, coming close to me. The love-struck look about her fortunately seemed to have vanished, and she was back to her normal self. 'To make sure your uncle thinks you're here the whole night.'

I would have asked, but Prince Caleb strolled up at

that moment and put his hand on the small of Sid's back. 'Is there anything I can do for you, Princess?' He asked, pointedly ignoring Bryn.

'No, thank you,' She said brightly. 'We have some-place we need to be for a time.' She hesitated, then turned and placed a hand on Caleb's arm. 'Actually, could you possibly find Alois, my maid? I haven't seen her all night and would like her assistance with something.'

'At your service,' Caleb said with a bow and a smile that most women, myself not excepted, would have killed to have aimed in our direction. Sid didn't seem to notice. Bryn did, and his mouth twitched into a frown.

'He's a good person,' I said quietly to Bryn.

He swallowed and drained his drink. 'He's a coward.'

'You've known him for less time than it took you to drink this.' I took the tankard from his grip and set it on the table behind us. 'You shouldn't judge him or Sid so hastily.'

'I'll judge people however I want.'

'On your own head be it, then,' I said loftily and turned to Sid, who was scanning the room on the lookout for Alois.

'Once we have Alois we'll head to Philip's tower,' she said, and motioned for us to start making our way to the door. 'We can see what he has to say and then we'll make everything ready for you to go.'

Alois appeared out of the crowd not far from us, and Sid waved for her to join us. None of us bothered making introductions, but made our way directly out of the packed great hall and toward Philip's tower.

Philip, of course, had not come down to the festival. As was tradition, he had overseen the lighting of the fireworks before going off to bed with a small cask of fine ale. He wasn't one for crowds, though he didn't mind a late night. It didn't surprise me to see that there was still a light at the top of his tower.

Rue answered the door of the tower sleepily and let the four of us in with a confused look. I couldn't blame him; normally he would only ever see me alone, but lately I kept bringing more and more people by the tower.

I dropped a kiss on Rue's forehead and he blushed, shutting the door behind us. I led the way up the stairs, this time going past Philip's workshop to the top of the tower, where I had seen the light.

The top room of Philip's tower was his observatory. At the top of the stairs I pushed open a trapdoor in the ceiling and stepped up onto the floor, which was less like a room at the top of a tower than a platform with some columns holding up a ceiling. Wind cut across the platform at high speeds, but it was a warm wind, a friendlier kind than I had encountered at this time of night since autumn.

Below the edge of the platform on which we stood the whole of Gydrocc Castle was laid out before us, brightly lit like a sea of stars in the darkness, and beyond that what seemed like the whole of Clovia, silhouetted against the moonlight and stretching on for an inky black eternity.

'This is beautiful,' Sid said the moment she had both feet situated on the floor. I made a noise of agreement but there were other things to worry about now.

'Philip,' I called gently, seeing the old man bent over a telescope near one of the railings. Aside from the telescope and a table beside it upon which Philip's notes resided, the platform was empty.

Philip looked up and smiled at me, though his expression grew somewhat strained when he saw that I had brought a crowd.

'Is there something going on?' He asked, straightening up and closing his book of notes swiftly. 'Am I wanted below?'

'Not by anyone else,' I said. 'This is Bryn.'

Philip's defensive look suddenly brightened into something more welcoming. 'Ah, my dear boy!' He reached out with both hands and toddled over, age and alcohol making him a little unsteady on his feet. 'I've been so looking forward to meeting you!'

'And I you,' Bryn said genuinely, though a little hesitantly, as he accepted Philip's handclasp.

With the smile of a teacher who had been waiting for a pupil, Philip raised a twisted old hand to point to the stars. 'Tonight marks the beginning of the warmer seasons,' He said, tracing constellations with his gestures. 'The last of the winter stars have risen and begun to fall. The first of the summer stars will be seen just before dawn and there will be no more heavy winter until those summer stars return to their long sleep.'

I exchanged a glance with Bryn and Sid, who looked just as confused as I did. It wasn't exactly the kind of comment that came off as being helpful, or as reflecting well on Philip's continuing sanity. Surely he didn't think Bryn had come here just for a social call.

'Philip,' I said, drawing his attention again. 'We need to know whether or not you've found anything about the stone man. Is there any way to destroy him?'

'Only what I told you before.' Philip glanced through his telescope again. 'Dragon fire seems the way forward. I keep finding references to water but as we saw before, that wasn't very effective.'

The hope that had grown in my chest over the last few minutes dissipated like mist at this admission from Philip. I had hoped for something more definitive, something more helpful.

'Bryn and I are going to the mines tonight,' I explained, my voice coming out flat. 'They seem to be finished and closing the tunnels. We have to find out what they're planning now. Those stones will be dangerous wherever they end up.'

'I see.' Philip turned to face us with a worried look and set down his book of notes on the table. 'I do see.'

'Is there anything you can give us to help?' I pleaded, hoping for some charm that we could simply show to the stones to keep them from awakening.

Philip shook his head. 'All I can tell you is that if a dunking in the lake didn't help there probably isn't anything other than dragon fire that will.'

'I think we should go,' Bryn said, inching his way impatiently toward the trapdoor. 'If it takes us too long to get to those mountains, we might be the ones guilty of waking up the stones when we try to put things right.'

'How are you supposed to put things right?' Sid demanded, shaking her head in utter disbelief. 'They've already taken rather a lot of those stones from the mountain and it's not as if they can just be put back.'

'At least if they're underground they won't be exposed to the sunlight.' I shook my head. 'I don't know how much it will help but at least we can try to put all of the stones back before dawn.'

When no one made any other suggestions, Bryn and I started down the ladder. The others followed, including Philip, who directed us down the stairs to his study. Inside, Sid ushered us all to have a seat.

Apparently she had been thinking on the way down, because the first words out of her mouth were, 'You can't leave without something to keep Lord Ruben from noticing your absence.' She pointed to my necklace. 'Especially considering that he may have laid a spell on that jewellery you're wearing.'

Philip noticed for the first time that I was wearing jewellery. 'Ah, those? Yes, those do have a spell on them,' He said offhandedly as he sat.

'What do you mean?' I asked, turning to face him. 'What sort of spell did Lord Ruben put on them?'

'I don't know.' Philip looked at the pendant with tired, watery eyes. 'I can see that there's a spell, and that it's not taken hold of you yet, but other than that I can't be certain without doing some further investigations.'

'We don't have time for that now,' Sid reminded us. 'What we do have time for is to get Alois to dress up in your things, Tara, so she can pass for you.'

A single glance at Alois' slim frame made an easy sceptic of me.

'Sid, I don't care how much you know about painting faces and dressing people, there is no way anyone is going to be deceived by Alois wearing my dress.'

'Oh no?' Sid gave a secretive smile. 'Go. Both of you. Alois, put on all of Sid's things. Philip, can Sid borrow something of yours to wear?'

In a moment Alois and I had been ushered upstairs to change. It didn't take nearly as long to switch dresses with her as it had taken to get dressed originally, which made me wonder exactly why Lady Aisnley bothered employing Ivanna. It wasn't much use to get dressed more slowly with help than without.

I fixed my veil in place on Alois, who looked far

lovelier in my clothing than I ever managed to in spite of the poor fit. Philip had offered me a pair of trousers and a tunic, along with a cloak, and in his clothing I once again looked more like a man than a woman.

'You look better in that dress than I ever did,' I commented as Alois and I headed down the stairs again. 'How no one is supposed to notice I can't imagine.'

'Princess Amanthea has a way of surprising people when it comes to that,' Alois said cryptically.

When we stepped back into Philip's study Sid was waiting for us. She took Alois by both hands immediately, pulled her into the light of the fire and smiled at me.

'This will do just fine,' she said, tucking Alois' hair a little more tightly behind the veil.

'No one is going to be fooled,' I commented, and was met with silence. I looked around at the other four, all of whom seemed unconcerned. 'Just look at Alois,' I continued. 'She's far prettier than I'll ever be.'

Alois reddened, but said nothing. Sid shook her head and said in commanding tones, 'you are beautiful, Tara, just not in the conventional way.'

I scoffed. Sid held up a hand. 'No, stop. I need to concentrate.'

Sid furrowed her brow and stared at Alois' face, holding both of her hands. Occasionally, she would glance at me, then back to Alois. After a few moments, she began to examine the rest of Alois, again throwing the occasional look in my direction. Strangely, she never seemed to blink, as if she was concentrating too hard to be distracted by such a meaningless thing.

It had been nearly five minutes by the time she released Alois' hands and stepped away. 'Is that it?' I asked, looking from Sid to Alois.

I didn't bother saying anything else for fear of sounding more like an idiot than I must have already.

Alois was—well, different. She looked like a completely new person. No, not a completely new person; she looked like *me*.

If I hadn't known it was Alois standing in front of me, I might have thought I was looking at a particularly fine portrait of myself.

'Her jaw is too long,' Bryn drawled from the chair in which he was sprawled.

Another glance and I could see he was right. In fact it reminded me very much of my most recent portrait. A little different here, a little different there; if someone didn't know me very well, or didn't look too closely, they could be convinced it was me. However, anyone that knew me well was likely to see that things weren't quite right.

'I'm afraid that's the best I can do,' Sid said apologetically, tilting her head to one side to examine Alois' new features. 'It should last the night, as long as I'm awake. So don't let me fall asleep before Tara gets back,' she added to Alois.

'What did you do? How did you do that?' I asked,

stepping up to Alois, whose face—my face—was turning red at the close scrutiny. 'How did you make Alois look like me?'

'Um, well,' Sid managed astutely before Bryn cut her off.

'Haven't you heard of the Fairy's Glamour?' He said from the extremely comfortable depths of one of Philip's cushioned chairs. He sounded disgusted. 'There's a reason fairies are known for being so beautiful, and it's not because they're born that way.'

There was an awkward silence while I waited for someone to dispute that, but no one did. Sid shifted uncomfortably while Philip sat nodding in agreement from his own cushioned chair.

Finally, Sid looked at me apologetically and explained. 'One of the few gifts of the fairies that has been passed down through the generation is the Glamour. We can make things look different than they actually are, if we're concentrating and if the thing stays close to us.'

'It's usually used as a tool of vanity,' Bryn added.

'Wait,' I said, confused. 'Do you use this on yourself?'

Sid gave a broad, painful smile. 'Usually.' She hesitated. 'Almost always.'

'So have I ever seen what you actually look like?'

'I look like this!' She said with a pained expression, motioning to her perfect face. 'Mostly. I just get rid of the spots and make my nose look a little smaller. And my eyes aren't quite this blue, usually.'

A glance at Alois said that wasn't the whole story, but this wasn't the time to ask. I shook my head to clear it. 'Right. So you can make Alois look…well, *mostly* like me for the whole night? As long as you concentrate?'

'Yes,' Sid said with certainty. 'Once she looks like you I can pretend it really is you. That will make it easier to hold up the illusion.'

'Great.' I was suddenly at a loss for words. Not only was she beautiful, she was magical as well. I felt suddenly inferior, as if Sid and I were strangers once again. What other skills was she hiding?

'Wonderful.' My voice sounded flat, even to me. 'Bryn, we need to go.'

He stood immediately and headed for the door. I hesitated, though, worried both for Sid and Alois if Lord Ruben found out what was going on, and for what might happen to Bryn and I at the mines.

'You'll be alright without me, then?' I asked, looking at Alois once more and thinking that she would probably make a better me than I would. She would certainly be more graceful on the dance floor. Perhaps it would be attributed to Lady Ainsley's lessons.

'We'll be fine,' Sid reassured me.

Alois nodded. 'I won't talk to anyone.'

I could see why. It was unnerving to hear her voice coming from my face. 'Avoid my uncle. And Lady

Ainsley.'

She nodded again and smiled. 'It'll be fine. I've done this before.'

That opened up a whole world of questions, but I couldn't ask any of them now. Bryn was obviously aching to get out of here and back to the mines.

'I'll see you in the morning,' I said reluctantly, and closed the door behind me.

THIRTY

At the bottom of the tower I let us out into the night air, which was rapidly turning cool now that the sun was fully set. 'Which way?' Bryn asked as we looked across the courtyards.

'Here,' I said, climbing out one of the empty archways of the outdoor hallway and heading straight for the door near the stables. 'I always go this way when I sneak out at night.'

The courtyard was not as dark as it usually would be when I was sneaking out, though. The kitchen was still well lit, and servants were everywhere, not to mention revelers that had spilled out into the courtyard from the Halls inside.

To avoid being spotted I took Bryn the long way

around the stables and kept to the shadows. It wasn't nearly as cold as it had been even a couple of weeks previously, but the ground was wet with dew already and soaked through my thin dancing shoes quickly.

The gate in the outer wall gave us no trouble on the way out as the guards were as busy with the spring festival as anyone else. I took the key from the hook on the wall and unlocked the door with almost no fear that we would be spotted.

Gate shut and locked behind us, I pocketed the key and started off across the wide open space between the castle and the forest. Bryn gave a sigh of relief as we left the lights of the castle behind.

'Your human dwellings always make me uncomfortable,' He said as we walked quickly toward the woods. 'Too many walls and never enough windows.'

The admission was surprising, and I said so, adding, 'Which is strange considering that you live in a mountain.'

'The mountains are different. Mostly we stay close to the cave entrances. We don't go deep into the mountain. Not to live.'

To me the cold seemed so much sharper out here than it had in the castle walls, and I thought how different our views of the world were. While the dark openness of the fields at night didn't terrify me, it did make me feel considerably less secure than the warmth of the castle.

The thought of the mines waiting for us with their

dark, close tunnels made me feel even colder.

Nervous now, I started to run toward the edge of the forest. The feel of my feet pounding hard into the ground shook out some of my nervousness and distracted me from a growing terror that something bad was going to happen tonight, something that would result in my exile or death.

Bryn adjusted quickly to my sudden change of pace and kept up with ease. I didn't slow down until I'd come to a clearing, the same one Sid and I had stopped at on our return last time. Breathing heavily, I looked around to see if this was enough space for Bryn to take off.

'Is this enough room?' I panted.

'It should be.' Bryn watched me closely, and I thought I could see a hint of concern on his face. 'Are you ready?'

'Is anyone ever ready for something like this?'

Bryn grinned, breathing as heavily as I, and returned to the trees. I turned my back and looked for the crossbow that I had left here before. I had no intention of going to those mines unarmed again. It was barely a minute before I heard the slithering of scales across the forest floor. Bryn crouched beside me, red scales glinting even in the darkness. I motioned for him to wait a moment and crouched down in the bushes.

There, where I had left it, was the crossbow and bolts, along with a few other now-filthy things from the last time we had come out. The crossbow looked a little worse for wear having been left out in the elements, but there hadn't been any other option than just leaving it here.

With the crossbow safely strapped around my shoulders, I clambered onto Bryn's back. Considering it was only my third night riding a dragon, it was far less intimidating now to climb onto his back ready to fly away into the night.

Bryn spread his winds with a snap and lumbered into a run, wings rising and falling with elegant force as he lunged across the clearing. With no room to spare before we hit the trees, he gave a great leap as his wings thrust downward. It gave just enough lift that his clawed feet only just brushed the treetops below.

Our climb through the cold night air took what seemed an eternity. In fact, we were still low enough as we passed over Gydrocc Castle that I could almost make out who individuals in the courtyard were. I could have sworn I saw Hawkins dancing around one of the many fires with a pair of large women; the thought made me smile as we rose higher into the night sky.

We left Gydrocc behind swiftly, and soon there was only darkness below us, with the occasional point of light coming from a village hosting their own spring celebrations. I turned my eyes ahead to the dark silhouettes of the Gray Mountains. They rose like teeth from the dark horizon, forbidding and treacherous.

The only indication that we were moving at all was the wind in my face and the pinpricks of tiny fires at the mines that eventually became visible on the side of the mountains.

In some ways it was like reliving our first flight, except that this time I hadn't bruised my face on takeoff. We landed in the same place in the forest below the mines, with that same strange controlled fall into a space that seemed far too small for a dragon to land in.

Once on the ground, I slid from Bryn's back and reached for the crossbow to trigger it. I didn't want to be caught off-guard, and chances were, after the last time we had visited, there were going to be more patrols around the camp and far more suspicion on the part of the guards. If they got the slightest whiff we were there we would be dead before Bryn had a chance to take off.

At least, I would be dead. Bryn would be protected by those inch-thick scales. Another disadvantage of being a small, fleshy human.

We crept silently through the cold forest, aware of every noise and snapping twig. I drew Philip's cloak tight around me to guard against the cold, but left enough room to hold the crossbow out in front of me. I had left it unloaded for fear of shooting myself in the foot, but it would take less than a moment to notch an arrow into the space and pull the trigger, which might be all the time I had if we were noticed.

My toes started to feel frozen as we walked and I wished that I'd had a bit more foresight in at least putting on an extra pair of stockings. Much longer and I would be shivering.

I shook my head at myself; of all the things to be uncomfortable about tonight, I was worried about my cold toes.

We were only halfway to the mining camp when a childlike giggling echoed out from the trees.

It was here again.

I swept the crossbow up, turned, and looked into the forest behind me for any sign of movement. There was nothing, the same as the last time. Before, the strange giggle had disappeared into the night without a trace; it looked as though the same was going to happen again.

Bryn puffed at me, and I glanced at him. He was turned around to look at me, his sinuous body forming a u. His gaze was not scornful this time, but curious, searching, just as mine were.

'Did you hear that?' I demanded.

The giggle sounded again before he could answer, off to one side. Both of us snapped to attention, tracking the sound. This time, there was the slightest suggestion of movement amongst the leaves far enough away it was barely discernible in the darkness.

I looked to Bryn and he looked back. Then, with an unmistakable twitch of his head, he motioned for me to take a look.

Stunned, my mouth dropped open. 'You're the dragon,' I hissed. 'You're not supposed to be afraid of anything!'

Bryn shook his head and shoulders all together at one time with a rustle that I didn't know what to make of. At my obvious confusion, he plopped his hindquarters down on the forest floor a little too noisily and shook his great head once.

'Fine,' I said, offended and surprised all at once. 'But you're just being stubborn. It's your fault if I get killed doing this.'

If Bryn could have spoken, I don't think he would have. Instead he stared at me in stony silence that was so human I could see his disdain.

With a deep breath, I notched an arrow into the crossbow and carefully advanced on the source of the shaking leaves. Though I placed my feet with care, I knew I was making enough noise that whatever was hiding in the trees could not fail to notice my approach.

The leaves rustled again, but much closer now, and on my left instead of straight ahead. I turned swiftly, crossbow at the ready, but only heard the childish giggling one more time.

'Come out,' I said clearly, though not so loudly that my voice might carry as far as the mining camp. 'I know you're there.'

The rustling stopped, and there was a stillness in the forest around me. The trees seemed close and simultaneously very far away as I focused on the source of the human-like giggling, which was dying away now.

I could do nothing but wait, and finally, my patience was rewarded after what seemed an interminable amount of time. From behind one of the large pine trees stepped a child.

THIRTY-ONE

It was not a normal child. For one, I could not tell if it was male or female though it was not wearing any clothing. While it had the head and face of a human child, the body was roughly cast, as if out of clay, sexually ambiguous and devoid of nipples or a navel. Its skin was strange even in the darkness, a mottled patchwork of brown and green that looked so like the trees and bushes around it that I could barely tell where one stopped and the other began.

It was smiling at me, with a strange closed-mouth smile. I lowered my crossbow, uncertain what to make of this thing. It had been following us, that much was certain, especially when it looked at me and giggled once more.

'What do you want?' I demanded. 'Tell me.'

The child did not speak, but advanced, one step at a time. Each step seemed to swallow up far more ground than it should have, and in four steps it was almost level with me. I snapped the crossbow back up to my shoulder.

'Speak, or have a bolt through your chest!' I threatened, too loudly. I was scared, and the threat was empty. My concentration was not good enough at this moment for me to hit anything I aimed at.

The thing came to a halt in front of me. What was it about this strange little cherub that Bryn was unwilling to face it? Was he afraid of it? I swallowed past a dry throat. Anything that could make a dragon fear was well worth avoiding.

'What are you?' I demanded, my voice a whisper.

The little child-thing stared at me with wide dark eyes, wispy green hair floating out around it like leaves. I stared back, unable to find any more words now that the thing was near enough to reach out and grab the end of my crossbow.

The dragon does not want to offend us.

I jumped, nearly dropping the crossbow in shock. The creature was speaking to me with its eyes. My hands unconsciously lowered the weapon, and I couldn't help my wide-eyed stare.

'What do you mean offend you?' It was the first response that came to my mind.

The little creature ignored my question and tilted its

head to one side, watching me. When no response was forthcoming, I went back to my earlier questions.

'What are you? What do you want?'

The little thing smiled more broadly, though it still did not open its lips to truly smile. Neither did it blink. I licked my lips and took another deep breath, racking my brains for any information that could possibly help me.

My mind caught hold of Fionnuel's History of the Dark Woods, and what Sid had said about her reading therein. What had she said? Will-o-the-wisps? Unicorns? Tree spirits?

'Oh,' I breathed, my confusion ebbing away like the tide. 'You're a tree spirit.'

The giggle sounded again, issuing forth from the thing in front of me without it making a single movement. I shivered and looked back to where Bryn was standing, his ears perked up to hear what I was saying from this distance.

My mind raced. 'The dragon wouldn't speak to you…because it is a creature of fire and knows better than to speak with a creature of the forest uninvited,' I said slowly. The pieces were building up into a coherent picture. 'Why have you shown yourself to us?'

You can help.

Those wide eyes did not change as it continued to stare at me. My confusion must have been evident in my own gaze, because gradually words formed in my mind, almost as if the tree spirit could guide my thoughts in the same way it could plant words in my mind.

'The miners have destroyed a part of the forest. Your forest' I chose my words with great care. 'You have not forgiven them. Do you want revenge?' I asked, wondering how on earth a tree would exact revenge without help.

I supposed that was where the dragon came in.

The tree spirit shook its head, and the smile dropped away a little bit. It reached out to me, offering a hand of what I thought must be friendship. I went to take it before realising that I was still holding the crossbow in a white-knuckled grip.

With a grimace, I hastily unloaded the bolt and lowered the crossbow, though I kept hold of it with one hand. With the other, I took the childlike hand offered to me. It felt like the smooth bark of a young birch tree, with only the smallest bit of roughness, cold as a tree might be on a night like this.

The spirit led me back toward Bryn, who stood as it approached, perhaps out of respect. The tree spirit stopped in front of Bryn but did not release my hand.

There is danger under the mountain.

Bryn's head snapped up, and I knew the tree spirit was speaking to him as well. I made a hushing noise at him and gestured to the strange child. Bryn lowered his head to look at the thing. He wisely kept his distance, and kept his mouth clamped shut.

'We know of the danger,' I said to the spirit. 'The

stones pulled out of the mines will waken in the sunlight and begin to destroy the things around them.'

The spirit shook its head. *That is not the danger.*

Bryn and I exchanged a glance. 'Then what is?'

For centuries the trees have calmed the mountain. Now the trees have been stripped away, and tonight is the night of awakening.

An image of the now-barren mountainside filled my mind as the tree spirit gave me images to view that were not my own. I could see, as if overlaid on top of that, an image of what it used to be. The trees that had once covered every spare inch of the mountain were gone, leaving only a few bits of brush covering the rocks and soil.

More than that, I could see a pulsating life in the image of the trees that extended deep into the mountainside with the root systems, completely intertwined with the rocks. I could feel the calming pulse of the trees, too slow and steady to be heard or felt by any animal.

In the image without the trees, that pulse was slowly ebbing away. The roots that remained under the earth were now no more than twisted bits of wood, no longer a living thing.

Then, in my mind's eye, there was the image of the rocks. Not the ones that had been removed from the mountain that we had been so worried about, the ones meant for King Stephen's enemies, but the ones under the mountain, the ones that had remained undisturbed by the quarryman's pick.

I could see a mental image of the moon and stars moving across the sky as the night wore on. Unseen from aboveground, the rocks would begin to vibrate, the tree spirit told us in the images. They were the same vibration Bryn and I had seen before, when one of the miners had struck the wrong place on the rocks, a bone-shattering kind of rattle that threatened to bring the whole set of tunnels and caverns down around our heads.

The vibration would build and peak, the tree spirit seemed to tell us, until finally the rocks would loose themselves from their footings, wakened by the spring sunlight and the lack of life around them to hold them down.

The last thing I saw before the images drained away was the side of the mountain exploding as a rock giant the size of Gydrocc Castle smashed its way out of its cage.

My wide-eyed horror was matched by Bryn's as we came back to ourselves.

'I don't think Lord Ruben was prepared for that,' I managed breathlessly. My mind raced as I sought for explanations and solutions. 'Why tonight?' I asked, confusion mounting. 'The trees have been gone from the mountainside for weeks. Months.'

The little tree spirit did not reply, but looked up to the sky. Suddenly, the cryptic words Philip had uttered earlier came back with full force to my mind. *The first of the summer stars will be seen just before dawn and there will be no more heavy winter until those summer stars return to their long sleep.*

That was why the mining had stopped so suddenly, on tonight of all nights. The miners, or the ones who had hired them, had worked out that they were approaching something deadly, just as Bryn and I had, but there had been no tree spirit to tell them that simply stopping their work would not be enough to quiet the mountain.

Bryn looked at the little tree spirit with intense concentration, as if willing the thing to understand what he could not say in his current form. The little spirit seemed to understand him in spite of the lack of words.

The fire of a dragon is powerful, but it would take a hundred dragons to calm this creature.

Were there even a hundred dragons left in this world? It didn't matter. We would never gather enough of them in time. Bryn obviously thought the same thing as he gave a worried glance in the direction of the mines. Suddenly the issue of seeing that none of the small carts of rocks made it out of the mines seemed trivial.

'What can calm it?' I demanded. 'What can we do?'

There must be a pulse. The rocks do not live, but they crave life; they will move if nothing moves on them.

It made no sense. I couldn't tell what the spirit was trying to say. Regardless, we were running out of time

307

to figure it out. With a glance at the sky, I said, 'Will you come with us? Help us?'

The broad grin returned, and the spirit took my hand once more.

I took that as a yes.

THIRTY-TWO

The three of us stared at the mining camp from the edge of the trees, counting fires and soldiers.

'There are more of them now,' I commented, though I knew Bryn could see that for himself. 'I guess you frightened them last time.'

Bryn snorted quietly in response. I smiled a little. It would be the only spot of humour in tonight's escapade.

I looked back toward the camp. 'All of these men will die if they stay here tonight,' I said quietly. It was chillingly obvious in light of what the tree spirit had shown us. When the stone giant broke free there would be a rain of boulders and mud that would completely destroy anything on the surface of the mountain. That would include the entire camp and probably a good number of the trees that remained downslope.

I mentally outlined a plan. 'First we need to scare off all of these people,' I said with a significant look at Bryn. 'I'm sure you can manage that with a few well-aimed bits of fire. Then we need to get the carts of rocks that are out in the open back into the mine somehow. Then...then we need to calm the rocks so they don't animate themselves.'

Bryn gave me a look. I grimaced. 'No, I'm not sure how we'll do that yet.'

We have faith in you.

I looked at the tree spirit, surprised. It looked right back at me with that unnerving, unblinking grin.

'Well, I'm not sure your faith isn't misplaced,' I said shortly, unsure how else to respond. 'This isn't something either of us ever done before.'

The little tree spirit put its hand through mine and squeezed gently. I could feel a sense of warm calmness radiate from the spirit. As I felt my fear ebb, I realised this was how the trees had calmed the mountain for so long.

Feeling considerably calmer, I nodded to Bryn. 'We don't have time to waste. Do you mind scaring them off?'

This time it was Bryn that grinned at me, and he grinned with all of his teeth showing. That was considerably more unnerving than the tree spirit not blinking.

With sparks leaking from between his teeth, Bryn slithered up the nearest tree and was gone.

I readied the crossbow, in the event that any of the fleeing soldiers came in my direction, and huddled down to wait.

I didn't have to wait long. Once Bryn got to the top of the tree he must have taken flight, because it was only a few spare moments between him leaving my side and his appearance in the sky above the mines, breathing out columns of flames as thick as a tree trunk and long as three houses put together.

Screams wakened the camp, followed almost immediately by the sound of bowstrings twanging. Bryn rolled and dived, blowing fire all the way, first lighting up the ground between two of the campfires, then the air above the soldiers' heads as he flew low over the top of them, swinging a lazy leg to knock over swordsmen like toys.

The difference between last time, when we had fled from the soldiers like rabbits from a hunter, and this time, when it was safe to expect the soldiers would run, was threefold: first, Bryn wasn't in human form to start with; second, he had the element of surprise; and third, he was in flight, and a dragon in the air is a hundred times more difficult to harm than a dragon on the ground.

The sight of a dragon sent the miners running for cover, screams on their lips. If any of them had harboured ideas of returning to this place to continue mining outside of Lord Ruben's control, those financial dreams were now very effectively dashed. This was the second dragon sighting in the same place in a month and that did not bode well for future work here. The miners ran for their lives in whatever direction they thought would lead to escape fastest.

The soldiers, on the other hand, only had a few moments of panic before they grouped together to fend off the creature that descended on them. There must have been thirty guards, presumably enough to match a dragon in a fight, if all of them were lucky and sufficiently brave.

Unfortunately for them it is a rare man brave enough to face a dragon, even when the dragon is out-numbered. As Bryn circled and came back at the column of men, spouting a jet of flame aimed at their feet instead of over their heads, some half a dozen of them dived for cover and did not return. They fled for the trees in understandable panic, some of them with boots aflame.

I was ready with the crossbow but did not need to use it. The soldiers scattered in other directions than towards me.

More of them dived for cover at Bryn's second round, and by the third, when he came at them jaws gaping and claws extended, not only were there less than ten soldiers left, but none of them had anything more than a sword as all of their bowstrings had burned up in the heat.

There were screams but no blood as the last of them ran for it. No one would blame the soldiers for fleeing; ten men were a nice, easy feast for a dragon, according to the old stories. I briefly hoped that Bryn had never actually eaten a man. It might make future family dinners awkward. I waited with my crossbow until all of them had gone, then headed for the camp. Some of the soldiers might return, after all; we had time, but needed to be quick in disposing of the carts of stones.

As I hurried to the first cart of stones, still covered with a tarp, I addressed the tree spirit.

'Which tunnel will take these stones deepest into the mountain the most quickly? Do you know?'

The tree spirit pointed to the first tunnel to have been boarded up, which Bryn and I had seen on our previous visit. I hurried to it, and motioned for Bryn to follow me. If there was any chance of keeping the stones from animating, we needed them all in one place to start with. Once that was done we could worry about how to keep the mountain asleep.

Bryn landed heavily next to me, his sides heaving from the exertion of his aerial acrobatics. I pointed to the boarded up tunnel. 'Can you please open that?'

It took two swipes of dragon claws to reopen the tunnel. Without another word, Bryn blasted a fireball down into the depths of the tunnel. I looked in after the fireball had gone to see lingering light showing that, rather surprisingly, the tunnel went several meters into the side of the mountain before dropping off abruptly.

It was a natural shaft that plunged deep into the mountain. The tree spirit sent a visual into my mind of a long enough drop that light would never penetrate the depths to touch the rocks we put down this tunnel.

'Perfect,' I said as I hurried back to a cart of the rocks. 'Bryn, can you push this into the tunnel? I'll find the others and we can get rid of them.'

Bryn pushed the first cart easily into the tunnel, where it rolled down the gentle slope until it came to the end, where the wheels no longer came into contact with the ground. Cart, stones and all fell down into the depths of the mountain, tumbling noisily the whole way.

The racket was enormous as Bryn repeated this feat, and I hoped it wouldn't wake the rest of the mountain. The tree spirit seemed unworried, so I tried to push the thought out of my mind. It surely would warn us if we were doing something dangerous.

There were a dozen carts to be found spread across the entire camp. By the time Bryn had collected the last one to push into the tunnel, we were both exhausted, me from running, he from a combination of scaring off the soldiers and moving several tons of rocks.

Once the last of the carts had been cast into the depths, Bryn flopped down on the ground in front of the tunnel and let out a smoky sigh.

My legs were wobbly as I hurried over to his side. At least I wasn't cold anymore. Wiping sweat from my brow, I knelt next to him. 'Are you alright?'

Bryn puffed at me and closed his eyes briefly. When he opened them, he looked tired, ready to fall asleep. I couldn't begrudge him this chance to rest and turned my attention to the tree spirit.

The tree spirit stood completely still next to me, radiating impatience, eyes on at the sky. It was well past midnight now. If the tree spirit was right, we didn't have very long to find a way to soothe the mountain before it would wake up on its own.

'What now?' I asked, exhausted myself. I dropped to a seat onto the ground next to Bryn's head, my legs shaking with nervous exhaustion.

The mountain must be soothed.

'Yes, but how?' Despair was building in my chest. We had come all this way and successfully driven out the soldiers and miners, but I still had no idea what we were supposed to do to keep the mountain from waking with the dawn and going on the warpath.

'Bryn is exhausted. I'm exhausted. We don't have anything but a crossbow and a couple of charms to try doing the impossible.'

The trees have always kept the mountain calm.

'Yes, but there aren't any trees here now.' My irritation must have been audible as I waved a hand at the naked mountainside. 'And they take more than a few hours to grow.'

The little tree spirit smiled at me again, but this time the smile was less reassuring. Perhaps this had something to do with the fact that its lips stretched so far out to each side—nearly reaching its ears—that it was obvious it was only pretending to be human.

The full light of day has not yet risen, the tree spirit said. *If the mountain wakes now, tree spirits can keep it calm. It could be led to a place where the light of dawn will not wake it.*

Of all the things the tree spirit might have suggested, this was undoubtedly the worst.

'You mean you want to purposely wake the mountain?' This was turning more surreal every moment that passed. 'Instead of waiting to see whether it will wake up on its own you want to wake it now?'

The tree spirit watched me, expression unchanged. I assumed this was confirmation.

With a glance at Bryn, then at the mountain, I could see that we had very few options. Either we followed advice from the tree spirit and hoped it was right that it could calm the stones, or we consigned ourselves to dealing with a rampaging stone giant.

'So you can keep the rocks calm until the sun comes up?' I looked to the sky. If that was the case we didn't have very much time.

You can wake the mountain, and I can calm it until the sun rises. We will take it to a place where it can sleep again safely.

'And what sort of place do you have in mind?' I asked wryly. 'It's not like we can bury it under a forest in the next four hours.'

The tree spirit's smile widened, if that was even possible, and it reached a hand out to place it gently on my chest. *You smell of waterfalls.*

With the tree spirit's touch, I could see the waterfalls of Gydrocc, cascading down toward the lake in a constant flow, year round. Unusually, the falls never dried and had been flowing constantly for as long as there had been people to see them.

'Philip said water wasn't effective,' I said quietly to the tree spirit, all of my hope draining away at the simple but flawed plan. 'He tried. The little stone man walked right out of the moat.'

The tree spirit didn't respond, only looked at me with those wide, guileless eyes. I stared back, waiting for a response. If I was looking for some assurance that this really would work, I would be disappointed. The spirit said nothing.

I considered our options. If—or rather, when—the mountain woke up, it would lay waste to everything around for miles, including Gydrocc and the rest of the kingdom.

From what I had seen, and from what both Philip and the tree spirit had said, the next few hours were the last chance we could have to even make an attempt at calming the mountain.

Undoubtedly it was terribly unsafe to lead the thing straight back to my home and leave it there, sitting under one of our waterfalls. This was assuming that a waterfall would keep the creature calm when a dip in the lake wouldn't.

But, all things considered, wouldn't it be less safe to let it wake up on its own, without anything to keep it from going on a rampage?

'I'll go into the mountain,' I said finally to the tree spirit. The options were stark and limited.

I reached out to touch Bryn's snout. 'I'm going with the tree spirit to wake the mountain. Will you be ready to fly again when we come out?'

Bryn lifted his head a little off the ground, ears perked up and eyes narrowed into what I took to be a worried look.

'I'll be fine,' I said, though I didn't believe that myself. With a grimace I added, 'If the mountain wakes up we're both dead, not to mention a lot of other people. Someone has to do this. At least we know what's going on and we have someone on our side.' I nodded to the little tree spirit.

Bryn huffed again, but nodded his big head. I hesitated, and dropped a little kiss on his scaly nose. 'If I don't come out of there, know that I've enjoyed your company. In spite of the bruises. And the danger.'

The big coal-bright eyes focused on me, and I could have sworn that the heat radiating from Bryn increased suddenly. I laughed, completely taken off-guard.

'Are you blushing?'

This time the huff was embarrassed. I kissed his nose again, suddenly sentimental, and stood. With one last glance at Bryn's scaly red face, I turned to the tree spirit.

'Let's go.'

THIRTY-THREE

The tree spirit led the way to the mouth of one of the mining tunnels. It was not the one Bryn and I had been down before, but a slightly wider one that looked to be near the centre of the mining action. We couldn't have come to this tunnel if we had wanted to on our last visit; the miners' tents were all pitched out front.

The spirit stopped at the mouth of the tunnel and pointed to a bag of miner's tools.

You will need those.

I hesitated, wondering whether this was really a good idea, but hefted the bag anyway. There was the heavy metallic clinking of picks and chisels against each other as I slung it over my shoulders, fifteen or twenty of them. It was a lot to carry, certainly heavy enough that I wasn't going to be able to carry it indefinitely.

'All of them?' I asked hopefully. When the tree spirit only looked at me, I assumed a positive answer.

'I hope it won't take long to get where we're going,' I added as the tree spirit started into the mountain.

The tree spirit continued walking and smiled at me. This would have been less unnerving if it hadn't turned its head almost completely around on its shoulders to accomplish this.

I tried to smile back but failed miserably. The tree spirit did not slow down to wait for me, but memories of the darkness of the mines held me back.

The darkness last time had been as crushing as a physical force. There was no way I was going to rely only on the small amount of light radiating from the tree spirit. I picked up a nearby miner's lamp and lit it with a stray ember from one of the destroyed campfires. Lamp lit, I stepped forward into the dark tunnel.

As I entered I was immediately glad for both sources of light. The light from the tree spirit was not insubstantial in comparison with the darkness all around, but it was hardly enough for me to feel comfortable as we descended into the bowels of the earth.

Again I had the feeling of being swallowed alive as I descended into the mine. The walls and ceiling seemed to press down on me the farther we got from the entrance.

If I had been alone, I doubt I would have taken more than twenty steps down the tunnel; the tree spirit walking ahead of me was the only thing that kept me moving forward, partly because I knew now how much relied on my actions here.

As we followed the tunnel around a bend and the exit was completely lost to view, I wished Bryn was by my side. His brash lack of worry about anything was more of a comfort than the silent presence of the tree spirit.

Gradually the tunnel narrowed. There was a prickling at the small of my back as the walls grew closer to my shoulders and I had to continually duck to avoid knocking into the ceiling. Claustrophobia had never been a companion of mine, but here there was no avoiding it.

Though the passageway did not actually get any narrower past a certain point, it felt as if the space was growing smaller every passing moment, or that I was growing larger. An irrational fear that I would never leave this place accompanied the dead echoes of my lone footsteps on the stone floor. Cold sweat prickled at the base of my neck.

The tree spirit seemed unworried as we descended deeper into the mine, and it led the way through the tunnels with great confidence. At least this route was straightforward, with no twists and turns. If it came down to it I could find my way out again on my own this time.

It surprised me when the tree spirit came to a halt ahead of me at the edge of a cavern. When I stepped forward to see, it was almost identical to the cavern Bryn and I had seen before when we came down into the mines. The only significant difference was that there was no stream running through the centre of this chamber.

Breath rushed back into my lungs in the relative openness of the chamber, though my relief at the sudden vastness of the space was tempered by the knowledge that I still had to go through the tunnels again to get out.

Glossy, crystalline stalactites reflected and refracted the light from my lantern into a dazzling display of rainbow hues across the floor and ceiling. It turned the little light from my lantern into something magnificent. The cavern was aesthetically equivalent to Princess Amanthea, and in spite of the danger I wanted to do nothing more than bask in the radiance surrounding me for a long moment.

The tree spirit had different ideas. It immediately crossed the cavern to the other side, where I could see even from here the scars of mining.

The cuts in the stone were not as brutal as they might have been, but I knew now that the miners had been cautioned to take extra care with their task or risk waking the mountain.

With a deep breath I followed the tree spirit. My footsteps echoed loudly in the chamber as I crossed. It made me feel more alone than the descent had. The tree spirit's footfalls did not echo. Only my own movements made any noise, and they were magnified just as the lantern light was, so it seemed that I was a noisy giant in this large space.

The tree spirit stopped in front of the other wall of the cavern. As I approached, the scars of mining were thrown into sharp relief by my lantern, and I could see something of a pattern, though it didn't make sense to me entirely.

In some places the gouges were deep where large chunks had been taken from the mountain, these deep cuts usually surrounded by a host of shallower marks that barely scraped the surface. In other places there was nary a scratch on the stone wall.

Sometimes, there would be great chunks taken out of an otherwise untouched area, and occasionally there was a long swathe of wall left completely untouched in the middle, while the rest was carefully chipped away.

'Why did they stop here?' I asked, pointing to one of the places where the pick marks suddenly stopped.

Some parts of the mountain are more sensitive than others.

I thought back to when Bryn and I had come down into the other cavern. On that night one of the miners had obviously touched a sensitive spot and the cavern had started to shake as if ready to collapse. The memory sent a shiver down my spine as I remembered the fear of being crushed underneath the mountain.

'So now what?' I asked, looking down at the little spirit.

The trees cannot calm stones that have been woken by summer light. The tree spirit looked at me, and somehow the fact that it was not smiling was far more frightening than any of its inhuman grins. *You must wake it first with the tools you have brought before it can be calmed and led away.*

I looked up at the side of the cavern, and the feeling of claustrophobia and fear I had felt since entering the mountain suddenly burst like a volcano in my chest, sending shivering chills down my arms and legs that set me shaking.

'I have to wake it *here*?' I asked, my voice hollow. My nervous question echoed all around me. When the tree spirit didn't respond, I felt my heart sink.

Visions filled my head of the mountain waking and collapsing first this cavern and then all of the tunnels before bursting out the side of the mountain. Alongside these thoughts came a detached curiosity about what it would feel like to be crushed to death by falling stones and a certainty that I would soon be experiencing it firsthand.

'There's no way I'll make it out alive,' I whispered, despair crawling through my veins. 'I'll die, and then Bryn will burn down your precious forest, and then this thing will go on a rampage and kill everything in its path.'

The tree spirit didn't offer any sort of comfort as I might have expected. Even the obvious lie of, 'You're not going to die in this cave,' would have been more comforting than the dead silence that greeted me. The tree spirit only stared at me, waiting.

My voice echoed around the chamber, filling the empty space long after I finished speaking, and it seemed to me that the echoes became more and more panicked every time they bounced back to me. Looking around I felt suddenly frantic and dropped to my knees in front of the tree spirit.

'I will die if you make me stand in this place and wake the mountain.' My voice sounded unnaturally flat in my own ears. 'I will be crushed to death. My body will never again see the light of day. Please, tell me there's some other way. Some way to wake the creature from another place, somewhere closer to the surface.' My mind reeled, panic like fire in my blood. 'Why can't you wake it?'

The tree spirit only continued to look at me. As its gaze held, a feeling of deep disappointment that was not mine filled me up slowly from the soles of my feet to the top of my head. The emotion was old, as old as the trees, and spoke of duty that could not be avoided. *Who*, the disappointment asked, *could do this task, if I would not? The tree spirit could not. Bryn could not. Who else could?*

I thought of Bryn, lying exhausted outside the mines. He had already done what I could not do in first driving away the miners, then in getting rid of the stones that had been taken from the mines.

That was something completely beyond my strength, and he was not done for the night; he would still have to fly back to Gydrocc as a guide for the tree spirit to take the stone creature to the waterfalls.

I thought of the tree spirit, who had waited for someone to come that would help. It had finally found myself and Bryn. It had helped us this far, and had long hours ahead of it keeping the stone creature calm so it would be willing to walk as far as Gydrocc without destroying everything in its path.

Both of them had, or would soon, face great danger in their part of this plan. What made me think I should be exempt? There was no one else to do this part of the task. We would all fail, and their efforts would be in vain if I didn't now do my part.

Even if it meant that I might die in the process.

I blinked. There were no tears. There could be none. My panic gradually subsided as I stood and faced the wall. The panic was replaced by a sense of destiny.

It wasn't the kind of feeling that made me think I had a great future in front of me. It was the kind that made me think that this was the whole point of my life, that nothing I could do in the future could ever live up to the importance of following through with this one decision.

All of my worry about someday being disowned and exiled by Lord Ruben seemed laughable. Of course I was going to die here. One didn't simply run with dragons and expect to live through the adventure. I had been a fool, naïve and optimistic in the light of a life that was only cause for pessimism.

With sudden determination I tied the lantern to my belt. If I wanted any chance at living through this—and I did—I needed to be able to run, and to run, I needed to be able to see my escape route.

I pulled a pickaxe out of the bag of tools and briefly considered leaving the tools here. After all, I would be able to run better without them.

On the other hand, if I got trapped alive in a cave-in, I was going to need all the tools I could get to dig my way out.

I kept the bag on my shoulder.

Addressing the tree spirit, I said, 'Where should I hit it?'

The tree spirit did not smile, for which I was grateful. One more of those smiles or giggles and I might have turned around and run for the exit. At this point I was not in the mood for cheer.

Instead, the tree spirit pointed to a large stretch of untouched rock. The miners had obviously avoided this part of the wall. Apparently there had been a good reason.

I situated myself in front of that section of the wall, feet shoulder width apart, the pickaxe held tightly in both hands.

'Ready?' I asked. The tree spirit didn't respond. I

grimaced and shifted my grip on the pick.

The pick seemed light in my hands as I drew it back to one side and swung with all my might at the wall. Metal met stone with a loud chink and a little shower of dust came away from the wall.

I almost closed my eyes, waiting for the inevitable, but after several seconds nothing happened. I looked to the tree spirit, who continued to look at the wall.

The wall was silent. I licked my lips nervously.

'Again, then?'

The second swing didn't wake the mountain either, nor did the third. Anxiety growing, I began to swing the pick more rhythmically.

What if I wasn't actually strong enough to wake the mountain? All those miners hadn't managed it before, and here I was, a single person, trying to do the unthinkable.

On one particularly heavy swing, the pick stuck into the stone. I pulled, but it didn't come loose. I glanced at the tree spirit, who said nothing. With a sigh, I pulled another pick out of the bag on my shoulder and started again a few inches away.

My arms began to ache as I kept swinging the pick, and I could feel where I would have blisters in the morning if this kept up much longer. The pick felt like it was growing heavier by the moment, and I lost count of my swings somewhere after twenty. By thirty, I was sweating heavily and out of breath, every swing weaker than the last.

Pieces of gravel and stone had now built up around my feet. I kicked them away when I wanted a break from swinging the pick, until eventually I couldn't lift the pick again for another blow.

'I can't do it,' I breathed, wiping my forehead with the back of one hand. 'I just can't.' The pick hung loosely from my other hand.

You must.

I didn't even look at the tree spirit. I knew it was right.

The pick seemed to weigh as much as a broadsword now, and my shoulder chafed from the bag of tools. The lantern swung at my waist, and the crossbow that hung useless off my back was only a deadweight that I was foolishly sentimental about leaving behind.

'Will this ever end?' I cried, swinging almost blindly at the wall with the pick.

I was so tired I almost didn't feel the shift beneath my feet, but I certainly heard the low rumble above me. I didn't need the tree spirit to tell me that I had finally hit on something. Something sensitive.

Something that could wake the mountain.

Energy renewed, I pulled back the pick as the groaning stone quieted and drove it again into the wall. I struck the stone again, as hard as I could.

The stone wall in front of me gave a shudder. I drew back, this time swinging so hard I nearly overbalanced with the force of the strike and a large chunk of stone dropped out of the wall.

I thought it was enough when there was a mighty crash behind me and my back was pelted with hundreds of tiny stones. I turned to see that one of the crystal stalactites had fallen from the ceiling and shattered against the floor.

'Let's go!' I cried, triumphant.

No.

The coolness of the simple word stopped me. The tree spirit stood beside the wall, shaking its head. *Not yet.*

I gave one look at the ceiling, which was now full of cracks, and listened to the hum of stone vibrating, which was constant all around me.

'Surely it's awake now!' I cried. The hum was so obvious that it was painful to listen.

No.

It was the last straw.

If the ceiling was already caving in but the mountain still wasn't awake, there was no way I was getting out alive. By the time the thing was awake I would be crushed by a stalactite.

Certain death made a brave fool of me. After a moment's indecision, I dropped the pick on the floor with a clatter and dug through the bag of tools. I found a chisel and a mallet and immediately put them to work.

The chisel went into the deepest part of the little hole I had already made. After a little shifting, I drove the hammer home onto the back of the chisel. It took three strikes to get the chisel firmly embedded in the wall.

Another stalactite crashed down to the floor behind me with a deafening sound. This time as it shattered a large piece of the crystal hit me in the back of the thigh.

Pain radiated up and down my leg and I nearly fell as the blinding stimulus added to the bundle of pain and exhaustion I already felt.

Concentrating for all I was worth, I swung the mallet at the chisel. Metal struck metal firmly enough to drive the chisel an inch into the stone. The stone itself seemed to be giving way more now than it had at the surface of the wall. It was almost as if I had dug through the tough skin of a great creature and was now to the soft flesh beneath.

With the next blow of the hammer, the sound around me shifted. Before, it had been a rumble. Now it was becoming higher pitched, and louder.

A deep crack appeared in the wall above me and to my right, and for a terrifying moment I thought the whole wall was going to collapse on top of me.

There was a cacophony of sound behind as several stalactites fell at once, and I was pelted with debris from all sides as the ceiling and wall in front of me shifted.

This time the tree spirit did not hesitate.

Run.

THIRTY-FOUR

I didn't need telling twice. The mallet went to the floor with a clatter and the chisel stayed deeply embedded in the wall. I took one look at the ceiling to check for falling stalactites and darted away across the chamber.

There was no way I wanted to run under any stalactites that were still suspended from the rapidly fragmenting ceiling. At the rate they were falling, one of them might come down directly on the top of my head as I went under it. The only safe way I could think of to cross the cavern was to run where the stalactites had already fallen.

The first pile of felled crystal nearly proved my undoing. I stumbled up the near side of the pulverised stalactite, barely able to keep my footing as the stone shifted under my feet. The crash of another stalactite falling to my left was enough distraction that I lost my footing. I skidded down the other side of the pile, sharp stones embedding into my palms on the way. There wasn't time to take stock of myself, but I did check the lantern. It was thankfully undamaged, and I could still see my exit ahead.

The pain in my hands was not a priority as I picked myself up and ran for the door. I pumped my legs as quickly as they would go and jumped over the remains of one of the smaller stalactites. The crystal shards slid under my feet as I landed but I miraculously stayed upright.

The largest rumble came just as I arrived at the door to the cavern. I did not turn, but cast a glance back over my shoulder at what I had wrought. I immediately regretted it as my knees almost gave out in terror.

The place that I had been digging had cracked itself out from the wall, the shape so clear it was unmistakeable. It was like a massive human hand, less one finger, as wide as Bryn's wingspan.

The cracking sound was stone breaking as the hand and its associated arm came away from the wall of the cave.

With one massive, earth-shattering crack, an arm came away from the surrounding stone completely and the hand crashed to the floor, one part of a massive stone man preparing to lift himself from lying down on his front.

Run.

This time it wasn't the tree spirit saying it.

It was me, thinking about the consequences if I waited any longer to get out of these mines.

Already I could see that the tunnels ahead of me were not going to stay stable. There was as much noise of falling rock from ahead as there was from behind. If the tunnel caved in ahead of me, I would have no choice but to find an alternative route, and there was every chance I would get lost in the tunnels until it was too late; I would either be crushed by the final collapse or starve to death in a small pocket of air.

I ran.

I'm not sure how I managed to run when I was so exhausted from everything else that had come during that night, but I ran. It was almost as though I could no longer feel the pain and fatigue in my limbs. I could only feel the terror at being trapped in these tunnels, and it propelled me along with no thought for what my body felt.

At least once I scraped my head on the ceiling, but I barely noticed, and certainly didn't care. There was nothing now but the terror that lent me speed as the tunnel began to cave in around and behind me. I would run or I would die.

My legs and lungs burned with the effort of maintaining speed. More than once the tunnel collapsed directly behind me to send out billowing clouds of dust that made me choke and cough.

It seemed an eternity before I saw the mouth of the tunnel. The stars were visible, and with them my escape.

With a final burst of energy I launched myself through the opening at a run, a trail of dust and gravel just behind. I couldn't stop; my legs were going now and they seemed to have a mind of their own. I heard a massive crack from where I had just been and felt a shower of stones on my back.

This time I fell, the small shower of gravel enough to knock me down where nothing else had.

I heard a low rumble from Bryn and rolled onto my side, knocking the lantern loose from where it was tied to my belt. The destruction inside the mountain was only visible now from the outside as several tunnels collapsed internally and sent clouds of dust out their entrances. Most of the mountain still looked unchanged. Even the rumbling was so quiet from outside that it could be overlooked.

With what seemed to be the very last of my energy I scrambled to my feet and hurried to Bryn, who was watching the mountain with an unreadable expression.

'We need to go,' I said hoarsely, my throat full of dust. While I still couldn't feel any of the pain I knew should be there, I could now feel that my legs were like lead. It was almost impossible to make myself move faster than a walk.

Bryn stood slowly, obviously still exhausted, and turned to let me climb onto his shoulders. He looked haggard, and I knew I would feel the same the moment I had a chance to stop moving.

A loud rumble made us both turn, and we could see clouds of dust shooting out of all of the remaining mine entrances. My eyes widened; the collapse inside had caught up. I scrambled up Bryn's shoulder and wrapped both arms around his neck.

'Go!' I cried.

Bryn did not hesitate but ran down the mountain at full speed with wings outstretched to catch the wind.

I turned my head to look back, never loosening my grip on Bryn's neck. What I saw was unlike anything I could have imagined. It was the vision the little tree spirit had showed me in the forest, but a hundred times bigger, a hundred times worse.

The mountainside grew, pushed up from the inside as cracks formed all across the surface. What few trees and shrubs were left on the surface fell into the cracks, which widened with every passing moment.

Before my eyes, with a sound that made me wish I could cover my ears, the mountainside exploded in a hail of debris.

Boulders the size of houses went flying through the air, along with smaller, sharper pieces of rock and crystal from the once-beautiful caverns inside the mountain, all of them now undoubtedly destroyed. Dust billowed out as an impenetrably thick wall.

Rising from the middle of the destruction was a tall, spindly man made of stone, so tall that it looked as though he could have plucked the moon out of the sky. The great stone man stretched out his arms to either side, less like a yawn than the stretch of one cooped up in a too-small space for far too long. It was the same gesture the little stone man had made just before he attacked Philip.

'Fly!' I cried to Bryn, tears of fear coursing down my cheeks.

I hadn't died in the mines, but Bryn and I could both just as easily die now, flying along at treetop level with this thing following behind us.

Bryn launched himself into the air with such speed my arms were almost torn from his neck. I scrambled to maintain my grip and buried my face in his scales. All I could do was hold on and hope for escape.

As fast as Bryn was, it only took a single one of the stone creature's massive steps to put us in danger again. I watched as it lifted one massive leg out of the hole that had been the mountain and stepped forward almost in slow motion. As it moved, it reached out to snatch Bryn from the air.

I'm not proud of the way I screamed.

Those massive fingers closed in the air just behind Bryn's tail as he dived and rolled away to one side. The muscles that connected to his wings flexed under me, pumping with a mad speed that I hadn't thought Bryn capable of as he fought for altitude.

I was nearly sick as Bryn engaged in the kind of aerial acrobatics that would have put a housefly to shame.

He was impossible to catch, impossible to hit, writhing through the air with such speed and unpredictable changes of direction that it seemed impossible for the stone man to catch up with him.

When the stone man finally did, it was the end for us.

The great stone fingers caught up with Bryn's wingtip in a crippling blow that made Bryn scream in so much pain that I thought he was going to die. In a single moment we went from flying at great speed to being sent hurtling to the ground in a death spiral.

THIRTY-FIVE

Somehow Bryn stretched his damaged wing out sufficiently that we stopped spinning just as we reached treetop level, and he scrambled to grab at tree branches with all four legs as he fell, breaking off a dozen before finally catching one that slowed us down. The jolt as he caught hold of the tree almost knocked me free again, and I scrambled for purchase against his scales and pack, clinging on for dear life.

The branch snapped under the weight of our fall and Bryn had to grab desperately for another. This one held, but bent and swung dangerously.

We hung from the tree, as still as we could manage, waiting for death to descend from above, for one of those massive hands or feet to come down to crush us both in a single movement.

It didn't come.

Eventually, I managed to take a deep breath.

I caught an exhausted sob before it escaped and stroked Bryn's neck.

'The tree spirit must have managed to calm it.' I hiccupped, holding on to Bryn like he was the only safe thing in the world.

Bryn let out a whimper in reply. Embarrassed at myself, I remembered the reason for out fall. I looked back at his wing to assess the damage and immediately wished I hadn't. A dragon wing has two major joints, one near the body and one halfway out the wing; at least, it does normally. Bryn's right wing looked like it had a brand-new extra joint not far past the second, and almost the entire outermost half of that wing was completely mangled.

He was frozen in position, unwilling to move at all. I looked down to the forest floor far below and stroked Bryn's neck, my mind racing at the thought of a fall from this height.

'It's okay,' I said in soothing tones, trying not to let any emotion show through. 'Just climb down to the ground and we can stop to check on your wing. I'm sure everything is fine.'

It was a lie, but a necessary one at the moment. A fall from here could kill both of us as easily as a blow from the stone man.

Slowly, painfully slowly, Bryn crept down the tree,

whimpering every so often. When he finally reached the ground, he backed into a little clear spot and stood high up on all four legs, his back arched like a frightened cat, his neck coiled back and chin tucked in.

I slid from his shoulder carefully and moved to look at his wing, making soothing sounds all the while. It did not take an expert to see that the fine, strong bones that held the scaly skin of his wing taut had been completely broken on that side. I couldn't see how the bones could be expected to heal in a way that he would ever fly normally again.

'Everything's fine,' I said, as I took hold of his wing behind the first joint with both hands, far from where the damage was. I slowly pulled the wing close to his body to help fold it up. 'Everything should heal just fine. Don't worry about it. Let's get through tonight and then we can worry about it in the morning.'

I was a terrible liar, and perhaps it was not the right approach to the situation, but I couldn't think what else to do.

While Bryn didn't seem like one to give up simply because things were becoming difficult, I didn't know how he would manage to continue in this task if he knew that he would be permanently injured for all his trouble.

Bryn looked at me, so much in pain that there was only the barest glimmer of scepticism at my comments. He did not move yet, only stood stock still, blinking occasionally. Perhaps he was in shock.

CHAPTER THIRTY-FIVE

There was still work to be done. Bryn would, like it or not, have to wait.

I looked up through the treetops. 'Tree spirit!' I called, unsure how else to get its attention. 'Tree spirit!'

What I saw next was a massive stone hand descending through the trees, and after an initial jolt of horror that I had just called down death on the both of us, I realised that the hand was coming to rest beside us, palm up.

The hand stilled, waiting a foot off the ground, an open, welcome platform that we could climb onto. I looked up through the trees to see the arm and body the hand was attached to, immense and terrifying in spite of the benign gesture.

Well, at this point we were dead anyway if the tree spirit hadn't managed to fully calm the giant stone man, so I turned back to Bryn, took his snout in both hands, and led him to the stone hand.

Bryn didn't even protest as we climbed into the giant palm. He crouched in the cradle of stone beside me, slow and still, wings and tail overflowing from the sides of the giant's stony hand. His eyes had a glazed look to them as pain drove away all thought.

The hand lifted away from the earth again, up high into the sky until it was level with the stone man's massive chest. I watched the stone man, holding on to Bryn for reassurance, and was relieved when I saw the forest spirit sitting atop the great boulder of a head.

The mountain must meet the waterfall before dawn.

I turned to face Gydrocc. 'Then we should go.'

The stone man ate up miles with ease, his massive stride covering the distance faster than Bryn could manage in flight. Looking below and behind, I could see the massive craters where the stone giant's feet had been, ready to provide a great mystery to anyone that came across them. Briefly, I hoped that we weren't stepping on any homes, then shuddered and put it out of my mind. It was no good worrying about it now, when everything could still go very wrong.

Bryn dissolved into a shivering pile of scales as we travelled. He released the occasional fiery sniffle, exhausted and wounded, leaving me to direct the tree spirit back to my home.

I did my best to avoid human habitations while still taking a direct route, working from memory of the maps I knew of the area. We didn't have as much time before dawn as any of us would have liked; it had taken far longer to drive away the miners and wake the mountain than any of us had planned.

'We're nearly there,' I called out as I saw Gydrocc and the lake in the distance. 'We'll need to avoid the castle. It may be dark but if anyone sees this thing they may attack and we'd just lost time.'

The forest spirit didn't respond, but it hadn't at any point in the journey so far, other than to follow my directions. Apparently, concentrating on keeping this much stone calm enough to walk non-violently across a kingdom was only just within its realm of capability.

The first and only time it spoke since telling me to get out of the mines was as we neared Gydrocc to say, *Dawn is coming*.

Bryn and I both turned to the east to see the earliest grey light of the dawn rising over the far mountains.

'Can this thing go any faster?' I asked, looking at the tree spirit.

The blank look I got back said that this was already pushing it.

'Almost there,' I repeated, looking to the lake. It would only take a dozen more of those massive steps to reach the side of the lake, then the thing could just walk into the lake and we could lead it under the falls. If we went to the largest of the falls, near the centre of the cliffs at the other side of the lake, I hoped that the stone man would be almost completely under the water, and his head might even be hidden by the falls.

The first sign of trouble was a little hesitation in the stone man's step as we drew level with the lake. He lifted his foot to take that first step into the water, and slowed down so much that I thought he might have completely solidified again.

'Just a few more steps!' I called, looking up to the forest spirit.

The forest spirit wasn't there.

The sky wasn't grey anymore. It was blue.

And there was a ray of sun shining directly onto the

stone man's head.

'Bryn!' I screamed, scrambling up Bryn's shoulder to riding position, 'Get us off!'

My urgency, combined with the strange hesitation in the stone man's movements, must have been enough to bring Bryn back to consciousness. He managed to lunge forward onto the stone fingers and jump, stretching his left wing out easily. His right wing, on the other hand, did not cooperate. It stretched out halfway before Bryn released a loud cry.

We hung in the air in front of the stone man's hesitant fingers, and I clenched my teeth in preparation for our fall and ensuing impact with the icy lake water.

Somehow, though, Bryn managed to keep his wings open. He glided across toward the cliff face, dripping pained flames from his mouth the whole way.

I alternated worried glances between the rapidly approaching cliff ahead and the receding but still enormous figure of the stone man behind, who did not seem to understand what was happening yet.

Gliding might have been something Bryn could manage on a busted wing, but a safe landing was simply not going to happen. He knew of only one good landing spot on the cliff side, and went for it; the clearing that we had met in before.

However bad his first landing there was, this was going to be infinitely worse. I braced myself for impact as we approached.

He didn't so much land as crash into the side of the cliff just below the clearing. The jolt nearly knocked my teeth out. His front legs caught a boulder sticking out and we tumbled head over heels, momentum carrying us forward onto the clearing. Bryn's neck hit the rock first and his body rolled over with him in a kind of somersault.

I launched myself away the moment I thought I wouldn't fall from the cliff, and it was none too soon. My boot caught under Bryn's back as he rolled, though it came free almost immediately, and I was mercilessly driven into the ground by the impact of Bryn's wing across my back. I saw a tumble of dragon legs overhead out of the corner of my eye as Bryn continued to roll.

Somehow, I avoided tumbling in my hasty dismount, which probably saved my life. The sharp point of a pick dug into my side from the bag of mining implements still hanging from my shoulder as I picked myself up off the ground. It could have impaled me if I had moved any farther.

I sat up, my entire body aching, and took stock of myself.

The crossbow was slightly bent but unbroken, which was more than could be said for my leg that had ended up under Bryn. Searing pain shot through my ankle as I moved to rise. Eyes watering, I looked over to Bryn to see him crumpled against the wall, his limbs splayed out in unnatural directions.

He was worse off than I was.

It was up to me to deal with the stone man.

From across the lake I could hear the tell-tale cracking as the stone giant prepared himself to move. I had woken him before in the mountain, but the sunlight was waking him again, and this time no tree spirit would be able to calm him.

Everything else—pain, exhaustion, confusion, fear—seemed trivial in light of the fact that I had just brought this enormous, violent creature to the very doorstep of Gydrocc Castle.

There could be no defence against something this large. I crawled miserably to the cliff edge to see what was happening.

The giant stood at the edge of the lake and slowly stretched out his arms to both sides, his great hands clenched in tight fists. He was doing that strange sort of yawn again, waking himself for another round of destruction.

My hands scrambled for something, anything that could help. I had the mining tools and the bent crossbow with its ridiculous, ineffective accuracy charm, but that was all. The only thing I could think was to try distracting the creature. Perhaps I could somehow lure it under one of the waterfalls?

I could barely move from where I was sitting on the edge of the cliff, my leg growing more painful by the minute. The only thing I could think of was to shoot at the stone giant with the crossbow and hope it would come towards me rather than head off to destroy Gydrocc Castle.

I grimaced. Now that I'd thought of it I couldn't just ignore the idea, especially given that it was the only one I had. I strung the crossbow with the leg that wasn't broken, loaded a bolt, and took aim.

My hands shook as I sat with the crossbow held out in front of me. Every ounce of energy had already been wrung from my body. I was completely spent physically. The only thing I had left was Philip's charm, and his promise that it would allow me to hit my target as long as my concentration was good.

If ever my concentration had been good, it was now. My home was in danger, as was everyone I knew. Mind sharpened by fear and danger, I stared down the creaking stone giant as it completed its stretching and became aware of itself.

With a light squeeze, I released the first bolt into the morning air. Even with my thoughts of the destruction of my home to spur it on, the bolt only made it halfway across the admittedly massive distance between myself and the giant. It fell in the lake to start a ripple that I couldn't see from this height.

I had seen for myself that this charm was not very reliable. Perhaps the small charm alone wasn't enough to make up the shortfall of the enormous distance and my poor aim.

Dark thoughts tumbled over one another in my mind. We were going to die. All of us. Philip. Sid. The king, the queen, Prince Caleb. Even the thought of Lord Ruben and Lady Ainsley meeting their death sent a pang through me.

I loaded another bolt. The fear of death that had dulled since I escaped the mines sharpened again, a knife hanging over not just me now but all of my loved ones as well.

This time when I squeezed the trigger the bolt flew farther than I ever would have imagined possible. It soared across the width of the lake as if it were a quarter of the distance, fast and true.

It struck the stone giant in the leg.

I looked down at the crossbow, surprised and pleased, but the single crossbow bolt to the knee wasn't enough to attract any of the stone giant's attention. The monster was, ever so slowly, turning toward the castle, and I recognized the posture from what seemed an eternity ago, when the miniature stone man had wound itself up to launch itself towards Philip's head at inhuman speeds.

Without even thinking, I grabbed one of the heavy chisels out of the bag and loaded it into the crossbow.

I'm not sure what part of me thought that was a good idea, because the logical part of my mind said, *there is no way a crossbow can launch a chisel. No way. Not going to happen. You're going to pull the trigger and that chisel is going to fall on your foot.*

I had a look at Philip's charm on the butt of the crossbow one more time and thought of him. *If this chisel doesn't do exactly what I need it to, Philip is going to die.*

The kind, aged face of the alchemist filled my mind. His was a goodness I had not encountered in anyone else since coming to Gydrocc. I was not about to lose him to a situation of my own making.

I lifted the crossbow and took aim, less with the bow than with my thoughts. I looked right at the stone man, staring hard at a point on the boulder that made up his head. I thought viciously, I'm going to hit you so hard I knock that pointy block right off your shoulders.

I pulled the trigger.

The string twanged.

The chisel flew across the lake as if propelled by the hand of God.

I couldn't see where it hit, but it hit the stone giant.

I knew because he straightened up as if stung, and his shoulders rotated under his head to face me.

The next thing I knew, the stone giant leapt across the lake, directly at me.

THIRTY-SIX

The stone man hit the surface of the water halfway across the lake and there was a roar as water splashed out in all directions. Seated where I was on the cliff above, I was instantly soaked in the splash, which nearly knocked me from my perch. Before the initial splash settled, a wave several feet high swept out in all directions, and the river leading out of the lake swelled so quickly it broke the banks to sweep the fields below.

The stone man sank to the bottom of the lake. His head was not visible above the surface of the water for a long moment, but I knew better than to think that he would be soothed by the still water of the lake. Another chisel found its way into my hand and I loaded the crossbow again. Perhaps it would be no more than an annoyance, but if I was going to die here, my last act would be one of defiance.

It was at this point that I realised I was sitting directly above one of the six waterfalls of Gydrocc. There was no better place to be situated, and I silently thanked mother for finding this place, and Bryn for coming here when he jumped off the stone giant.

Perhaps I could do more than annoy the stone man. If I could annoy him enough that he came for me, he would end up directly beneath the flow of the waterfall. If the tree spirit was correct, the waterfall would lull the stones back to sleep.

The giant head of the stone man broke the surface of the lake before long, and I directed another chisel at his head. It flew straight and true, directed by my intense concentration, and I saw it strike the stone man's head hard enough to chip off a large chunk of stone.

The stone man's shoulders turned toward me and the cliff, and he began to move.

With every one of his great strides, the stone man displaced more water from the lake. It flowed over the banks in great gushes, flooding the forest, the fields, and nearly reaching the castle itself in slow, rhythmic waves.

I realised as the stone giant approached that if the waterfall didn't soothe him straightaway, he was likely to climb up the cliff and crush me to a pulp.

Oh well. It was too late now. I was dead one way, I was dead another way.

Part of me wished that fate would just let me know which way I was going to die so I could stop worrying about the things that weren't going to kill me.

Another chisel went onto the crossbow and I fired.

All I could do was fire chisel after chisel at the stone man as he walked slowly across the bottom of the lake, fighting the surge of water as he did so. His head was just visible over the surface and I was briefly thankful that Gydrocc Lake was so deep. It certainly slowed the stone giant down better than anything else could.

He reached the edge of the lake below the cliff where I sat at the same time that I ran out of chisels and was left with a few mining picks. They were useless, but at this point most things would have been.

The stone giant reached one hand up the cliff, halfway to where I sat, as if it meant to climb. This hand went right through the waterfall and released a spray of deflected water across the lake. The hand took hold of the cliff behind the waterfall, and he sidled over as if to climb up.

There was nothing else for it. I closed my eyes and waited to die.

I had woken the mountain, led it across two kingdoms, crashed into a cliff and managed to get the stone creature to the only place that the forest spirit thought would put it back to sleep. I was exhausted. If it was going to get me now, it was going to get me. There remained nothing I could do.

With my eyes shut, the sound of the waterfall next to me was the only thing that mattered. It was a soothing rumble, more constant and calming than the scraping cracks of the mountain that I had been hearing all night. My body relaxed against my will. Stiff, sore muscles and my broken leg tried to rebel against me for staying sitting up when all they really wanted was for me to lay down and let go of all the stresses of the night.

I opened my eyes, ready to face death in the form of sentient rocks.

There was nothing in front of me, so I looked down over the edge of the cliff. Water from the falls was still spraying out oddly from the stone giant's outstretched arm, which hadn't moved since it was placed there. I leaned forward a little more to see the head, still and silent as a boulder should be, nearly level with the surface of the lake, the water from the falls a cascade over it.

The stone man wasn't moving.

The last act of the stone giant had been to step under the waterfall in a bid for a better place to climb the cliff. It was now immobile, asleep under the waterfall, just as the forest spirit had promised.

Without another thought, I lay back on the ground and joined the stone man in unconsciousness.

THIRTY-SEVEN

When I woke, it was dark. I could see that much through slitted eyelids, but little else. I closed my eyes completely again and basked in the feeling of warmth and softness all around me, not daring to move for fear of what I might find.

I turned my head a little and grimaced. The top of my scalp burned. It took me a moment to remember I had scraped my head in my desperate escape from the mines.

'Tara?' Sid's worried voice cut through the fog in my brain. 'Tara, you're awake.' She breathed a sigh of relief. 'I thought you were never going to wake up.'

'Where…?' I breathed, my throat dry.

'In the castle,' she said quietly. I opened my eyes

just a little to look at her. Sid was seated next to me in a high-backed chair with a book hanging limply from her fingers as she leaned forward to speak. There was a fire going on the other side of the room, and I was in a comfortable bed, though things seemed strange, unreal; it was like a dream.

'Philip and I went to the clearing this morning to find you since you hadn't come back. We were afraid something had happened to you, what with everything else going on, and I knew you would go there before you came back to the castle.'

Awareness came to me slowly. The image of Bryn's crumpled body lying atop the cliff blazed into my mind, real and painful. 'Bryn?' I whispered hesitantly.

'He was persuaded to turn human again so we could bring him down,' Sid said with a blush. 'He's worse for wear than you are.' She put a hand on my cheek. 'What happened? You both look terrible.'

'We did it,' I managed to say

'I take it your success has something to do with the fact that half the country got flooded this morning,' Sid said with a wry smile.

I smiled weakly in reply. 'I guess.'

Sid reached over to the bedside and lifted something up for me to see. Through my haze of exhaustion, the swinging gleam of the pearl from Bryn came into view.

'We retrieved it from Lady Ainsley at the end of the night,' Sid explained. 'She was more than happy to give it back, though she's now convinced someone tried to break in and steal from her during the night.'

I didn't have the energy to reply. Sid gently put the pearl down at the bedside again.

She stood, and I fell asleep again before she was gone.

When I finally did wake up properly the next day, I had no recollection of my conversation with Sid, so she had to tell me all of it again, as I sat up stiffly with a bowl of stew in what I now recognised was her bed.

'Philip is suspicious of what your uncle has done to your room,' Sid explained. 'He thought Lord Ruben might have a way of spying on you. Bryn is in Philip's tower. Philip and Rue are taking care of him.'

'How is he, really?' I asked, dreading the answer. Even the most basic part of his recovery could take weeks.

'Not well,' Sid said honestly. 'But Philip is doing his best. He sent a message to the dragons that Bryn was injured and we think they're going to come for him.'

I nodded, feeling terrible. I wondered if the dragons were going to deem me unworthy now, or too much of a troublemaker, after having almost gotten one of their own killed. If they decided what I did was too injurious, they might just come and destroy Gydrocc themselves; a horde of angry dragons was easily as destructive as a stone giant.

Apparently my troubles were not over.

My thoughts gradually came around to the last time I had seen Sid, just before Bryn and I left for the mines.

'What happened at the festival? Were they fooled by your trick with Alois?'

Sid smiled, looking mischievous. 'I would say so. By the end of the night you had two marriage proposals and your uncle was looking rather pleased. He sent up a note with his congratulations yesterday morning, asking that when you're feeling better you go speak with him about your options. I told him you were feeling unwell after the party. I'm putting them off now saying it's your time of women.'

I laughed at that. 'Perhaps they'll be fooled enough to think that a broken leg is part of the time of women?'

Sid shrugged. 'You never know.' She patted my unbroken leg gently. 'Perhaps if you simply sit still and act ladylike they'll never notice?'

By the end of a week, I could walk, though not very far, and only with the help of a splint under my skirts. The first time out of my tower I went to find Bryn, only to discover that he had gone from Philip's tower in the night, retrieved by two of his cousins.

'And no one noticed?' I asked sceptically.

'The two cousins in question were an ink black and midnight blue, not like Bryn's rather more colourful hue,' Philip said, pouring me a cup of tea. 'Bryn left you a note.'

I took the note from Philip and opened it. Sid leaned over my shoulder to read along.

Lady Tara,
My congratulations on your first kill.

Sid gasped.

I put up my hands defensively. 'He must be talking about the stone giant, because I swear I didn't kill anything else.'

As I seem to have missed the most exciting parts of our adventure, Philip relayed to me the details he got of the incident from your vile faerie.

Both Sid and I snorted.

I am very impressed and would like much to hear the story from your own lips. Please do me the honour of visiting my home later this summer. My father would very much like to hear the tale as well, though for different reasons.

Send word to your mother of when you plan to arrive. She will contact us.

Bryn

'Well what do you say to that!' Sid straightened up. 'An invitation to dine with the dragons!'

CHAPTER THIRTY-SEVEN

'Dine with, rather than be dined on, I should hope,' I added.

'Two betrothals and popularity amongst the dragons?' Philip leaned back with a smug smile. 'Perhaps you should do this kind of thing more often.'

I looked at the letter, and shifted in my seat. Pain shot down my broken leg, and my sore muscles screamed for rest. That was not to mention the nightmares that now haunted me every night about being crushed to death under a mountain.

'Perhaps,' I said quietly, 'Perhaps not.'

ABOUT THE AUTHOR

J M Beevers developed a lively imagination growing up in the Rocky Mountains of the United States and now lives in England with family.

This is the author's debut novel.

Made in the USA
San Bernardino, CA
12 April 2015